SEA OF *Rescue*

SEA OF *Rescue*

Restored

Part 2

Mary E. Hanks

www.maryehanks.com

Suzanne D. Williams Cover Design
www.feelgoodromance.com

Cover photos:

micromonkey @ iStock;
narcisopa @ Shutterstock

Author photo: Ron Quinn

Visit Mary's website:

www.maryehanks.com

You can write Mary at

maryhanks@maryehanks.com.

For Mike,

My sweet brother who led me to Jesus many years ago.

For Jason,

The guy whose green eyes still make my heart flip-flop.

When anxiety was great within me,

your consolation brought joy to my soul.

Psalm 94:19

Basalt Bay Residents

Paisley Grant – Daughter of Paul and Penny Cedars

Judah Grant – Son of Edward and Bess Grant

Paige Cedars – Paisley's younger sister/mom to Piper

Peter Cedars – Paisley' older brother/fishing in Alaska

Paul Cedars – Paisley's dad/widower

Edward Grant – Mayor of Basalt Bay/Judah's dad

Bess Grant – Judah's mom/Edward's wife

Aunt Callie – Paisley's aunt/Paul's sister

Maggie Thomas – owner of Beachside Inn

Bert Jensen – owner of Bert's Fish Shack

Mia Till – receptionist at C-MER

Craig Masters – Judah's supervisor at C-MER

Mike Linfield – Judah's boss at C-MER

Lucy Carmichael – Paisley's high school friend

Brian Corbin – Sheriff's deputy

Kathleen Baker – newcomer to Basalt Bay

Bill Sagle – pastor

Geoffrey Carnegie – postmaster/local historian

Casey Clemons – floral shop owner

Patty Lawton – hardware store owner

Brad Keifer – fisherman/school chum of Peter's

James Weston – Paul's neighbor

Penny Cedars – Paisley's mom/decease

Sal Donovan – souvenir shop owner

One

Ice-cold adrenaline raced through Paisley Grant's veins as she leaned against the pantry door, an empty quart-sized Mason jar clutched in her right hand. She ignored her shaky breaths, her throbbing heartbeat, and the heat rising in her flushed cheeks, because her nemesis, Craig Masters, was out there, somewhere, maybe just a few feet away.

Was he waiting to hurt her? Terrorize her? She couldn't put her finger on any other motive for his late-night arrival.

Swallowing past the bitter taste in the back of her mouth threatening to choke her, she clamped her mouth shut lest she make a sound and give away her hiding place. She gripped the jar tighter, mentally and physically preparing herself to hit the intruder, if it came to that. *Please, God, don't let it come to that.* In her left hand, she held two long skinny wooden frame pieces from Mom's old busted canvases. It was an odd collection of weapons, but she'd do what she had to do to survive.

She pressed her ear against the crack of the door, listening for the next sound that might alert her to Craig's location. Was he in the kitchen? Farther away in the living room? She didn't shuffle an inch, afraid her boots might make a ripple in the standing ankle-high water left by the flood following Hurricane Blaine. How long could she stand statue-still like this without him finding her?

A shiver raced along her nerves, imploding in her brain, or so it felt, as she thought of another time when Craig caused a terrible fear to rise in her. Her hand clutching the jar shook. Her heart hammered double-time against her ribs. Lightheaded, she blew out a breath. Had she locked her knees? She flexed her leg muscles. Inhaled silently.

Why was the man who worked with her husband, Judah, at C-MER, Basalt Bay's Coastal Management and Emergency Responders, being so quiet now? Moments ago, he yelled her name over and over. White fear had spasmed up her breastbone, leaving a spark of pain in her chest. Now, waiting in the pitch dark, with nothing but silence and her wild imagination, was nearly as terrifying.

If she could figure out how to run through the flooded house and escape without him seeing her, she would. But charging through the swamped kitchen, and dashing through the living room where Mom's paintings still floated in seawater, without Craig catching her? Impossible.

She swallowed hard. Kept the jar clutched to her chest.

Even if she could elude him, what then? It was late. Dark outside. The whole town was without power. No streetlights. And thanks to overcast skies, no moonlight. The neighbors had covered their windows with sheets of plywood, and probably locked their doors, before fleeing town prior to the hurricane. She'd have a hard time breaking into any houses.

Her thoughts rushed back to Craig and how she could get away from him. He was a solid man. Muscular. A football player in his high school days. Still, she was gritty and wily. She'd kick, swing her elbows, flail at him with her Mason jar and the broken frame. Then run like crazy. What if she couldn't get away? If he grabbed her wrist. Forced her—

No! She'd stay alert. Watch for her chance. Her previous altercation with him flashed through her mind. That time she fought him, kicking and scratching—a losing battle. He overpowered her, even drunk as he was, until Mayor Grant came along. That her father-in-law wound up being a hero *and* a scum revolted her still.

A door squeaked open, then thudded closed. The front door? Had Craig been outside looking for her?

The muscles in her fingers contracted around the Mason jar's neck. She could do this. Protect herself. God was on her side—if Judah knew what he was talking about. *Please, please.*

The man's boots made a thwump-thwump rhythm as he strode across the kitchen where the floor wasn't carpeted, coming toward her. She pressed her weight against the door. Lifted the glass weaponry. How hard would she have to hit the man to knock him out?

As a kid she was a pro at throwing mud balls. Had a good aim. If she hurled this jar at Craig—to protect herself—she was going to make it count. He'd probably need stitches. A visit to the ER in Florence.

"*Paishley?*"

Why did he slur her name like that? Her heart skipped a couple of beats.

"I been *lookin'foryou.*" His gruff voice ran the words together. "You think you can hide from the *mashter* of search and *reshcue?*"

He made a snarky laugh. Something thudded as if he ran into the wall. He said a foul curse word. Was he drunk?

Something crashed. She jerked, then wished she hadn't. Did he see water swirling on the other side of the door?

What if his broken speech and bumping into things were an act? A lure to get her to come out of hiding. She had to be careful. Cautious of his tricks.

"I foun' your ole man's *shtash*." He sounded like he was pickled.

What stash? What was he talking about?

"Daddy's an alcoholic, hmmm?" He crashed against the wall right next to her hiding place.

I don't want to hurt him. But if he comes in here, I'll do whatever it takes to stop him.

"Women drive men to drink. That what happened to your dad?"

Her dad wasn't an alcoholic. An image of him barely able to walk up the front steps yesterday pinged in her thoughts. She never knew him to be a drinker. He used to say he hated beer. Was he drinking to bury his grief over Mom's death?

Then again, maybe Craig was hoping for her lapse in attention. Her distraction. She stiffened, leaned firmly against the door.

"*Paishley* Grant!" He rattled the doorknob.

She gripped the jar. This was it.

"Funny how *thingsh* work out." His tone changed. He sang a couple of muddled lyrics from a country love song.

Why didn't he just open the door?

"*Paishley?*" His loud voice came through the crack between the door and the doorframe. A flashlight beam blasted through the narrow space, creating stripes of light across her clothes.

She froze.

"Peek-a-boo! I *shee* you."

Two

Ever since the phone connection with Paisley went dead, Judah Grant had been tromping around the perimeter of the parking lot of the storm shelter in Florence, Oregon, praying one second, ranting the next. He needed peace. Paisley needed a miracle. Despite the darkness and the late hour, he hobbled past the cars outside the high school gym, rehashing their phone conversation.

"Someone's here."

That made him crazy. *"What? Who?"*

"I . . . don't . . . know."

The staticky exchange left him with haunting questions. How could she not know who was there? A stranger? Looters?

He asked her about a weapon. Told her he'd be praying. Did she hear the worry in his tone? Sense his love for her in his voice?

God, please protect her. Rescue her even though I can't be there.

His thoughts leapfrogged over the events of the last thirty hours. His notifying Basalt Bay residents of the approaching storm. His search for Paisley. Violent winds. The window exploding. The glass impalement in his calf. His and Paisley's separation. Tonight, they were only twenty miles apart, but that distance seemed more like a hundred miles.

What if looters were in his hometown? Judah hated that a few lowlifes might take advantage of people in distress, invading homes, stealing, causing havoc. If that happened with Paisley there by herself—

His heart throbbed so hard it felt like it could burst out of his chest.

What if it was Craig? Hadn't the man driven Judah to the ER, then disappeared? What if his coworker—

No! He could not think the worst, or the terrorizing thoughts tumbling about like circus acrobats in his brain would drive him mad. He had to have faith, building up his confidence that God was working in their lives. Yet, Judah couldn't control every troubling imagination that pulsed through his mind over what might be happening. He should be there with his wife, his arms around her, protecting her. He should be the one fighting off an intruder. Not her.

His footsteps pounded the damp, uneven pavement, and his newly stitched calf caused an odd rhythm as he walked. Each step made him grimace, but he kept going, wouldn't stop.

A little while ago, he tried calling Paisley back with James Weston's—a neighbor who lived across the street from Paisley's father—phone. No answer. Went straight to voicemail. Useless. Frustrating.

As he plodded along, passing vehicles he recognized—the bakery delivery truck, Mia Till's sports car, another coworker's SUV—he begged God to save his wife, to protect her against evil, including looters, Craig, or Dad. Although, now that he knew the truth about Craig's past behavior with Paisley, he considered his father the lesser of the three evils. He even hoped it might be him coming to her aid. Not causing her grief the way he had last time.

Oh, God, be with my Paisley. Keep her safe.

What if she experienced another panic attack? Alone. Around some stranger. Judah walked faster. His leg burned with intense pain, so he slowed down. Kept praying. Waiting out the night. Questioning God's will. Then praying for more faith.

A war battled within him. Trust versus anxiety. Doubt versus faith. A double set of arch enemies. What-ifs resounded in his mind. What if Dad lured Paisley away with money again? What if Craig pressured her to do something against her will like he did before? What if it were strangers, looters, too numerous for her to fight off? What if they—

"No!" He would pray and believe that God was greater than his worst fears. Come morning light, he'd find a way back to Basalt Bay, even if he had to walk the whole way. With his limp? Yeah, right.

He trudged around a low spot in the pavement that was still flooded with water. He passed the entrance to the gym that had been built since he went to high school here. The toe of his shoe tripped over a surface crack. He caught himself, grimacing at the tug in his calf. If he couldn't take one lap around this parking lot without stumbling, without being in pain, how could he walk all the way to Basalt Bay, twenty miles away? He groaned.

The displaced residents were told they might have to stay here for a week, or longer, until the roads leading into town were fixed and utilities restored. Surely it wouldn't take that long. He had to find a way back. Someone would drive him. James

Weston. Or one of his coworkers. If none of his friends could help, he'd rent a car or hire a driver.

He gritted his teeth and kept trudging forward. He didn't care how late it got. Didn't care if anyone heard him calling out to God. "You tell us in Your Word to love our enemies." He glanced up at the dark sky. "The thought of an enemy hurting my wife is more than I can bear. Please, protect her. Help me too. I don't want this awful fear boiling in my spirit. I care for Paisley so much, and I know You love her too."

Inwardly he quoted Scriptures. *Even though I walk through the valley of the shadow*— Wait! No reciting verses about the Valley of the Shadow of Death. *I will sing of your strength, in the morning I will sing of your love; for you are my fortress, my refuge in times of trouble.* He quoted the verse from Psalms again. That was better. Comforting. *You are my refuge, God.*

He wanted to trust the Lord to be with Paisley, just like he believed for two of the three years she'd been away from him that God would bring her back. Finally, hallelujah, she returned. Then the mega-storm hit. His world turned upside down with his injury, her confession about Craig, and her refusal to get into that man's truck. Their separation—again. Now, this dreadful waiting and wondering. The doubting.

Lord, I'm sorry for my doubts. You are a good Father. With good plans for us.

"Judah?"

Mia? *Ugh.* He'd rather keep a football field's length between him and the flirtatious receptionist from work.

The click of her high heels crossing the pavement in an otherwise silent night preceded her. "There you are, Judah."

His name on her lips sounded soft, sultry. Made him want to run like Joseph ran from Potiphar's wife.

"What's wrong? I can see something is bothering you."

Her intruding on his quiet time bothered him. "It's nothing that I want to talk about. You should go back inside the gym."

"Has something happened?" Her voice sounded more caring instead of coy, this time. "Did you get bad news from Paisley?"

"I'm not discussing it." He was being abrupt, but someone might see them out here, alone at night, and misinterpret what they were seeing, draw the wrong conclusion. Basalt Bay's rumor mill was a force to be reckoned with, especially when it came to Paisley and him.

Mia wrapped her arms tightly around her middle. "It's cold out here. How can you stand it?" She shivered dramatically, her teeth chattering.

Was she fishing for him to find a way to help her get warm? Maybe offer her his coat? He wouldn't do anything that she might interpret as romantic. "I didn't notice. You should go back inside where it's warmer."

Not many hours ago, he put a gym's length between them. He'd wanted to reassure Paisley that he was doing the honorable thing as her husband, but he was also frustrated with Mia.

The receptionist didn't heed his advice about going back into the shelter. She stood in front of him with her shining doe eyes peering up at him. She might not mean to come across so flirtatiously, but she seemed schooled in the art. Her soft tone of voice, her being here with him in the middle of the night, felt suspicious.

"What have you been doing out here all this time?" She glanced over her shoulder as if checking to see if someone else might be out there too.

"Walking and praying. Waiting for morning."

"So, something is wrong. Are you okay? I'm here for you, Judah." She put both of her hands on his arm, gazing up at him.

He stepped back, disengaging her fingers from touching him.

"If you want to talk or need someone just to be with you . . ."

Her words put him on edge the way fingernails scraping across a chalkboard would.

"If you'll excuse me, I'm going to continue walking." He resumed his limping stride, hoping she'd take the hint and leave him alone.

Her high heels clicking behind him let him know she didn't. He stopped suddenly to speak to her again. She bumped into him.

"Oh, sorry." She giggled. Another scraping sound on that mental chalkboard.

"Why don't you head back inside? You've got to be freezing."

"You're sweet to be worried about me." Mia leaned into him, shivered, as if drawing from his warmth. "Judah, you must know that I care about you."

Whoa. "What do you mean?"

"You've got to know how I feel." She reached her hands toward his chest.

He backed up several steps. "I don't know what you're implying."

"We care for each other as friends, right?"

"Okay, yeah."

"Colleagues, and maybe more?" She grinned as if she expected him to agree.

Oh, good grief. "Friends and colleagues, yes. There's no 'more' to it. Return to the gym, Mia. And stay there." He hobbled away from her. Would have run if he could.

Her little confession meant her previous flirtations weren't just his imagination. Or Paisley's. That knowledge slammed into his chest like a rock. A warning.

Mia's heels clicked faster, closing the gap between them. "What's wrong with you, Judah? You can talk to me."

He didn't want to talk to her. He'd all but commanded her to go into the storm shelter, and she acted as if his words were an invitation for her to keep walking with him. Where was the disconnect? What else could he do? He trudged forward.

"Is something wrong with Paisley? Is she sick?"

"No."

"Injured?"

"Just leave it alone, will you? Leave me alone." His voice rose and he didn't try to hide his exasperation with her.

"I'm sorry about earlier when I touched your cot." She sighed. "I was confused. Getting mixed signals. You know?"

He stumbled over an uneven chunk of pavement. Came to a complete stop. "Mixed signals? Are you kidding me?"

"I thought you were interested in me. Really, I was flattered." She gave him a wide smile. "I knew you and Paisley weren't together anymore."

Her words were a dagger twisting in his gut. "You're wrong. Paisley and I are still married."

She squinted like she didn't believe him.

"When did I ever act as anything other than a friend and coworker to you?" He'd never flirted with her. Never would while he wore his wedding ring. That silver band was a constant reminder of his faithfulness to his wife.

"I just thought that you were handsome. Friendly. A nice guy. Sweet smile. Lonely, maybe."

Her giggle made him feel dirty. Like he really should run.

"I assumed you felt the same way about me." She splayed her fingers through her blond locks.

"Look. I'm a married man, Mia. I'm sorry you thought that I returned your feelings. You were wrong. I have no interest in you as a"—he didn't even know what to say—"as anything other than a coworker. If you can't see me as a friend, and only as a friend, we cannot even talk." He pivoted sharply and marched through the center of two rows of cars, limping toward the front door of the gymnasium. Once he got there, he counted vehicles to alleviate his annoyance with her.

Finally, the sound of her heels alerted him to her presence. *Twenty-nine. Thirty. Thirty-one.*

"If you ever change your mind, or, you know, things don't work out between you and Paisley"—she drew in a breath—"I really like you, Judah."

"Don't ever say that to me again."

"But—"

"Go inside." He yanked open the front door. How could she think he cared for her in that way?

"I'll always be here for you, Judah Grant." As if she didn't hear one word of his denial, her fingers trailed along his hand on the door before she slipped inside the building.

He couldn't pull back his hand fast enough. He plodded around the parking lot again, working off his frustration. How many more minutes until daylight? How many more laps around this parking lot until he could find a way back to Basalt Bay and the one woman he couldn't bear to be away from any longer?

Three

"You know how I know where you been hiding, Little Red Riding Hood?" Craig kicked the pantry door.

Water swirled near Paisley's feet. *Little Red Riding Hood?* Did that mean he thought he was the Big Bad Wolf? Her heart pounded like a bass drum beneath her breastbone. Her breathing became tight and shallow.

Don't panic. You're going to be okay.

Would she be okay? How long did Craig know her hiding place? Was he toying with her fear? Manipulating her? Her hands clenched the protective items a little tighter. She needed something to focus on, something to ground her. She concentrated on the cool glass held in her sweaty palm, the curve of the round jar against her fingers.

"Here's a fact for you"—he snorted—"our extinguished mayor knows everything." He didn't correct his improper English. "He's watching you. Big Bad Daddy-in-law *shees* you."

Craig was out of his mind, on alcohol or drugs. How could

Edward know anything about her, let alone see where she was hiding? Yet, standing here in the dark with shards of light criss-crossing her clothing, shivers raced over her skin. Even if her father-in-law knew something about her, why would he inform Craig? The two were hardly buddies.

Craig rammed into the door. If he kept doing that, he'd dislodge the old hinges from the frame. She wouldn't be able to hold the door against his weight.

"Judah's with Mia Till." He belched. "Can't call out to him for help. Mayor Grant, n-neither."

Like she would ask Edward for anything. She could take care of herself. And Judah wasn't with Mia. He called Paisley earlier to inform her that he moved away from the wanton flirt. She trusted him more than she trusted anything Craig said. Besides, Judah was praying for her right this minute. Hadn't he said he'd keep praying until she called him back?

She heard a strange noise. Heavy breathing. Or snoring. *Wait.* Did Craig fall asleep standing up? Probably faking. Yet, for several minutes she listened to his deep, nasally inhaling and exhaling. If he had conked out leaning against the door, this was her chance to escape. But he blocked the exit.

Earlier, when Judah's cell phone light still worked, she noticed the wooden slats nailed to the outside of the small window frame. Could she kick them out and slip through? She didn't have a hammer. And if she made too much noise, Craig would hear it.

Feeling more confident that he might actually be asleep, she stepped away from the door. She crept to the shelves in the dark, then set down the wooden boards. With the Mason jar still secure in her right hand, she shuffled to the window, keeping water movement to a minimum. With her left palm, she reached into the window area until her hand brushed against rough wood. Applying pressure to the boards, she tested them. One edge felt loose. She set the jar by her feet, close enough to grab quickly. She shoved her shoulder against the wood. Nothing gave. She pushed again, clenching her teeth.

A rustling came from the other side of the door. *Oh, no.*

She whirled around, flailing her hand near the floor, searching for the jar. *Where is it?* Her fingers clutched the top just as the door burst open. Blinding light from Craig's flashlight blasted her. She stood and pulled the jar back over her shoulder, her heart pounding in her ears. If he took one step closer, she'd let him have it. Then she'd grab the other jars and hurl those at him like mud balls.

"*Shurprishe!*" He stumbled forward. "About time you and I had a little dish—" He paused as if to think. "Talk." He swung the flashlight beam back and forth in the small space. "What d'ya say, Paisley-bug?"

How did he know her dad's pet name for her? She hated hearing the endearment on the skunk's lips. She glowered at him even though she couldn't see his face in the bright light.

"You gonna throw that or what?" The light bobbed toward the jar, then back at Paisley's face.

"I will if you don't back up." A twist of her wrist, that's all it would take, and he'd have a lump on his head the size of Mt. Hood.

"I don't mean any harm."

Right. All this fear churning in her middle that he'd caused, and he didn't mean any harm?

He wobbled as if he might fall over, the light bobbing with his drunken movements. "I mean, I didn't come here to hurt you. Or cause you any trouble." The last phrase sounded like a whimper.

She didn't, wouldn't, believe anything he said.

The flashlight's glow pulsed toward her makeshift bunk. "You been *shleepin'* here?"

She wasn't going to talk with him about sleeping arrangements. Should she throw the jar then try to get past him?

"Don't look at me like that. I'm not a *monshter*." For a second, the light flashed on his face. His goofy smile was an oxymoron to the man she knew him to be. "I'm a nice guy."

"Stay back."

"I'm not the enemy." He lifted his other hand, palm out. He filled the narrow doorway. No escape. "Aren't you gonna ask why I came here?"

She knew what men like him were after. Cad. Rattlesnake.

"Don't believe me? I'll show you. You can go to *shleep*." His hand lowered to the doorknob. "*Notgonnado* anything you don't want me to do. Never would."

He had a short memory. Unless he meant "never again."

Slowly, the door closed until total darkness surrounded her. A breath caught in her throat.

Was he really going to leave her alone? Then why did he sneak through the house after dark like a criminal returning to the scene of a crime to finish the job? Maybe he was stalking her just to make her fearful. Why do all of this and then walk away?

The sound of his footsteps got quieter, more distant.

She blew out her breath but kept her arm raised, the jar ready. Terrorized, yet conflicted, she shuffled through the few inches of water, stopping at the closed door. She lowered the jar slowly, then leaned against the wood as before, listening.

Somewhere out there, he crooned another country tune, slurring the words. He belched. Guffawed. *Disgusting man.* Cupboard doors slammed. Several thuds made her think he might be throwing wood chunks to the floor, probably off the washer and dryer, or the kitchen counter—places she contemplated sleeping earlier.

"G'night, *Paishley*. We have more in common than you think. *Shweet* dreams."

Yeah, right. She wouldn't close her eyes tonight. And they had nothing in common. She lowered the jar to her side. What now? Stand here until morning?

How could Craig even go to sleep? He had to be soaking wet. Freezing. Although, the alcohol he must have consumed might keep him warm, for now. When that wore off, what then?

This whole go-to-sleep routine might be a subterfuge. Or, if he was wasted, he might sleep soundly. React slowly.

A few minutes later, the sound of throaty snoring reached her.

Was this her chance to escape?

Heart galloping beneath her ribs, she clung to the Mason jar. With her other hand, she reached out into the dark and grabbed hold of the comforter she used earlier. She'd need it to survive the cold night. In cautious movements, she pulled up on the door handle and inched it open. She froze. Waited a few seconds. Craig still snored. If he was faking, he was a good faker. If he made an aggressive move, she'd stick to her previous plan of throwing the jar at him.

The house was pitch dark as she shuffled through standing liquid, hoping she wouldn't bump into any floating objects. Even though she couldn't see, she knew the way. How many times had she crept into the kitchen late at night to grab a snack when she was young? Although, there'd never been seawater on the floor before.

She heard water rustling around her boots, felt the wind blowing through the window. Craig's rhythmic snoring propelled her forward.

Being careful not to fall over the branches of the apple tree that crashed through the window during the storm, she half crawled, half lunged through the gaping hole, trying to soften her landing on the porch.

"*Paishley?*" A loud thud. A groan. Had he fallen off the counter? She didn't wait to find out.

She slid off the porch, into the darkness beside Judah's white pickup. She sneaked across her dad's watery front lawn. Glancing back once, she didn't see any movement on the porch, or in the window. Carefully, she waded across the street, pausing only to crawl over a downed tree.

Since it was too dark to go far, she strode across James Weston's yard, stepping around debris and the travel trailer laying on its side. Then she crept up onto his porch, ducked down, and waited tensely for several minutes that felt like an hour. Finally, when Craig didn't follow her, and she didn't hear any suspicious sounds coming from the other side of the street, she sighed.

Thank You, God.

She shuffled over to the bench that leaned against the front of James's house, sat down, and wrapped the comforter around her shoulders. Her insides shook. Her teeth chattered.

But she was safe, for now.

Four

After stumbling in the dark too many times, Judah trudged inside the gym, plopped down on the floor in the corner where he was before, and fell asleep sitting up. Although he'd determined to keep his all-night vigil, the spiritual and emotional wrestling matches, and the aching in his calf, took their toll.

Now, with his forehead propped against his folded arms, which were braced against his bent knees, he awoke to an awful neck kink. He leaned back against the wall, wincing as he stretched out his leg, and turned his neck slowly back and forth. He sighed, and the murmur of early risers huddled around the coffee table reached him.

"How long can they force us to stay here?"

"As long as they want."

"I think it's a conspiracy to keep us away from our homes."

"Maybe they want looters to get our stuff!"

"I'm finding a way back today."

That idea snagged Judah's interest. He stood, moving in increments, feeling the effects of not only having slept on the floor, but having walked around the parking lot too many times on his injured leg last night. Maybe that had been a mistake. But he couldn't regret the time he spent praying for Paisley. For their marriage. He glanced at his watch, clicked the digital display. Six a.m. Time for coffee.

And another pain pill. But if he took one, he might be too groggy to be of much good. He wanted to stay alert, hoping for a chance to return to his wife.

How was Paisley doing this morning? What was she doing? His thoughts raced to prayer. *Lord, be with her, keep her safe.* How many times would he pray those words before he saw her again? What if something bad happened to her last night? A rush of worry hit him. But he reminded himself that trusting in God's faithfulness was the only way he could stay in the right frame of mind. Yet he kept struggling with that. *Lord, help me. Bless Paisley. Keep her safe. Please, let me find a way to get back to her today.*

He trudged toward the table loaded down with two large coffeepots, a dozen stacks of Styrofoam cups, various creamers, and a bowl full of sugar packets. He gave the platters piled high with donuts a once-over. Another unhealthy breakfast. His stomach roiled as he imagined the grease-laden pastry. Even so, he grabbed an apple fritter and downed it in four bites. The first chance he got to eat a real meal he'd take it.

He filled a disposable cup with steaming coffee. Forget creamer. He needed the pungent bite of full-strength caffeine.

James Weston stepped up beside him and reached for a cup. "Morning." His white hair stuck up in random tufts. His face appeared even more wrinkled than yesterday. Didn't look like he slept well last night, either.

Judah swallowed a gulp of the strong brew. "Good morning. Thanks for letting me use your phone last night. I appreciate it."

"No problem." The older man sipped his drink. "Everything turn out okay?"

"Not sure." Judah lifted his cup to his lips, wishing he had more information. "You didn't get any calls from Paisley, did you?"

"Nope."

Judah doubted the cell he gave her had battery power left, anyhow. If only he made different choices yesterday. Not going to the ER with Craig. Staying with Paisley. Too late for regrets. He needed to face facts and act quickly. Take every opportunity. "Oh, uh, James."

"Yes?" The man lifted his shaggy uneven eyebrows.

"Any chance you could drive me as close as you could get to South Road?"

"You heard the police report." James's mouth turned downward. "No one can go back 'til the road's fixed. Sorry excuse, if you ask me. Nothing to be done about it, though."

"I thought if I could get near enough, I'd hike overland across the dunes, then follow the beach. The Guardsmen would be none the wiser." Judah didn't want to cause trouble for James, but his wife's safety was more important to him than following the local emergency rules and regulations.

"Highway's impassable, they say."

"Impassable?"

"Mudslides are the topic of the morning." James nodded in the direction of a group of men huddled near the entryway, coffee cups in hand. "All of us are in the same boat, chomping at the bit to get home." He made a tsk-tsk sound. "Hate this waiting." He shuffled over to the group.

Judah had to find someone willing to drive him to the dunes. He grabbed a maple bar and stuffed a couple of bites in his mouth. The frosting soured in his stomach. Or maybe his reaction had more to do with his anxiety level. If he had his truck, returning to Basalt Bay wouldn't be a problem. He'd park south of town and hike in, the way he explained to James. Who else could he ask for a lift?

A couple of coworkers approached the coffee table. As soon as they made their selections, Judah stepped forward and questioned them about the possibility of catching a ride. Both said they wouldn't be going back to Basalt until the evacuation ended. A couple of other guys seemed interested in off-roading. However, none were willing to risk getting in trouble with the law. Apparently, Deputy Brian wielded a long arm of fear in the community.

Judah understood people's reluctance to get involved. They'd fled from a second, unprecedented hurricane strike on the western seaboard. Were temporarily outcast. At the mercy of strangers' kindnesses. Unsettled over what damages may have happened to their houses and businesses. But where did that leave him? He couldn't hike twenty miles. Not with his injury. Why couldn't things work out easier? He rubbed his free hand over his whiskered chin and groaned. Then downed his cool coffee.

"Something wrong?" Mia's unexpected voice so near him made the hair stand up on the back of his neck. "Anything I can do to help?"

"Uh, no." He automatically stepped away from her. Why did she think something was wrong? Was she eavesdropping on their conversation? "Thanks, but there's nothing you can do."

She winked. "You'd be surprised how resourceful I can be."

Ugh. Her early morning flirtation made him want to growl out a rebuke. Would she never stop?

"Need a lift somewhere?" She reached for a cup. "Because if you wanted me to drive you somewhere, I would."

You've got to be kidding me. The only person willing to help him get back to town was Mia? Why would she even offer after what he said to her last night? After he rebuffed her flirtations. Maybe she felt badly. Or was this just another ploy?

"You want to go back to Basalt, right?"

"I do."

"Well, then." She filled her cup with dark coffee. Smelled it, grimaced. "I'm your girl Friday." She giggled as she poured in creamer, then more creamer, stirring rapidly with a plastic stick.

How would he explain this twist in his plans to Paisley? And what if Maggie Thomas, Basalt Bay's gossip queen, found out that Mia called herself his "girl Friday?" He'd be the talk of the town. Accepting Mia's offer would solve his immediate problem but might create a whole slew of other ones.

He thought of an excuse. "Your car might not be able to get back to Basalt Bay."

"Why not?"

"It sits low. Heavy rainfall during and after the hurricane caused mudslides." A blessing in disguise? He'd ask to use her phone to call about a car rental, but he knew her cell was out of battery power.

"What else am I going to do today? Sit around here doing nothing?" She shook her long blond hair off her shoulders. "They'll probably have the roads cleared by the time we get up there, anyway, don't you think?"

"Hard to say."

"The Guardsmen might not let you through, but I'll drive you as far as I can." She smiled. "I can talk my way out of most anything if we get stopped."

He didn't doubt that.

"Your call." She seemed to be trying to help, and not acting overly friendly. Maybe she took his words to heart last night. "I'll keep my hands to myself. Promise." She winked.

Inwardly, he groaned. How could he even consider taking her up on her offer?

"I'm going to finish this coffee, then I'll meet you at my car." Her gaze danced toward the front of the gym. "A drive will be a perfect way to spend a few hours, don't you think?"

"Oh, sure." If he could endure the twenty miles with her. Hopefully, he wouldn't regret it.

"Good." She grinned and pumped the air with her fist.

Now, why was she so enthusiastic about driving him north? Maybe he should tell her he was having second thoughts. Third thoughts. But he wanted to get back to Paisley as soon as possible.

He strode to the restroom to wash up. When he returned, Mia stood by the door, her fingers rapidly tapping the screen of her zebra-striped phone. Last night she got angry with him when he used up the remaining battery power. Had she found a way to recharge her phone?

"Ready?" Mia dropped the device into her purse. "I'm heading out." She curled her index finger for him to follow.

Like a puppy on a leash, Judah trailed behind her through the rain. Warnings shrieked through his brain—*Walk away. She's untrustworthy. Wait for someone else.* Yet, he didn't listen. This was an opportunity to get back to Paisley quickly. Even if he rented a car, the process would take time. Time he could be spending back in Basalt Bay with his wife.

In a second the sports car engine purred to life. He opened the passenger door and climbed in. When he shut it, the seatbelt automatically locked into place. The tug against his chest reminded him of a dungeon door closing, keeping him a prisoner. *Lord, help.*

Twenty miles, that's all. He'd direct their dialogue to work-related topics. Or to the weather. Maybe listen to music.

But as the car zoomed out of the parking lot, the windshield wipers going fast, Mia kept up a steady drone of conversation, filling in the awkward silence with prattle and giggles. "I can't believe how Hurricane Blaine destroyed the area. Can you? How could you stay in Basalt during such high winds? It's a good thing that more than your leg wasn't hurt." She nudged his arm.

He pulled his elbow in toward his side.

"I would have been scared out of my wits. Out of my mind. Not you. Oh, Judah, you're too good, too kind, to leave poor Paisley behind. How sweet and admirable of you. You're my kind of hero." She patted his wrist—reached over the center console to do so—then returned her palm to the steering wheel. "Sorry. I forgot." Her playful expression didn't contain any remorse.

His discomfort increased. "I'm not a hero. I wanted to be with Paisley during the storm. Still want to be with her. She's my wife." He placed his left hand with the silver wedding ring on his finger on top of his other hand, in an obvious position where she might notice.

"Oh, right." She rolled her eyes. "Your wife." She muttered something about an absentee spouse not being good wife material.

Annoying woman. At least she stayed quiet for a couple of miles. In a few minutes, he'd tell her where to drop him off, maybe a half mile before the cutoff into the bay. He'd hike through the brush, make his way over the dunes, and finally get to see Paisley. A tug in his calf reminded him that walking over the mountainous sand piles wouldn't be an easy task. Still, he'd do whatever it took to be with her before nightfall.

"You okay?" Mia must have seen his grimace.

"Mmhmm." Shifting, he adjusted his legs in the small confines of the front seat area. He'd much rather be riding in his truck than in this knee-cruncher. But each mile brought him closer to the woman he loved. Soon their separation would be over. *Thank You, God.*

"Those stitches must hurt something fierce." Mia reached over as if to pat his thigh.

He lifted his hand, intercepting her fingers before she could touch his leg. He glared at her.

"Habit." She made a pouty face.

"Just stop, will you?" Habit? *Come on.* Hadn't he told her that he didn't reciprocate her feelings? Why did she keep pushing herself on him?

"Okay, okay. Don't bite my head off."

He probably was testy after his short sleep, responding sharper than he would have on the job. But they weren't at work. And if she treated him romantically at C-MER, he would tell her to stop, also. Now that he knew how she felt about him, he wouldn't tolerate her flirtations even a little.

He had never led her on, never meant to. Although, he was an idiot for not noticing her interest sooner.

"Uh-oh." Her tone deepened.

"What?" He'd been staring out the side window.

"Trouble ahead." She muttered an unladylike word.

He squinted through the rain-splattered windshield. Just before the next curve in the road, a traffic control flagger held up a stop sign, waved it. "That doesn't look good."

"What now?" Mia brought her car to a slow stop.

The fluorescent-yellow vest the worker had on nearly glowed over his dark green raincoat. He approached Mia's side of the vehicle.

She lowered the window and gave him her typical wide smile. "Hi, there. Aren't you cute in that flashy gear?" She giggled.

Oh, brother.

"What's happening up ahead?"

"Washout. You can't go through. No one can pass until repairs are finished." The flagger nodded in a northerly direction. "Could be days."

"You're kidding, right?" A total closure of Highway 101? Judah couldn't believe it. Was the whole universe against him and Paisley getting back together? Of him coming to her rescue.

"Pavement's busted up badly too." The guy pointed toward the west. "Not to mention, another storm's on its way."

Judah groaned. Just what the area didn't need. More rain. More flooding.

"Thanks for the info." Mia passed the flagger something and laughed. What did she give him? A business card? To a stranger?

"Thanks." The guy stuffed the card in his raincoat pocket and grinned.

She closed the window. Waved at him for an awkward amount of time. "What should we do now?"

Judah would have commented on her unscrupulous behavior, but he already felt so frazzled, he just shook his head. "I don't know." He pinched the bridge of his nose. This morning's donuts glugged in his stomach.

Lord, some wisdom would be greatly appreciated.

One thing after another had gone wrong, barely giving him time to catch his breath. With no way of contacting Paisley and explaining the delays, what was he supposed to do? What would she think if he didn't come back today? A horrible sensation of being a failure as a husband, again, scraped through his insides. He'd determined to put her needs before his own, to be there for her in ways that he hadn't been before she left him, but how could he do those things when he couldn't even make his way back to her?

Mia did an abrupt U-turn. "Sorry it didn't work out." She touched the screen on the front console. Classical music filtered into the air. "I have an idea. Let's badmouth all the problems the hurricane has caused."

What good would that do?

"Stupid storm. Ruined everything. Left us homeless. Terrible food at the shelter. And the coffee? Don't even get me started. A national disaster right there!"

She was acting lighthearted, obviously trying to cheer him up. Instead, his thoughts raced down a dark avenue. *Paisley. Craig. Looters. Paisley. Dad. Craig.* Was his wife okay? Safe? How could he get to her despite the road closure? Even a rental car wouldn't help him now.

He groaned. Why had so many bad things happened?

A verse squeezed into the middle of his frustrations. *Trust in the Lord with all your heart and lean not on your own understanding.* He appreciated the reminder. He still wanted to trust God and believe for the best. *Have faith, Grant.* He sighed.

But if Craig or someone else was causing trouble for Paisley, Judah had to do everything in his power to get there. He couldn't just return to Florence and sit around in the storm shelter, eating donuts and drinking bitter coffee.

Lord, I promised Paisley I'd come back this morning. I want to keep that promise.

"Would you be interested in a homestyle breakfast? We could stop at a diner on the way back." Mia glanced at him without her usual frivolous gleam. "A real meal would help you feel better."

He had told himself he'd jump at the chance for a hot meal, but he didn't want to put himself in a compromising situation. Especially one where someone from Basalt Bay might see him with Mia and spread gossip. And he wasn't in the mood for chatting just to fill the time. His sigh came out more like a rumble.

"That does it." Mia smacked the steering wheel with her palm. "We're getting some honest-to-goodness food in you. Then the world won't seem like such a horrible place."

He didn't know about that, but he was hungry. After he ate something, he had to come up with a new plan for getting back home.

Five

Paisley opened her eyelids and squinted against the early morning light streaking across the sky. Where was she? She blinked a few times. Oh, right. Last night, she hid in the pantry. Escaped from Craig. Slept on James Weston's porch. Where was Craig now? She braced her right elbow against the wooden bench and peered over the railing, surveying Dad's house and yard that rested in shadows across the street. No sign of the intruder, other than his monster truck parked crookedly in the front yard. He must be either sleeping off his hangover or wandering the neighborhood looking for her.

She ducked back down. Had to stay hidden.

She ran her hands over her eyes, down her cheeks. Her nose felt frozen. Her muscles were stiff from her neck to her hips. But she was alive. Cold, but alive.

Would Judah make it back this morning? Or later in the day? How could she avoid his troublesome coworker until he arrived?

One thing was for certain, staying here on this porch in broad daylight wasn't an option. If she could figure out how to get inside James's house, she'd take care of her immediate needs. Use the facilities. Scrounge for food and water. But the windows were boarded up; the door had to be locked.

Too bad Dad didn't take similar precautions with his house. If he had, Judah wouldn't have gotten injured. Craig wouldn't have broken into the house. And she wouldn't have gone through those hours of terror alone.

But Judah *did* get hurt. Craig *did* invade her space. She *was* alone. Running for her life. Or hiding for her life. Even if Craig said he wouldn't hurt her, she doubted his intentions, his integrity.

If he was still sleeping, now was her chance to put distance between them. She had to find somewhere safe to stay until Judah returned. She might be able to hide inside her sister's art gallery. Or break into City Hall. But in this small town, if Craig was determined to find her, he probably would, right?

Not if she could help it!

She wadded up the blanket and shoved it to the end of the bench. Then, standing but hunched over, her nose barely above the handrail, she crept across the porch. She dashed down the steps, then waded over to a bushy tree in James's yard and hid behind it.

Everything seemed quiet. Too quiet, perhaps.

She shuffled through the water, her boots making a swishing sound that seemed exaggerated in the otherwise silent neighborhood. She noticed a watermark on the side of the next house that showed the water level had gone down a couple of inches since yesterday. A relief. But how long would it take for the receding water to make its way out to sea?

When she heard an odd sound, she dodged behind another tree. Was Craig following her? She peered around the trunk. A multi-colored beachball bobbed across the surface of the flooded street. It scraped against a dead-looking bush, skipped over some sticks and floating debris. She blew out a long breath and trudged forward, moving cautiously in the slightly downhill section where the frothy water reached her knees.

The hurricane's destructive force had affected most of the houses and yards in the neighborhood. Downed trees, outdoor furniture, tires, toys, trash, and shingles peppered lawns, driveways, and flooded streets. A canoe rested cockeyed on one porch. A motorcycle lay on its side on top of a flipped skiff. Porches were ripped off and separated from houses. Some sections of roofs were on the ground. A picnic table leaned through a broken window.

Seeing the damage to her childhood neighborhood tugged on Paisley's heart, made her feel sad for the people who would soon be coming home to the terrible mess and all the hardships. It also reminded her of the struggles in her own life. The losses that had squeezed the joy right out of her, and a few times even stole the breath from her body. This town needed a restoration. A healing. But so did she.

As her legs trudged through the water, heading toward town, the unnerving silence started to get to her. The sense of being the only person left on the planet was like an oppressive weight pushing down on her, making her more nervous with each step. Of course, Craig was in the ghost town, also, but that was far from comforting.

She kept her gaze on the water in front of her lest she trip over something unseen. The next time she glanced up, she saw a power pole leaning over at an odd angle, its wires dangling precariously close to the surface of the water. For a second, she froze. Judah warned her to watch out for downed power lines. She'd have to find a safer route.

Veering away from the danger, she shuffled to the curb, then stepped up using the lower edge of her boot to guide her footing so she didn't trip in the water. She skirted around a few houses, cutting across backyards and alleys, and ended up behind City Hall. Her legs ached from the effort of walking against the flow of seawater, and she hadn't even gone that far.

Compared to the other buildings in town, City Hall appeared to be in perfect condition. Boards tidily covered the windows and front door. Some trash floated in the parking lot, but nothing appeared broken or smashed in around the structure.

Should she try to get inside? There might be supplies. Water. Even, food. The mayor was still up at his house on the cliff, right? She didn't want him to catch her prying off a board from one of his precious windows. Although, she was still his daughter-in-law. He might understand her need to break in to find food.

She groaned. *What am I thinking?* If she caused any damage here, Mayor Grant would despise her even more. Just thinking of the man who had never approved of her caused her blood pressure to rise. And the things Edward said in the past about her not being good enough for his son, about her not being a good mother to her unborn daughter, and the way he paid her to leave Judah three years ago, burned in her thoughts. Each of those offenses still had the power to wound her heart and to create a greater schism between her and Judah. No, she didn't want anything to do with the horrible man or his place of business.

She couldn't get away from City Hall fast enough, although the floodwaters impeded her progress. Her boots felt like fifty-pound weights as she shuffled through the current, searching for someplace to get out of the muddy water.

On both sides of the city street, she observed more damages. Awnings dangled by threads. Signs were busted. Roofs gone. A sailboat had crashed into the front of Bert's Fish Shack, its stern the only part remaining outside. How would the quirky, but sometimes temperamental, owner react to that?

Across from her, the roof from Nautical Sal's Souvenirs lay broken and piled up like a beaver's dam. The heavy rains had surely ruined everything in his shop. Such a shame. She imagined Sal, one of the kindest, jolliest business owners in Basalt, stepping out of his store when she was a kid to tell her about an agate he found in a tidal pool. Would he be able to put his business back together after all this destruction?

Suddenly, she realized she'd been standing out in the open for too long. She was supposed to be hunting for a hiding place. Glancing over her shoulder, she perused the flooded street behind her. Didn't see anyone. She peered at the doorway of Paige's art gallery where she ducked under the awning before the hurricane hit. Beyond a pile of debris, the door appeared to be open, perhaps caved in. She wouldn't even have to break in. She hurried toward it.

What if Craig was in the gallery? Left the door open. She stopped. Apprehension twisted knots in her middle, but she couldn't remain out in the open on the street like this. And there might be food inside her sister's building. It had been a coffee shop, too, right? Besides, Craig was probably still back at her dad's, sleeping off his stupor.

Taking a deep breath, she tentatively entered the building. She paused until her eyes adjusted to the darker room, listening. She didn't hear anything other than the roar of the surf coming from beyond a glassless window. Fortunately, the room had an open layout, not lending itself to corners and easy hiding places.

A cone of light coming through the back of the building drew her forward. Uh-oh. A chunk of the roof was gone. She saw clouds through the hole. Several shingles dropped down and clattered to the floor, barely missing her. She leaped back. Was the building unstable? Was she safe here?

She strode away from the corner, keeping her distance from it. She waded through a couple of inches of water on the floor to reach the open window. The wind coming off the ocean blew hard against her, but she welcomed the powerful rush of sea air against her cheeks and hair. She breathed in deeply of the tangy, musty aroma. Sighed. Below her, gray turbulent waves charged over the sand, crashing against pilings, sending sea spray bursting into the air.

After the next wave abated, she studied the shoreline. Sandbags that C-MER employees and residents had piled up in the last minutes before the storm were torn up and scattered by the waves. Too bad those didn't hold.

Leaning farther out the window, her hands against the lower frame, she perused the parking lot on the far side of the beach where she'd left her purple Accord. It was gone! Had the sea swallowed it up during the storm surge? What else could have happened to it? The loss—yet, another loss—gripped her emotionally. Sure, it was only a car. But it seemed like more, like it had been a protective friend, her only friend, on her long journey home. She sighed.

Her stomach growled, reminding her that she needed to find food. Turning from the window, she crossed the room toward the coffee bar. Behind the counter, she yanked open several cupboard doors. Dishes. Serving utensils. Coffee supplies. She pulled open a couple of drawers. Snacks! She'd never been so happy to see packaged food. Breakfast bars. Granola bars. Cookies. She tore the wrapping off one, stuffing the contents into her mouth without checking the flavor. Chocolate mocha. *Delicious.* The next one was vanilla. *Mmm.* She tore into another package. Banana cream pie. She would have eaten them even if they tasted like cardboard, but this was much better. She found water bottles, opened one, and guzzled it.

Hunger and thirst abated, she peeked inside a narrow cabinet that resembled a locker and found several articles of clothing hanging on hooks. She grabbed a sweatshirt. Paige's? She slipped out of Dad's damp flannel shirt, tossed it on the counter, then tugged on the sweatshirt. Next, she fingered a long blue artist's shirt. She put that on over the sweatshirt—anything to help her stay warm. Finding pants would have been fantastic but wishful thinking in a place like this.

She felt around on the shelf above the hooks. Touching some fabric, she pulled it down. A kid-sized blanket? Maybe an employee of Paige's had a child. Paisley draped the square around her shoulders like a shawl. Sighed.

Now, she needed to find a hiding place in case Craig showed up. She stepped over chunks of wood and shells and piles of kelp as she walked the perimeter of the room. She opened a door and found a small bathroom with a lock on the doorknob. Perfect.

She came full circle, ending up at the window. She took in the spectacular view of the beach all the way to *Peter's Land*, her childhood name for the peninsula she'd dubbed after her brother. Seeing several gaping holes where giant boulders used to sit, she nearly cried at the changes to the landscape. For decades, the rocky barrier protected the town from fierce storms. Unfortunately, Addy and Blaine, nearly back-to-back hurricanes, had taken their toll on the city's fortress. The rest of the peninsula must be in Davy Jones's Locker, the resting place for sunken ships in some of her favorite pirate stories when she was a kid.

Part of her wanted to hike right out to the edge of the rocky outcropping, to sit on the point with sea spray dancing and exploding about her, to forget the difficulties and her fears of the last few days, but if Craig came skulking around, he'd see her. No, this gallery was the safest place, as long as she stayed away from the hole in the ceiling. She had food and water. A bathroom. She'd wait here until Judah arrived.

Or else, Craig found her.

Please, hurry, Judah.

Six

Judah stood in a line at an outdoor tent the National Guard and FEMA had set up for displaced residents to discuss problems and ask questions. Some folks ahead of him were complaining about a lack of food supplies. Others demanded to know when they could return home. A few even accused the Guardsmen of purposefully keeping them from their properties.

As an emergency worker himself, he felt sorry for the two uniformed men in the tent who were probably tired of the repeated questions, the demands for them to speed up the process, and having to deal with the frustrated evacuees in the long line. Judah also agreed with some of the disgruntled people. The authorities should do more to help, and yes, speed up the process. Wasn't that why he stood in line? Hoping someone would have mercy on his situation and help him get back to his wife? He heard the frustration building in the voices around him, and he doubted anyone in charge would have compassion on him, either. How could they assist him and deny others?

"Excuse me. Excuse me." Was that Mia again?

Judah turned to find her pushing past several people in line. She clutched two cups of coffee. Was one of those for him? If so, his annoyance at finding her still following him lessened a little.

"Sorry." She laughed and smiled as she squeezed past folks in line. Her grin seemed to disarm the grumpiest among them.

"No worries." "Come on by." "That's all right," some called out.

She stopped beside him. "Here you go." She handed him a to-go cup with a lid on it. "Vanilla latte, just how you like it."

"Uh, thanks." How did she know his coffee preference? He never talked about it with her. And they didn't have any specialty coffees at work. As soon as he sipped the brew, he closed his eyes. Sighed. He'd missed this.

"Have a plan?" Mia bumped his arm with her elbow. "Are you going to beg someone with a tank to get you around the closed road and into Basalt? Good luck with that."

"No plan. But I have to try something." He took another swig of the sweetened drink. "Can't sit around twiddling my thumbs."

"Well, you could." She chuckled. "I'm sure Paisley understands that you're injured."

Maybe. What he didn't understand was why Mia was here. They ate big breakfasts at a packed-out diner. Said goodbyes. She left to go shopping. "You don't have to wait here. Drive back to the shelter. Shop, whatever. I'll catch a ride with someone. Or walk." Besides, if a ride north didn't materialize, he wanted to check out a jewelry store, alone.

"No worries." She kept in step with him. "Want to take a drive after you're finished here?"

"A drive?" He wasn't leaving town other than to head to Basalt Bay.

"Maybe to Newport. Coos Bay." She shrugged.

"Why would I want to go farther south, farther away from my wife?"

Mia didn't meet his gaze. "Any place is better than waiting around the shelter. Besides"—she grinned—"I need a shopping trip." She slid her free hand down her slacks. At least she wasn't wearing that mini-skirt getup she wore during the storm. "I need warmer things. Jeans and a sweater."

He wasn't going anywhere else with her. "You should go do that. Thanks for trying to help me get home." No reason he couldn't be civil. They'd enjoyed a decent conversation about workplace policies over eggs and pancakes. Although, he noticed a few raised eyebrows from folks he recognized.

"No problem. I'd do anything for you, Judah. Help in any way I can." She sipped her coffee, her gaze dancing toward him.

Not liking her easy transition into flirty behavior, he changed the topic. "Have you spoken with Craig lately?"

"What? Oh, you mean, since the hurricane?" She turned, waved at a guy.

"Have you?" He shuffled forward in the line.

"I spoke with him yesterday." She stepped forward too. "He called to see how you were doing."

"When?"

"Beats me."

He could tell her to check her phone for details, but they weren't working. He didn't have authority to push for answers. However, the topic reminded him of another question that had been bothering him. "What about my father?" He kept his voice quiet so others in line wouldn't hear. She didn't know Dad personally, did she?

Her smile disappeared. "What about him?"

"Did you call him yesterday, too?"

She coughed. "Look, you were injured. Of course, I called him. What's the big deal?"

"Stay out of my family stuff. And stay away from my dad. I mean it." He gave her a stern glare. His father could probably be swayed by a younger woman's laughter and attention. Recently, Mia had said some things about the mayor that sounded suspicious. Things that made Judah question his dad's faithfulness to his mom. But it was probably nothing. Mia was just a flirtatious person.

For a few minutes, she acted hyper-focused on her drink. Each time Judah took a step forward, she did too. She didn't take a hint very well.

Judah was third in line now, and he recognized the man at the head of the group.

Brad Keifer, a local fisherman, gesticulated furiously. "I need to get back to my house tonight. How can we make that happen without a bunch of red tape garbage?"

"That won't be possible." The officer's voice sounded tense. Weary, most likely. "No one, and I repeat, no one is returning to Basalt Bay for a few more days, possibly a week." The guy behind the desk wore a crew cut and appeared to be in his mid-forties. His stiff upper lip and squinting eyes declared he wouldn't budge from his position. "Our men have the road barricaded. Anyone caught crossing the divide will face stiff penalties. The roads must be repaired for public safety. Utilities have to be restored."

"Oh, come on! That's the same malarkey we've been told for two days." Brad removed his rainhat, dashed his fingers through his dirty-blond hair, then slapped his hat back on. "I have to get my gear. Head out to sea. I've wasted enough time with this Blaine mess."

"That's unfortunate for you. Nevertheless, you'll have to wait patiently like all the others." The man in uniform gave him a brisk nod. "If that's all, sir—"

"No, that's not all." Brad punched the air with his index finger. "I've stood in this stupid line for over an hour. I demand answers!"

"Hothead." Mia smirked.

Judah felt empathy for Brad's exasperation. He wanted answers too.

"I've given you the only response possible." The man in green apparel crossed his arms. "Now, if you'll step aside, I'll talk to the next person in line."

Brad said something sarcastic and downright rude.

The Guardsman clicked his fingers toward a wide-shouldered security guy who immediately stepped forward.

"Yes, sir?"

"Escort this man—"

"No need." Brad growled and stomped away. "What a waste of time. I'll find my own way back."

How did the fisherman plan on circumventing the guards and getting into Basalt Bay? Judah had to find out. He strode from the line, following Brad's angst-filled footsteps the best he could.

"Judah, what are you doing?" Mia screeched after him. "After all this time waiting, you're walking away? It's almost your turn!"

He paused. "Goodbye, Mia. Go back to the shelter." Hopefully, she wouldn't follow him again.

Seven

As Paisley stood in the center of the art gallery, she smelled something, sniffed a couple of times. Craig's aftershave? She tensed. Made a 360-degree pivot, checking the room. No one else was here. Maybe the familiar scent was just her imagination.

She strode to the open window, watching the surf pounding the seashore. *Wait.* A man was on the beach! Craig? No, this guy didn't have that man's broad shoulders. He wore a raincoat and trudged through the sand, stumbled, seemed to be having difficulty walking. His back was to her; she didn't recognize him. But this meant someone else had stayed in Basalt!

It couldn't be Dad, right? He left with Paige the night of the storm. And yet—

The man tripped. Caught himself. Walked an unsteady gait across the soggy sand. She still couldn't see his face. He staggered, nearly fell.

What if that was Dad?

She dropped the blanket she was using as a shawl and charged across the gallery floor. She shoved the door open wider, scrambled over the trash pile in front of the building, and ran down the sidewalk, not caring what might happen if Craig came after her. If Dad had weathered the storm, and she didn't know if that was him, she had to rush down to the beach and talk to him. Why would he be staggering? Was he injured? And if it wasn't her father, someone else might be in distress and need help.

She raced around Sal's shop, leaping over driftwood and trash and seaweed. She reached the boulders she climbed up and down hundreds of times as a youth. Today they were wet and slippery, with water cascading down from the street above. Debris and chunks of wood were peppered between the rocks. Still, she instinctively knew where to place her next footfall.

Due to the nearly high tide, she didn't have much room to walk along the flat part of the beach. As the next wave receded, she ran forward across the wet shifting sand, staying closer to the big rocks than she normally would to keep from getting splashed.

Just ahead, the man tripped on a sandbag that had been washed away from the others. He flung his arms into the air and yelled as if talking to someone in the heavens. Paisley stopped and watched him. Couldn't make out his words. Still couldn't see his face. Then, he bent over, hands on his knees, and threw up on the beach. Poor guy. He stood upright, hacked a couple of times, turned slightly. With his face in profile, *his* nose, *his* thick black glasses, Paisley knew it was Dad.

"Dad! Dad! It's me, Paisley." She ran hard, her boots skidding in the sand.

He turned toward her, a scowl lining his face. He blinked

as if he had no idea who she was. He rubbed the back of his hand over his mouth. "It's you." His voice sounded gravelly. Dry. "It's me, Dad." She rushed right up to him. Threw her arms around him, hugging him tightly. "It's so good to see you." He didn't return her embrace. Seemed lifeless. Of course, he'd just been sick. Might be weak. She took a step back. "Are you okay? Why are you in Basalt? I thought you left with Paige."

His eyes flooded with moisture. "I thought you—" He flung his hand toward the sea. "I saw your car."

"You did? Where was it?"

"Submerged. Lost."

She gazed out toward the breakers.

"The purple roof. Waves rolling over it. I thought. I thought you might be in it. Gone too."

"Oh, Dad." She hugged him again. He patted her shoulder awkwardly. She stepped back far enough to get a good look at him.

His face was greenish. Probably due to his being sick. Scraggly whiskers covered the lower part of his face. He must not have shaved in days. His eyes looked bloodshot. Weary. His clothes were dirty and wet. Maybe smelly. Craig's words about having found her dad's stash of alcohol came to mind. Was that why he looked so unkept? So sickly?

"Where did you stay during the storm?" If she knew he remained in town, she would have searched for him.

He stared at the water with a dazed look, didn't answer. His teeth chattered. A dark cloud moved overhead, creating a shadow over his face.

"During the hurricane, where did you stay?" She asked again, but the wind seemed to grab her words and whisk them away. She linked her arm with his. "Come on. Let's find somewhere to get you warm. You need to dry out."

"Everyone left." He stared at her. "Where is she?"

"Who?"

"Paige."

"I don't know. I haven't seen her. Don't you know where she is?"

He shook his head, sighed, seemed confused. Was he in shock? Hungover?

"Come on." She led him to the parking lot. The only place she knew to go was back to his house, but what if Craig was there? "Where did you wait out the storm?" The pastor's words about Dad loading up Paige's car had reinforced the idea that he left town. Obviously, Pastor Sagle was wrong about that.

Dad's gray gaze met hers. "At your sister's."

"Is Paige here too?" If so, Paisley wouldn't have to worry about Craig pestering her. Safety in numbers and all that. "Is she at her house?"

Dad mumbled, acted as if he didn't know what she was talking about. "I want to go home." He pulled away from her grasp, trudged east, toward his house.

She ran after him. Stopped in front of him, holding out her hands. "Dad, wait. Let's go to Paige's, okay? Where does she live? Is her house around here?" The farther they got from Dad's, the better.

He turned in the opposite direction, scratched his head. He seemed to be trying to figure out which direction to go. In a small town there weren't a lot of options. He pointed south, then north. Why didn't he know where Paige's house was? "That way, I think." He pointed yet another direction. Was something wrong with his memory?

She recalled Pastor Sagle pointing toward the west side of

town when he said Dad was loading up her sister's car. "Show me where Paige lives, okay?" She tugged on his arm.

"She's not there." He pulled down on his knit hat, covering his ears. "Is she?"

"Probably not." Otherwise Dad wouldn't be wandering the beach alone in the rain, when he was sick, right? "Let's find Paige's house and get you inside." This time he moved in the same direction she did. Although, she didn't have any idea where they were going. She'd have to watch for his burnt-sienna Volkswagen.

"Piper isn't home, either."

"Who?"

Dad pointed east. "That's the way to my house."

"I know." Did he think she forgot the way to the house she grew up in? She kept leading him west, hoping he'd recognize the way to Paige's.

As if in doubt, he glanced back over his shoulder several times.

They passed the ice cream shop where he used to bring her when she was young. She spent many happy summer evenings chatting with him, there, about the sea, or showing him treasures she found on the seashore. Dad never seemed to tire of hearing her talk. Now, he barely seemed to know her.

He coughed hard, leaning over like he might be sick again. His lips looked dry and cracked. He groaned.

"You okay?"

He yanked his arm away from her grasp. "Where are you taking me?" He stumbled. His eyes had a foggy haze to them. He squinted at her. "Who are you?"

A sickening thud landed in her spirit. "It's me, Paisley." What happened to her father? Was he ill? Did he have dementia?

She felt terrible that this might have happened to him while he was alone, when she was away for those years. More guilt for her to bear.

His breathing sounded noisy. He was agitated, almost combative. "I don't want to go anywhere with you."

"We're going to Paige's, remember?" She tried to keep her voice sweet.

He stilled. "Do you know the way?"

"No. But you do, right? Where does Paige live?"

He shrugged, shook his head, then shuffled across the road toward Pastor Sagle's church. She kept in step with him, close enough to grab his arm if he stumbled. They walked a couple of blocks, wading through more water. They trudged past Aunt Callie's boarded-up house.

"Do you know where Aunt Callie is?" She was curious whether he remembered who his sister was.

"Gone. Same as everyone else." At least he knew that much.

"She's probably safe in a storm shelter somewhere."

He didn't agree or say anything else as they walked two more blocks, heading toward C-MER. There, on the right. She spotted his antique Volkswagen parked sideways in the driveway of a blue single-story house. Did the storm surge put it there? Or were Dad's driving skills that bad?

The windows on the house were all boarded up. Dad's doing? Maybe that's why he hadn't taken care of the windows at his own place. He probably assisted Paige, then it got too late. A tree lay on its side in the soggy front yard. Branches and garbage were scattered across the grass like everywhere else in town. Dad stuffed his hands in his coat pockets. "This is it."

"Okay." Paisley imagined her dad huddled inside the bungalow during the hurricane. "Is this where you stayed during the storm?" The image of how she'd been stuck in the upstairs bathroom at his house flashed through her thoughts. At that point, it would have been too dangerous, impossible, for her to go out and hunt for him.

He seemed troubled, like he couldn't remember. Couldn't stay focused. Maybe Craig was right. Maybe Dad's stupor was alcohol related.

"Let's get you inside and find some dry things." She tugged on his arm again. "Is there any food here?"

"No electricity."

"I know." If he was plastered, shouldn't she smell liquor on him? She leaned closer, sniffed. He smelled of the sea. Maybe of the vomit staining his boots. He needed a change of clothes.

He shuffled up the driveway. Then walked through the carport, toward the back of the house.

In the small subdivision backyard, a swing set with a built-in fort lay on its side, leaning against a back fence. The previous owner must have had kids. Maybe Paisley and Dad could get rid of the broken structure, clean up the yard, talk. She'd ask him what was wrong. Would he even know how to answer?

What happened to the dad she knew and loved? Did her three-year absence have anything to do with how he was acting now?

Eight

Paisley followed Dad into the back door of the house, trying to imagine this place as Paige's home. The blue walls of the kitchen were mostly covered with artistic sketches and paintings. Geese and duck knickknacks lined the countertop, along with a small pile of smashed, empty soda cans. A sippy cup lay on its side in the sink. Why was a kid's cup in Paige's house?

Dad strode into the dark living room and grabbed a flashlight off the coffee table where a pile of empty snack and candy wrappers were spread out. He flicked on the switch, creating a circle of light, then dropped onto the couch with a long weary-sounding sigh.

The beige carpet was wet, stained, and Paisley felt the squishiness beneath her boots. While seawater had found its way inside, thanks to someone's forethought in boarding up the windows, there wasn't standing water here like at Dad's place.

The presence of a rocking horse in the corner surprised her. As did the bundle of toys crammed into the TV cabinet. Was Paige babysitting? Paisley thought of the child-size blanket she found at the gallery. Perhaps her sister was watching a coworker's kid.

Dad closed his eyes, muttering something about being old and tired. Needing sleep.

"First, you need to change your damp clothes. Take off those boots. Did you bring any extra things to wear?" After not being present in his life for over three years, it felt weird to boss him around.

He gave her a dull look as if he were looking straight through her, not even seeing her. He closed his eyes again.

She sighed. "How about if I scrounge up something to eat while you go change?"

"Not hungry." He opened his eyelids and stared at the blank TV screen. "Wish ESPN worked."

Is that how he spent his days? Eyes glazed over, staring at the television. That would explain his house being in disrepair. Didn't he work at Miss Patty's Hardware anymore? He used to be everyone's handyman. The guy people came to for advice on how to fix things. This man, this apathetic person, she didn't even recognize.

"I'm thirsty. Soda's gone."

She pictured the pile of smashed cans on the counter. "I'll see what's here." She strode into the kitchen. Water would be better for him. She tried the faucet. It spit and sputtered. The town's water source must have been shut off. She opened the fridge and got hit with a blast of warm air. And something smelly. A couple of water bottles were on the shelf. She grabbed one, carried it back to Dad. Even though she opened the lid and handed it to him, he didn't acknowledge her or drink much. She secured the lid, then set the bottle on the coffee table within easy reach.

Maybe she could find him a blanket. Taking a couple of steps toward the hallway, she glanced back. A childhood feeling of love for him came over her, along with a wave of regret that so much time had passed without her having tried to make amends. But she was here now. "I'm so glad you survived the storm, Dad."

He didn't return the sentiment. Didn't meet her gaze. His cheeks seemed flushed. Did he have a fever? He got sick on the beach. Maybe he had the flu. "Why didn't you leave town with Paige?"

"Why didn't you?"

His gruff comeback surprised her.

"My car stalled on the beach."

He muttered something indistinguishable.

She noticed the flashlight's glow shining toward the opposite wall across from Dad, lighting up an electric fireplace with picture frames displayed on the mantle. Curious, she snatched up the flashlight and strode to the hearth. She aimed the light at the first image. Dad and Mom, ages ago when they looked happy. She splashed light on the next one. Paige, Peter, and Paisley as kids. Then Dad, Paige, and a—a baby? Paisley shone the light directly on the infant. A dark-haired newborn. In Paige's arms. Why did Paige have a picture of a baby with her and Dad? The next one was of a toddler with blond hair. Did the baby's hair lighten? Then one of a child playing on that swing set out back. Another of a Christmas tree with the girl, Paige, and Dad.

Paisley's heart beat a war dance in her chest. "Who's the kid in the photos?"

Dad didn't answer. She swung around. He stared at her blankly.

"Dad, who's the little girl?"

"Piper." The same name he mentioned earlier.

"And she's—?"

"My granddaughter."

A tug in her spirit turned over a rock wedged inside of her ever since she lost her own baby. Paige had a daughter? One who lived. *Breathe in. Exhale.* She blinked fast. This wasn't the time to get sucked into a tempest of emotion. It took a few minutes for her heart rate to settle. For her breathing to normalize. Inwardly, she buried the feelings alongside the pile already there. One of these days she'd have to face those things.

She glanced at the photos again, taking in the new information. Paige was a mom. Which meant Paisley was an aunt. In her three years away, she missed out on this too. On seeing her sister pregnant. Her sister delivering a beautiful baby girl. Piper's toddlerhood.

"Is Paige married?" She hadn't noticed a man in the photos.

"No."

So her sister was a single mom. That took grit and bravery. Her estimation of Paige went up a notch. Maybe Paisley wasn't the only Cedars girl the town gossips told stories about now. Not a kind thought, but one that gave her a measure of relief. A sense of camaraderie with her sister. "I didn't know she had a baby." She hadn't made any attempt to see Paige since she came back. Two days ago, when Judah tried to get her to help him at the art gallery, was this why? So she'd find out about Piper. Why didn't he just tell her?

The child in the photos was a mini-Paige with blond hair and a sweet smile.

Paisley swallowed that lump in her throat. *Don't cry.*

"Too bad you never called." Thick blame bled through Dad's tone.

Guilt settled beneath her breastbone. "I'm sorry about that." How many times would she have to apologize before he believed her? "I wish I had called." Him. Judah. Paige.

Setting the flashlight on the coffee table, she sighed and dropped down on the couch next to Dad. Not close. He did nothing to span the distance or to reassure her that he still loved her, even if she had disappointed him. It seemed he didn't have any emotion. Except, maybe for Piper. At least he was willing to talk about his granddaughter.

"Can you tell me about her?"

"Who?"

"Piper." She wanted to ask him if Paige was still with the father. And why they didn't get married. Instead, she asked a question he might be able to answer. "How old is she?"

"Two. Or three." He sighed as if the conversation were difficult.

"I still can't believe Paige is a mother." Paige, who never seemed interested in the sea, or swimming, or treasure hunting the way Paisley and Peter did, was a parent. Paige, the little sister who always stayed close to home, close to Mom, had grown up. A businesswoman and a mommy. Although, her gallery was in terrible condition, perhaps irreparable.

"She's a good mom too." Dad gave her a stern look, like he expected her to disagree.

She would have commented, but he was shivering almost violently. "You're freezing. How long were you on the beach?" Not waiting for an answer, she jumped up and ran down the hall, searching for a bedroom, a blanket. She came to a room decorated in rosy pinks. Must be Paige's. Paisley hunted for a suitcase that might be Dad's. Not seeing any, she yanked a floral comforter off the bed. She ran back into the living room, covered

Dad, tucking the edges around his shoulders. She kneeled on the wet carpet and yanked off his hiking boots and damp socks. He leaned into the corner of the couch, and she propped a pillow behind his shoulders.

"Don't need help." He still shivered. He clutched the blanket to his chin, his teeth chattering.

"You need to get warm, or you'll catch pneumonia."

"Just leave me alone."

She wanted to ask, *Why are you drinking? Why aren't you taking care of yourself?* Maybe she'd look for some food and give him a minute to cool down. "I'm going to hunt for sandwich makings."

"I told you I'm not hungry." He sounded belligerent. "You don't listen. Never did."

"I'm sorry." There, she said it again. "I am hungry. I think you should eat something too, but that's your choice." Two days ago—was it less than forty-eight hours since she heard that harrowing emergency alarm?—she was disappointed that Dad didn't need her help. Now he did, whether he'd admit that or not.

She strode into the kitchen, then scrounged around in the warm refrigerator. All the stuff in here probably needed to be thrown out. She hunted in the cupboards. Everywhere were signs of a child's presence. Sippy cups. Cartoon characters on plates. Child-proofing devices on the drawers. Fish crackers. Small packages of cereal treats. At least, Paige kept a supply of bread, peanut butter, and jam—Paisley's diet of late. She quickly made two sandwiches. Brought one to Dad.

He stared glumly at the food. He covered his nose and mouth with his hand. Did the strong smell of peanut butter sicken him after his throwing up on the beach?

"Sorry, there weren't many options." She set his portion on the coffee table before she dropped back onto the couch. She devoured her sandwich in a couple of bites. All she'd eaten for the last two days was PB and J, those breakfast bars at the gallery, and that sloppy joe sauce she shared with Judah.

"I n-need—"

She shuffled on the cushion to better see him. "Do you want to go back to the bedroom and rest? Get out of those clothes? I can hang them up in the bathroom to dry." Although, considering how cold the house was, they wouldn't dry quickly.

Suddenly, his eyes rolled back into their sockets. He jerked like he was having a spasm. Or a seizure.

That freaked her out. "Dad! Are you okay?" She shook his arm.

After several seconds, he coughed. "Where . . . am I?" He gazed at her dully.

Something must be terribly wrong with him, with his health. And she was alone. Without a cell phone or any way to contact emergency help.

"We're at Paige's, remember? Are you tired? Feeling sick again?" She snuggled the comforter around him where it fell from his shoulders. He must have gotten too cold down on the beach. "Do you have any spare clothes here?"

"I need my—"

"Clothes?"

His eyes watered. "Med-di—" He swallowed hard as if getting the word past his lips was painful, or too difficult. Was he choking? "Meds." He huffed out the word.

"Meds?" Something *was* wrong! His heart? "Where is your medicine? I'll get it for you." She jumped up. If he'd gone without a prescription that he needed, maybe that's why his thinking was fuzzy. Why he seemed grumpy and agitated. "Dad, where are the drugs you're taking? What are they for?"

His face scrunched up like he was trying hard to find the answer.

"Just tell me where they are, and I'll get them."

"H-home." He exhaled.

"Your medicine is . . . at your house?" At the same place where Craig was probably waiting for her?

Dad nodded. Let out a long shaky sigh.

"Where in the house? I'll, um, run over and get them and come right back." Not getting what her dad needed wasn't an option. A tenderness filled her as she stared at her childhood hero. "What's wrong with you, Daddy?"

He shuffled his shoulders back and forth as if seeking a comfortable position. "D-don't want . . . meds." He stared at something across the room. Or at nothing.

"How long since you took them?"

He licked his dry-looking lips. Shrugged.

She opened the water bottle again, held it out to him. "Was it before the storm? What kind of meds?" He clamped his mouth shut, so she set the water bottle back on the table.

"Don't—" He slumped over.

"Dad!" Was he asleep? *Please don't be unconscious.* "Dad! Wake up!" She shook his arm. "Can you hear me? Talk to me. Say something."

He mumbled incoherently. At least he was conscious.

"Dad, you okay?" She didn't want anything bad happening to him. She already lost her mom. She needed him. Wanted their relationship to be mended and restored. But first he needed to get well. For that to happen, he had to have his medicine.

Did she dare leave him alone, even to go after what he needed? And at her own peril? She would never choose to go back to the house where Craig might be. This was an emergency. No other choice.

"Where did you leave the meds?"

"F-fridge," he whispered hoarsely. "Maybe."

Maybe? "Okay. I'll be right back. You stay here. Don't leave." She didn't want him wandering down to the beach. With tidal changes, it could be dangerous. Deadly. She kissed his rough cheek. "I love you, Dad."

In a couple of minutes he snored softly, so she crept out the back door. This time, when she saw the swing set on its side, an affectionate feeling came over her. Her niece played here. Paige pushed her little girl in the swing the way Paisley had imagined doing with her own child. Sadness and joy mixed together within her, but she couldn't dwell on that. *Focus on Dad. On what he needs.*

Was Craig still lurking around her father's place? What were her chances of getting in, grabbing the medicine, and getting out without him noticing?

Nine

Paisley tread through her swamped childhood neighborhood, watching for any movement that might signal Craig's presence. In several low-lying places, she trudged around deeper water to keep the cold liquid from filling her boots. As she got closer to Dad's, she slowed down, peering around trees, stepping over debris, ready to bolt if she even saw Craig's shadow. Was he still nursing his hangover? Or searching for her?

At the corner of Front Street and Second, she paused to listen. Thud, thud, thud. A hammer? Who was in Basalt besides her and Dad? Or was Craig working on something in Dad's backyard?

She dashed behind the Shelton's gnarled spruce tree that was close to her father's property line. She got a glimpse of the front yard. Didn't see anyone.

If Craig was preoccupied behind the house, maybe she could sneak inside, grab the medicine, and slip out again. The possibility of him finding her, grabbing her, made her heart pound faster. But what else could she do? What other choice did she have?

Hunched over, she crept across the yard, her boots sloshing through the brackish water. If she could just reach the porch—

Craig rounded the corner of the house, a snarl on his face, muttering to himself. Was he still drunk?

She froze, startled to see him even though she knew this was a possibility. What now?

He stared straight at her, his eyes wide.

A pulse of white fear raced up her spine.

"Paisley." His arms were full of chunks of wood. At least, he couldn't grab her without dropping them. "You're back. Finally."

When he tossed the stack of wood onto the pile, adrenaline shot through her. She spun on her heels, charged around the Shelton's house, her boots flinging water and mud in her attempt to escape.

"Paisley!" He yelled from behind her. "Wait."

Not a chance. Determined to put distance between them, she barreled through the neighbors' backyards. Her old stomping ground. She knew the best places to hide. She ducked behind the tool shed next to Lucy Carmichael's parents' house. She pressed her body against the rough wooden wall, waited. Listening. Where was he?

"Paisley!" He sounded close

She didn't move, wouldn't give herself away, despite her throbbing heartbeat and the air burning in her lungs. But wasn't she putting off the inevitable? Dad needed her to hurry.

She felt a tickle in her throat like she just got a whiff of black pepper. Terrible timing. She held her breath, resisting the urge to sneeze.

"Paisley, I want to help." Was he on the other side of the shed? "I'm not here to hurt you. You have to believe me."

She didn't believe anything he said. She hunted for a chunk of wood, anything to grab for protection. There. A couple of branches. If she made a run for it, she could scoop up one to use if she had to.

"Why do you think I came all this way? Stayed with you all this time?"

Stayed with me? Stalked her, more like. The tickle in her throat increased in intensity. The sneeze expelled from her mouth before she could stifle it.

Craig stepped into view, his palms out. "Just stay calm."

Calm? Paisley glowered at him, then sprinted past him, not pausing to grab the branch. Mud flew off her boots, splattering her arms and face, as she dodged back the way she came. She leaped over a downed tree. Ran around the corner, heading for Dad's front porch.

Craig's boots clomped right behind her. "What's wrong with you?"

She went straight for Judah's pickup, and using the hood for leverage, heaved herself up onto the porch. Craig climbed up too. Got between her and the door.

She grabbed the old wooden rocker, keeping it between them. She'd have one chance to shove it at him, hopefully to knock him off the porch. Then she would dash for the fridge and grab the medicine. How she'd get past him on the way out, she didn't know. Unless she hit him hard enough to knock him unconscious. She shoved the chair toward him like a lion trainer.

"Settle down, Paisley." Craig spread out his hands toward her. His eyes looked tired, bloodshot. "We're the only two people left in Basalt. We need to help each other. Work to survive this ordeal. I didn't mean to scare you last night."

Sure, he didn't. "I don't need your help." And they weren't the only ones left in Basalt. "I want you to leave my dad's property. Now!"

"Or what?" A challenge leapt into his gaze.

There was the look of the man who forced her to kiss him once before. And she recalled his "Little Red Riding Hood" comment. Wouldn't forget that, either. "You don't want to know 'or what.'" She'd do whatever she had to do to help her father—and get away from Craig again.

"I've been cleaning up for you and Paul." He pointed toward the garbage pile. "I'm helping out the family. You can trust me."

Trust him? Like she trusted a rattler. She held the chair taut. How did he know Dad's name, anyway? Oh, right, small town. Everyone knew everyone.

"Let's work together, Pais."

"Don't call me that." How dare he act as if they were friends. Besides, she only allowed Judah to use that nickname.

"Paisley, then." He squinted. "I can't leave you here by yourself."

"Yes, you can. I've been on my own for a long time."

His eyes brightened. "You're a tough bird. I admire that about you."

"Don't admire me." She set the chair down but clutched the wooden cross pieces. "Judah's coming back today. You should go." Just mentioning her husband's name made her feel more confident.

"I doubt he'll make it back for a few more days. No one can enter the area until the National Guard allows them to."

Craig wiped his forehead with the back of his hand. "The entrance into town is badly damaged."

"He'll find a way. He promised."

"Like he got here yesterday?" He seemed to be baiting her. Why?

"Thanks to you, he couldn't." Anger replaced her previous fear.

"I came back to make sure you were safe."

What a liar. She shoved the chair forward a couple of inches, showing him she felt anything but safe around him. "As you can see, I'm fine. You can go."

"Can't leave a lady in distress alone."

"I'm not in distress!"

"I can see something's wrong. I can't leave you here." His gaze lied. As if he were a caring, thoughtful person.

She hated that. Wouldn't be deceived. "Because friends treat a pal's wife the way you treated me three years ago?"

His steely gaze didn't flinch.

She'd wasted enough time. Had to get inside the house. "For your information, I'm not alone. My dad's here. So you can get your sorry backside out of town without any fake remorse."

His eyes widened. Because of her vehemence? Or her news about Dad? "I care about your well-being. And your father's. That's why I'm still here."

"Oh, right. That's why you came here drunk last night? Because you 'care.'"

"I didn't come here drunk. I told you I found your dad's stash. I'll show you." He turned as if to leap off the porch.

Her chance! She clenched her fingers tightly around the wooden spindles and let out a growl as she plowed the rocker against his side. Craig flew off the porch, thudding against Judah's pickup. He dropped to the ground, rolled.

Paisley didn't wait to see if he was hurt. She barreled into the house, slammed the door and locked it, then ran for the fridge. She yanked on the handle. It didn't open, probably stuck because of the flooding. She pulled again, and it gave. A sour smell made her hold her breath. She shoved her hands between the lukewarm food containers and jars, searching for medicine. Her frustration mounted when she didn't find anything.

The front door rattled.

"Paisley!" Craig yelled. "Open the door. You've paid me back for my insolence three years ago. Can you let it go now?"

"No!" She moved aside butter, mustard, ketchup. There. In the door shelf was a narrow box. She held it up, shook it. Empty. "Oh, no."

Craig climbed in through the window—she'd forgotten about that access—clumsily tripping over the apple tree, sliding on the wet floor.

Ignoring him, she tried to read the label. She tensed at the sound of the man's boots sloshing through the standing water. Reaching into the fridge, she grabbed the first thing her hand touched—the glass ketchup bottle. She held up the jar threateningly like she did with the Mason jar the previous night. "Stay back! I mean it. I will throw this at you."

"Thanks a lot for shoving me off the porch." He rubbed his shoulder. Winced.

She kept the jar raised, imagining other things in the refrigerator that she could throw at him too.

"Who's the insulin for?" He nodded at the box in her other hand.

"Insulin?" Her jar-throwing hand lowered.

"Are you a diabetic?"

Diabetic? That's what was wrong with Dad? She stared at the box.

In her hesitation, Craig stepped forward and grabbed the empty container from her hand. "Who needs this, Paisley?" His voice took on a harsh tone. "Is this your dad's?" He stared at the box, squinting. "Paul Cedars." He must have read the faded prescription label.

Even though she hated him knowing anything personal about her or her family, she felt bewildered, dazed, and didn't answer. Dad was a diabetic? And she hadn't known?

"Is he acting lethargic? Sick?"

She nodded.

"Where is he?" He stood taller, his voice demanding. "He could be in grave danger without this."

"Don't you think I know that?" She didn't want Craig Masters involved in any aspect of her life. However, Dad's health was at stake. Since Craig worked as an emergency responder, if he knew something about this medicine, about this disease, she might have to swallow her pride. Her fear.

"Where's the rest of it?"

"I don't know." She turned away from him and yanked open cupboard doors, searching. "He said in the fridge." She grabbed the box from Craig, tried to read something that might give her a clue.

"We'll have to hunt everywhere." Craig opened and shut several cupboards and drawers. "These pens don't have to be refrigerated. Which means they could be stored anywhere." So he did know something about the medicine. Whatever he knew was more than she did.

She tugged open the rest of the drawers, trying to ignore

the proximity of her and Craig, side by side, working together to find the insulin. Every movement where their paths crossed created horrible tension within her. She couldn't believe she was in this predicament, depending on the man she loathed. But she couldn't focus on that. Where would her dad stash extra medicine?

"Maybe it's in his bathroom." Craig's voice sounded husky.

"That would be on the second floor."

"I know."

That's right, he rescued her from that room yesterday. Was it only a day ago? It already felt like a week.

She turned to look at the gaping stairwell where the stairs exploded the night of the hurricane. Craig turned at the same time. They bumped into each other.

"Stay back."

"Sorry."

She hated being in the same room with him. Wouldn't relax around him, wouldn't let down her guard. He might be playing the nice-guy card right now, but she knew the truth. He was a scoundrel.

She remembered something else. "When I was stuck in the bathroom, I checked the shelves behind the mirror. I didn't see any medicine. That leaves Dad's bedroom."

"Come with me." He stomped across the living room and rushed out the front door.

Like she'd do anything just because he commanded her to. Glad for the reprieve of his exiting, she scrounged through the fridge again. Her hands shook from tension and the horror of knowing she couldn't find what Dad needed. Something scraped against the front of the house. A ladder?

She ran outside, jumped down from the porch.

Craig was already at the top rung, climbing into Dad's bedroom window.

She didn't want to follow him up the ladder. But shouldn't she be the one looking through Dad's stuff? Not a stranger. Not him. Especially not him. Even in an emergency, she didn't want him handling her family's belongings. She trudged to the foot of the ladder, waited.

A couple of minutes later, Craig thrust his hand out the open window, holding a box. "I found this on his closet shelf."

She nodded, bit her lip. Dad would have his insulin. Craig could go away and leave her alone. They never had to speak with each other again.

She clutched the ladder to keep it steady while he climbed onto the upper rung. Their roles were reversed. Yesterday morning, she tentatively descended the ladder while he held the metal steady. Now, he barreled down like it was a slide. Paisley stepped back so he wouldn't touch her.

"Where's your dad? I can help him."

"What? No." She'd take the insulin to her father. She held out her hand to receive the box he found.

"I know what I'm doing, Paisley." He nearly growled. "I'm an EMT with C-MER. And my mother is a diabetic. I've helped her before." He held up the box, one eyebrow raised.

She lowered her hand. Dad's life might depend on this man's expertise and knowledge about a disease that Paisley knew nothing about. Because of the evacuation, they were isolated from any outside medical help. Was Craig Dad's best option in this emergency? *Ugh.* How could she agree to let this man who she didn't trust come with her to the other house? Nowhere would be safe from him. Or far enough away from him.

"I couldn't find your dad's blood sugar testing strips or

meter. But I have some in my emergency field bag." He strode to his truck, opened the door, then withdrew a dark-colored bag. He slammed the door. Faced her again. "Where is he?"

"He's at my sister Paige's." She despised having to tell him.

Craig took off, nearly sprinting in the direction of Pastor Sagle's church and the subdivision. Apparently, he knew exactly where Paige lived.

All Paisley could do was run after him and hope for the best.

Ten

"Brad!" Judah had been following the fisherman for about ten minutes, barely able to keep him in his sights. He thought the guy was heading to his car. Instead, he trudged in the direction of the river, maybe the marina. Brad, who had been a few years ahead of Judah in high school, didn't seem to hear him calling. Or else, ignored him.

At a coffee shop not far from the port area, Brad stepped inside, much to Judah's relief. His injured leg could use a much-needed rest. Another cup of steaming hot coffee appealed to him too.

The congested shop smelled of delicious coffees and pastries, and for a second Judah just wanted to inhale the scents. He gazed around the room at the varied populace—fishermen, businessmen, elderly folks, couples, groups of women, even children—lining the counter and clustered about small tables. There was Brad, sitting with his back toward the entrance. Judah strode across the room, then dropped into the opposite seat at his table.

Brad glared at him.

"I don't know if you remember me or not. I'm Judah Grant. I hope you don't mind if I sit here for a minute. The place is packed."

Brad sipped his drink that looked dark enough to be black coffee. Didn't comment. Didn't seem very friendly, either.

Back in high school, Judah knew of the Keifer brothers and their reputation for being brawlers. But their paths hadn't crossed much in the years since.

"I'm sorry to barge in on you this way." He stretched out his sore leg. "I've been following you since you left the information booth a while ago."

Still no comment from Brad.

"I overheard your conversation about needing to get back to Basalt Bay."

"What's it to you?" The man wiped his hand over his bushy mustache.

"If you don't mind my asking, what's your plan?" Judah didn't wait for small talk to ease the awkwardness between them.

"And if I do mind?" Brad's green eyes squinted at Judah as if he were a nuisance.

"I need to get back there. Today, if possible. It's urgent." Judah linked his fingers over his knee, trying to scale back his intensity, making it easier for the other man to do the same.

"Wait in line." Brad growled. He turned sideways as if terminating the discussion. Almost as an afterthought, he added, "Maybe you should call and ask your all-powerful, swindling father to bail you out."

Judah clenched his jaw. So, here sat another person with a beef toward Mayor Grant. He wouldn't be put off that easily. "This doesn't have anything to do with my dad."

"No?"

"No. I want to know how you plan on getting home." Judah leaned forward, his elbows on the table. "I'd like to go with you however you're returning to Basalt Bay."

"Not happening."

"Please. I'm desperate." Judah pinched the bridge of his nose. "I don't know what you have against my father, but I assure you, I am not him."

Brad shook his head. Squinted. Sizing Judah up, it seemed. Did he find him wanting? Weak? If it weren't for his leg—

"Why are you in such an all-fired hurry to get back to Basalt?"

Judah decided to go for the truth. "My wife is stuck there. Alone, as far as I know. Without a working cell phone. I need to get back to her. She may be in danger." He briefly described their stay in her father's house through the storm. Judah's accident. Her not going to Florence with him. Their last communication.

"Why did she stay behind?" Brad seemed more interested now. Even turned slightly toward Judah.

"That's not important. What I need is—"

"Hey, it's important to me." The other man's voice rose gruffly. "If I'm risking my life to bring another person along in an open skiff in rough waters, I want to know the whole story." His cup landed on the table with a clunk. "Especially with a guy who can't keep up. Can't fend for himself. I saw you hobbling back there."

Judah disliked that the fisherman perceived him as frail, maybe even crippled. But he stuffed his pride aside. "Okay, sure, I have this injury. I may be hobbling, but that means I'm moving forward. I'm determined to get back to my wife, with or without your help. I work on a skiff for C-MER. I know how to handle myself in rough seas."

"Why did you leave your wife behind?" Brad's question was blunt, his voice gruff, eyes glinting with judgment.

"I didn't 'leave' her." Judah sighed. "She didn't want to ride in the vehicle with the person who came for us. Refused, actually." Normally he wouldn't tell a stranger so much about their personal lives. However, Judah knew he had to give Brad the information he wanted, or he wouldn't even consider helping him.

"Family feud? Maybe she didn't want to go with *you*." Brad checked his watch. "Grants are notorious for stirring up strife."

Judah groaned. "Let's just call it an injustice caused by someone else. Not me." He didn't want to say anything about the matter between her and Craig. Small town gossip traveled far.

"Who's your wife, anyway?" Brad shuffled his hat on his head. Tapped the table. Apparently in a hurry to be on his way now.

"Paisley Grant. Was Cedars."

The man's jaw dropped. "Little fireball Paisley?" He guffawed. "I have been out of town too long. Pete's kid sister married a Grant?" He grinned and his white teeth contrasted with his reddish beard.

Judah didn't know whether to be offended or proud. "She did."

"The two were inseparable when we were kids." Brad chuckled. "High school changed that. They grew apart."

"Right. Peter left to go fishing in Alaska."

"Both of us did." Brad drained his mug. "I eventually returned to fish closer to the mainland."

A pause.

"About that boat ride?"

The fisherman's eyes gazed at something through the window. For a few moments, he seemed lost in thought. "I'm still waiting for a callback from a guy." He pulled a cell phone out of his coat pocket and thumped the screen. "Nothing yet. Give me your number and I'll call when I find out more details about renting a skiff."

"I don't have a phone right now." Judah stood and thrust out his hand to shake Brad's. "I'll stick around here until you hear something."

"Fine." The fisherman returned his handshake.

Judah shuffled across the room to the counter and ordered a latte, even though he'd had one earlier. He found an available bar stool and plopped down, hoping Brad would have good news for him soon.

Paisley didn't know that things had turned out rotten in his attempts to make it back to Basalt Bay. If there was any way to let her know, he would. He didn't forget his promise. He still wouldn't give up. Although, he had limitations. He massaged the calf muscle near his bandage, wishing it felt better.

The barista called his name. He raised his hand, waving to get her attention. She set the to-go cup on the counter in front of him. He sipped his hot drink slowly. Sighed. If only his circumstances were as pleasing. *Lord, could you—*

"Judah, that you?" Mia.

He groaned.

"I keep running into you."

"So it seems."

Did she follow him here, too?

"Any news?" She waved at someone across the room.

"Possibly. Just waiting to hear."

"Have you talked to anyone from C-MER? Oh, just a sec." She turned to the barista. "I'll have a half-caf, oat milk, extra-foam macchiato."

The frazzled, overworked twenty-something gawked at her. "Oat milk, really? We're swamped. Almost out of supplies. Definitely don't have any highfalutin—"

"Okay, okay. Fine. I'll take soy milk." Mia huffed as if it were the worst stepdown ever. "Oh, do you have stevia?"

The barista rolled her eyes. "No, we do not." Shaking her head, the young woman returned to her tasks.

"Someone isn't getting a tip." Mia scooted back to Judah, continuing the conversation like she hadn't stepped away. "I called Craig a couple of times."

"You did?" He tried not to overreact to the man's name. Still, his unsettled business with his supervisor fed his agitation. "Where was he?"

"He didn't answer." She grinned at someone. Waved. "Weird that he hasn't stayed in contact with his employees, don't you think? Seems he would have called by now."

"Maybe he's AWOL. Or his cell died." Any other reasons caused too much angst inside Judah's chest.

"Maybe." She nudged his arm. "Can you picture that? Our wonderful fearless leader without his cell phone?" She snickered. "Doesn't compute."

Judah didn't buy into her complimentary assessment of Craig. Her eyes shone too brightly. Were the two romantically involved? Or did their supervisor just happen to be another person she flirted with? He sighed. Not his concern. "When did you last speak with him?"

"Hmmm?" She leaned closer.

"Craig? When did you—"

Mia stepped back, bumping into Brad. "Oh, excuse me." She batted her eyes at the fisherman, grinning. "Why, if it isn't Brad Keifer. Funny running into you here."

Brad glanced at her with the briefest acknowledgement, then faced Judah. "Meet me at Wharf C. Two o'clock. Don't be late."

"All right, I will. Thank you." Did this mean he would be with Paisley today? A rush of joy danced through his heart. Things were looking up.

Brad strode out of the bustling café.

"What's with him?" Mia's lips creased into a pout. Apparently, she wasn't used to anyone ignoring her. "What's going on?"

"I'm catching a ride back to Basalt Bay with him." The less she knew, the better, so he added, "I don't know all the details yet."

"Two o'clock, huh?" She touched her lips with the matching red nail of her index finger.

Too bad she heard that. Nothing Judah could do about it now.

Eleven

Paisley kept ten feet between her and Craig as they rushed silently toward Paige's. If it weren't for her desperate awareness of Dad's medical problem, she would have grabbed the insulin container and ditched Craig. Did she really give him permission to treat her father?

The fact that Craig carried the medicine package like he was the one in charge bothered her. She could snatch it from his hand, but what good would that do? He seemed to know where Dad was, where Paige lived. He'd just find them. And what if he could help Dad? Would she deny her father medical treatment because of her own unease around the man?

"Your dad shouldn't be drinking alcohol, either." That was the first thing Craig said to her since they started walking.

Dad had never been a heavy drinker. But what did she know about his current lifestyle? Maybe after Mom died, he drowned his sorrows in the bottle. She wouldn't judge him. She'd found relief by running away. Temporarily, anyway.

"Alcohol can have unpredictable effects on a diabetic," Craig stated, his voice flat, monotone, like he was reciting data unemotionally. "It can mask symptoms, even those leading to a diabetic coma."

Was he trying to scare her? Did that happen to his mother? A diabetic coma sounded horrific. Paisley's heart rate accelerated, as did her worry for Dad. They were miles from a medical facility. Maybe they'd have to get him medevacked out. But surely his condition wasn't as bad as Craig made it sound.

"You should dump out all those bottles I found."

"Stop telling me what to do."

He glanced over his shoulder as if her sharp response surprised him.

Plenty more angst where that came from. She'd let him check Dad, since there didn't seem any deterrent to that happening. Then she'd tell him to hit the road, Jack. Whatever Dad needed from here on out, she was the one helping him. She wasn't an EMT like Craig, but she was his daughter. She'd make the decisions now. Her and Paige, once her sister returned.

Glancing at the ocean between the space of a couple of houses, she noticed the rough waves and charcoal clouds hovering over the bay. Was another storm coming? Would it keep Judah away longer?

Her thoughts drifted back to Dad. If he needed an airlift, how would they contact the authorities? What about Craig's cell phone? She hadn't seen him texting. Did it still have power? If it did, she could call Judah. Hadn't he called her using Mia's phone last night?

"Does your phone still have battery power?" She made herself ask, even though she didn't want to speak to him.

"No. It's dead."

"Oh." Then they were in trouble if Dad needed medical help that went beyond his need for insulin. Although, Craig's monster truck was still parked in her dad's yard. Maybe he could drive around whatever blockade the National Guard had set up and take Dad to the ER in Florence.

When they reached Paige's house, Craig strode up the driveway, past Dad's car parked sideways, and into the debris-strewn backyard. He seemed to know just where to go.

Entering the back door behind him, Paisley called out a warning. "Dad, it's me. I have someone with me."

No answer.

"Dad?" She pushed past Craig and ran into the living room. Her father was slumped over on the couch cushions. His mouth hung open wide. Was he breathing? Unconscious? Or—

"Dad!" She shook his arm.

"Mr. Cedars!" Craig rushed around her, pushed her out of the way, and dropped the insulin package and the bag he carried onto the coffee table. Kneeling on one knee, he put two fingers against the side of her dad's neck, checking for a pulse. He leaned his ear close to Dad's mouth.

"Is he—?"

"He's alive," Craig spoke tersely.

Paisley dropped to the edge of the couch beside Dad. She heard his breathing. It was shallow, barely noticeable, and had a catch to it like he was struggling to inhale oxygen. She knew what that felt like. How terrifying it was to breathe in empty-feeling air. "Dad?"

"His breath smells fruity. Dry lips. His skin isn't pale." Craig seemed to be speaking to himself.

She watched tensely, fearful they hadn't gotten back with the insulin soon enough.

Craig peeled Dad's eyelids back one at a time, peering into them. Then he yanked open his bag, withdrew a stethoscope. He pressed the circular chest piece against Dad's shirt, listening with the headset against his ears. "I don't have intravenous saline solution in my field bag."

"Okay." She didn't know why he told her that. Maybe he thought she understood more about Dad's problem than she did.

Craig checked her father's pulse again.

Dad twitched, jerked a couple of times, but didn't open his eyes.

"He did that earlier too. It scared me." She blinked rapidly, wouldn't give in to tears in front of Craig. "What's wrong with him? Can you tell?" Having to ask the man questions about her father, relying on him for wisdom and advice, was difficult for her to stomach.

"High blood sugar. Hyperglycemia, most likely." Craig dug in his bag and pulled out a small kit, probably the one he mentioned earlier. He tore open a package of wipes, filling the air with the scent of alcohol. He rubbed the cloth over the side of Dad's index finger. He withdrew other gadgets. A meter. A pen-like device. A small cannister. He inserted a narrow strip into the bottom of the meter. Twisted the top off the pen.

Even though Craig's eyes were bloodshot, and he probably had a hangover headache, his hands were steady.

Paisley didn't know what any of the paraphernalia was for, what Craig was doing as he pressed the pen against Dad's index finger that he just wiped clean. She had to trust him. Her immediate concern was for her father's health. *Lord, please touch my dad. Heal him. Give us a chance to work things out.* She wished he'd open his eyes, say something. At least, she could tell he was breathing, still alive.

Craig milked Dad's finger, drawing a droplet of blood to the surface. He picked up the meter with the test strip, touching the tip to the blood. He released Dad's finger, stared at the screen. He turned the device toward her. The display read "523."

"Is that bad?"

"Extremely high. I'll administer the insulin now."

"Okay." She didn't know what else to say, what to do. She was grateful she didn't have to face this crisis alone.

He set the meter on the coffee table, and his hand bumped the peanut butter sandwich she made earlier onto the wet rug. She'd take care of it later.

Tearing open the insulin box, he pulled out another pen-type object. He held it up; removed the cap. He opened a tiny package that had a smaller cap. He pulled a tab off that, and twisting the cap onto the pen, exposed a small needle. He worked with the insulin pen, squirting some clear liquid into the air.

"Lift his shirt at the waist."

She tugged up on Dad's flannel shirt and the stained white t-shirt beneath, exposing his belly, glad to have a task, something to do to help.

Craig held the pen like a pencil and pressed the needle into Dad's skin a couple of inches from his belly button. With his other hand, he pushed the button at the opposite end of the pen, releasing the liquid.

Paisley hated to watch, felt squeamish, but she wouldn't turn away. She might have to help Dad with this procedure. She needed to know what to do.

When Craig pulled the pen away from Dad's abdomen, Paisley tugged down on his shirt, covering him. "Will he be okay now?"

"We'll wait and see." Craig twisted the small cap onto the pen, turned counterclockwise, removing the needle. He recapped the top. Set both on the table. "As soon as he's alert, encourage him to drink water. He's probably dehydrated which is problematic with high blood sugar."

"All right." She tried to take in all the information as she watched, waiting for her dad to wake up. "How long will it take?"

"Varies. The insulin is working; give it time." Craig put some items back into his bag. The stethoscope still around his neck, he pressed the chest piece against Dad's shirt. "Sounds better."

"Good." She held her dad's hand, watching him, waiting. Praying.

A few more minutes passed. Craig stood, probably tired from the way he was squatting. He pressed his fingers against his temples, closed his eyes. It seemed she was right about the headache.

Dad's eyelids fluttered. "Craig, look. Dad!"

Craig squatted back down. "Paul?"

Dad moved slightly. His tongue wet his lips. His eyelids opened a little. He peered up at her through narrow slits. He winced. His gaze moved to Craig. Back to her. Did he recognize her?

"It's me, Dad."

"I'm Craig Masters from C-MER, remember me?"

Dad didn't respond to either of them.

"He gave you your insulin." She rubbed her father's hand, hoping he'd squeeze her fingers, say he knew who she was. He didn't. His hand was still limp.

Craig checked his eyes again. Took his pulse. Listened with the stethoscope on his chest.

Finally, Dad's gaze met hers with a foggy look, his eyebrows quirked. Was he wondering how she knew about the insulin? About his illness?

She gripped his hand tighter. "You're going to be okay. We're here to help you." She remembered what Craig said about the water. She let go of Dad's hand, then reached for the water bottle she'd given him earlier. Uncapping the top, she leaned the ridge against his lower lip. "Drink some of this, okay?"

He swallowed a little bit of water. Grumbled. Shook his head.

She glanced at Craig. He nodded as if telling her to keep trying.

"Can you drink a little more? It's good for you to drink as much as you can." She pressed the bottle to his mouth again. "I want to help you."

He took some water in, then pressed his lips closed tightly. "Don't . . . need . . . your . . . help." He turned his head away from her.

She felt his rude rejection all the way to the bottom of her heart.

Craig eyed her, but she ignored his unspoken question. "Paul, how long has it been since your last dose of insulin?"

Dad shrugged. "A week, or so."

"You should test yourself regularly, every day."

"Yeah, yeah. Leave me alone." Even though Dad hardly lifted his head off the pillow, he seemed combative.

"How long since you last ate something?" Craig asked.

Dad huffed. "Don't know. Don't care. I've been too sick. Sick and tired."

Paisley held the water bottle out to him again. "Can you drink some more?"

"No. Let me be, will you? You had no right to give me that insulin."

Why was he acting this way? As if he didn't want to get better. As if she'd done something wrong.

Craig frowned. "Do you know what day this is? Who's the president?"

"Who cares? Leave me alone . . . to die in peace." The last words were huffed out on a shaky breath, barely audible. He shut his eyelids as if closing himself away from them.

To die? "I won't leave you alone." Paisley smoothed her palm over his sleeve, fighting the urge to weep. "I love you, Dad. I want you to get well. I want us to talk and share our lives again. Things are going to be better between us. I promise." Her dad didn't even want to live? How long had he felt so hopeless? "Think about Paige. What about Piper? Don't you want to see her grow up? She needs her grandpa."

"Papa," he muttered gruffly.

"Piper calls you Papa?"

He nodded, still not opening his eyes.

"That's so sweet. See there, you need to get well so you can spend time with the little girl who calls you Papa." She sniffed, fighting her battle with tears.

Craig pointed at the water bottle, reminding her of her task.

She picked up the plastic container again. "You need to drink more water." She uncapped the lid. Held it to his stubbornly clamped lips. "Please? I want you here with me for a long time. I need you."

"You don't need anyone." His voice sounded raspy.

"Yes, I do."

Craig threw her a curious glance. "You should try to drink the water, Mr. Cedars. In a few minutes, I'd like to retest your blood sugar."

"No."

"I strongly recommend that you test yourself and take the needed doses of insulin daily." Craig squinted at Dad. "Your reading from a few minutes ago was over five hundred."

Dad opened his eyes. "That bad, huh?"

"How are you feeling now?"

"Tired." His breathing didn't sound as shallow and broken as before.

"We'll drum up some food for you, too." Craig nodded toward the water bottle.

Paisley held it out to Dad again, but he didn't open his mouth. A memory from when she was a kid came to mind. "Remember when I fell on the boulders at the peninsula and gashed my knee? I didn't want stitches. Yelled at you to use duct tape. It fixes everything, right? I told you I wasn't going to the ER. You said if I planned to run on Basalt Beach for the rest of my life, I needed my leg fixed good as new. I want to hike on the beach, search for treasures, and enjoy the Pacific with *you* for a long time. Please, get well and give us a second chance." She begged him with her gaze, and her heart, if only he could see into it.

She avoided Craig's glance. Didn't want him privy to her family's pain. But he was here. Silently observing.

She knew she'd hurt Dad by leaving Basalt without telling him goodbye three years ago. And he never understood about her not attending Mom's funeral. But she longed for a real father-daughter relationship with him again, somehow.

Craig checked Dad's pulse. "Will you let me test your blood sugar again in a few minutes?"

"All right, stop pestering me, both of you." Dad glared and crossed his arms.

Maybe they'd gotten through to him. She should thank Craig

for his help. What if he hadn't been here? What if she had to deal with this all by herself? But even with those thoughts, she didn't have the words to say to him.

Dad sighed and closed his eyes as if he were going to take a nap. She pulled the comforter up to his chin.

"We'll have to watch him closely." Craig picked up the used needle cap and nodded for her to follow him into the kitchen.

She grabbed the soggy sandwich off the floor, then left the room to give her father some peace and quiet. When she had internet access, she'd study up on diabetes and find out how she could help him more. She walked to the trash can and tossed in the sandwich.

"If he's drinking alcohol on top of the diabetes, that's a bad combination." Craig picked up an empty soda can, dropped the used needle cap into it, and set it in the garbage.

"You should lay off the sauce too."

His face flushed. "We all have our vices."

And he was mean under the influence of his. Although, today he seemed different. Not that she trusted him.

"It might be a week until we get electricity." He stuffed his hands into his jean's pockets. Maybe he felt awkward too. "Your dad needs to drink lots of water, eat healthy food, fresh vegetables, and get daily exercise for his recovery."

A whole week without electricity? She couldn't imagine living in the dark, cold dampness that long. And where would she find fresh vegetables and healthy food in this devastated town? Even locating fresh water might be challenging. She swallowed what felt like a wad of cotton, wishing he'd go. Leave her to think. But what if something else went wrong with Dad?

"Guess we'll have to focus on survival."

We'll? Did he imagine she still wanted his help? Needed him? He was delusional. And yet, Dad might very well need him for the next hours. Days, even?

Ugh.

"There's a barbecue grill in the backyard."

"So?" She hadn't noticed one. She'd seen the messy yard, the wrecked swing set.

"Why don't you check the freezer for usable meat?" He strode to the back door. "I'll see if there's propane to fire up the grill. Then I'll come in and check on your dad." He exited quickly.

She should have told him she didn't want him here. He was a horrible human being. A cad. That's what she still considered him, right?

She sighed.

He was correct about one thing. Their survival depended on food and water. A clattering noise came from the backyard. Probably him dragging the barbecue grill across the patio.

She tugged on the freezer handle above the standard-sized fridge. She found packages of hamburger, steak, and chicken already thawing out. She grabbed two pounds of hamburger, noticing the grass-fed stickers. That should be healthy enough for Dad, for all of them.

Craig deserved a meal too. Afterward, she'd thank him for his help, and that would be the end of this weird little interlude of dependency on a man she couldn't stand to be around.

Twelve

After they finished eating charred hamburgers and cold canned beans, Paisley noticed that Dad seemed more alert. Even talkative, mostly with Craig. She hadn't worked up the nerve to tell that man to leave yet, but she would soon if he didn't take the initiative.

Now, Dad was stretched out on the couch with his eyes closed. Craig was still doing something outside.

Dusk had settled in, making the rooms less inviting, full of shadows. After a perusal of the house, using the flashlight, she found it had two bedrooms. A queen-sized bed was the centerpiece in Paige's room. Dad had probably slept here. The second bedroom contained a child-sized bed. And a futon lined the opposite wall—the most obvious place for Paisley to rest. Either that or she'd sleep on the living room couch. Without electricity, there wouldn't be a night-light for either place; she always kept one going after dark.

So far, Judah hadn't arrived. It seemed unlikely that he

would this late in the day. If he was detained due to the road closure, he must have tried everything he could to get back to her. He was injured. Probably couldn't walk far. And the conditions must be bad everywhere along the coast.

She wouldn't allow herself to imagine him hanging around Mia at the storm shelter, possibly trapped in her flirtatious web. Right. The woman's face repeatedly popped up in her thoughts every time she wondered what Judah might be doing.

She needed a task, something to distract herself. Maybe she could find enough candles to stave off the coming darkness. This flashlight wouldn't last forever. She grabbed a cinnamon scented candle from the mantle of the electric fireplace. Too bad that wasn't a wood stove, instead of it being electricity dependent. She set the candle jar on the coffee table. After scooping up the snack wrappers and throwing them away in the kitchen garbage, she checked the cupboards for matches. She found a box, then grabbed two medium-sized candle jars from the windowsill. She smelled the pumpkin and vanilla scents before setting them on the coffee table in the living room.

One other place might have candles—Paige's room. She discovered two more. She placed them all together in a cluster. That should be enough wick power to keep the room lit for a while.

"Good job." Craig paused at the doorway. "It will be dark soon."

He didn't have to remind her of that.

Dad stirred from his catnap. "What's going on?" He squinted at Craig. "Who are you?" Apparently, his mind was still fuzzy.

"Craig Masters." The tall man thrust out his hand and shook Dad's like he was a caring neighbor, a friend.

Paisley grumbled as conflicting feelings battled within her.

"I work with Judah, remember?" Craig smiled widely. "I'm here to offer my assistance to you and Paisley in his absence, however either of you might need help."

He sounded so noble, and he didn't meet her gaze, her glare.

Dad sat up. "Got any soda?"

Paisley handed him a water bottle. "Try this."

He complained about not liking water, but he took a sip.

"How are you feeling, sir?" Craig squatted beside him.

Dad inhaled and exhaled, rubbed his palm over his stomach. "Some better, I think."

"That's good to hear." Craig stood and rocked his thumb toward the door. "I should probably get going."

Paisley was relieved he came to that conclusion himself.

"I'll head out to my place." Craig took a couple of steps. "I'll check back in the morning."

"Where do you live?" She probably shouldn't have asked that, since she didn't want him thinking she was interested in his life.

His eyebrows lifted. "I live on the south side. Not far from Judah's cabin. Oh, um, and yours, of course."

They were neighbors? Maybe he'd purchased a place since she went away. "That's a long walk." On second thought, his staying a mile away sounded perfect.

"I'll just—" He strode to the door. Stopped. His back toward her, he seemed reluctant. "You sure you'll be okay? Maybe I'll sleep in my truck. Stay closer."

"Why?" She preferred his first plan—his going somewhere far from her. Tonight she'd like a good sleep, knowing he wasn't going to barge in on her and make her fearful.

Dad's health problems kept her from making a disparaging comment. He might need Craig's help with another insulin shot. When would he require the next one?

"I feel responsible for you."

"Don't. You aren't." How could she forget how afraid she was last night, hiding in the pantry? Even if Craig acted differently today.

"Why don't you just sleep here?" Dad patted the couch. "Plenty of room."

"Dad—"

"I'll head back to the bedroom," he continued. "No reason to hike all that way in the dark."

Plenty of reasons. "Dad—" She shook her head, glared a warning.

"What? It's the Christian thing to do. Provide shelter. We're all in this disaster together." He was speaking more coherently now.

For her to state her opinion of Craig would require her to explain about their past. Something she didn't want to do with him standing right here.

"It's settled then."

Nothing is settled!

Dad pushed off the couch. Wobbled. Paisley leaped forward and grabbed his arm. Craig crossed the distance in two strides and held onto her father's other arm. Dad's voice sounded stronger, but his body was still weak. Together they led him back to Paige's room. Helped him get out of his damp clothes and into bed. How would she have done all that by herself? She grudgingly admitted to herself, again, that she appreciated Craig's assistance.

"I can leave," Craig said as soon as they entered the living room.

"Probably for the best."

"But your dad—"

She looked at him sharply, guessing what he might say.

Dad might need his help in the night. Craig had EMT training. She didn't.

"Okay, fine. You can stay on the couch like Dad said. Tonight, only." She hated acquiescing. Hated giving this man permission to stay in the same house with her.

His eyes widened. Her acceptance of the situation must have surprised him too.

She blew out all but two candles, then grabbing one, stomped back to Piper's room. Her nemesis sleeping under the same roof? She slammed the bedroom door and leaned hard against it. She shined the light from the candle onto the doorknob.

No lock? She groaned. How would she ever get to sleep in this room without one?

Thirteen

At two o'clock, Judah had met Brad at Wharf C, only to discover that the boat the fisherman planned to rent from Richard was gone. Someone else offered the owner more money.

Richard attempted to placate them, promising they could rent the boat in the morning. He said he was sorry. That the other client had an emergency. What else could he do? However, if there was a serious situation—one more serious than Judah's—why would the boat owner even mention the higher payment? Could they trust that he was telling the truth about the next day's use?

Frustrated, Judah left the wharf, nearly dragging Brad along with him. The fisherman was beside himself, railing at the owner's business ethics, then threatening to steal one of the other boats tied to the dock. Although, Judah couldn't see any worth committing a crime over. Several skiffs were damaged from the storm. One upside down on the wharf. A couple half sunk. None were boats he wanted to use to travel twenty miles in unpredictable, possibly rough, waters.

Brad said he'd never rent from the guy again. But they still needed a boat, even if they couldn't get one until morning.

Judah had failed Paisley, again. That's what bothered him the most. He assured her he'd be with her today. And he tried. Man, he tried. Now, it was too late. What must she be thinking? How was she? Was she safe? Agitation gripped him in the gut until he felt physically sick. Sometimes things just all went wrong. So frustrating. Maddening. His sigh came out like a moan.

Finally, exhausted, discouraged, and with his leg needing a break, he plopped down on the low cot in the storm shelter.

Closing his eyes, he sighed and reminded himself that he and Paisley were in God's hands. But what if his wife thought he deserted her? What if she was still in trouble? Or waited eagerly for his arrival, only for him to let her down, again.

He groaned. Massaged his face with his palms.

"You okay?" Mia spoke from somewhere that felt too close.

"Yeah, fine." He growled the words. Then regretted his short fuse.

"Judah?"

He leaned up on his elbow. "I'm okay. Just trying to sleep. Forget this day."

"Sorry things didn't work out for you to return home." She stared at him from her cot. "You tried. Paisley will understand."

"Thanks. I hope so."

"Tomorrow will be better."

"I know." He laid back down. A little while later, fatigue overrode his churning thoughts, and he relaxed despite the hum of noise in the crowded gym.

Hours later, he opened his eyes to light coming in through the upper windows. Did he sleep all night? He checked his watch beneath the blanket. Almost six in the morning. He stretched his calf muscles. Winced in anticipation of pain. It still hurt, but not as badly as yesterday. Good. He might have a lot of walking to do today.

He sniffed, smelled coffee, and his thoughts raced to Paisley. How did she survive another night? Was she still at her dad's? She probably didn't have any coffee to drink like he did, since the town was without electricity. She might even need food or water. A troubling thought.

Today, nothing would stop him from getting back to Basalt Bay. *Please, God, let it be so.*

But first he'd locate Brad and check on the boat arrangements. If there was a snag, maybe Dad had connections. He might know someone who would loan a skiff to two desperate guys in Florence. Not that Judah wanted to call and beg his father for a favor. Especially not after what Paisley told him about the mayor paying her off to leave town three years ago. He still struggled with that. His own dad taking such malicious steps to intrude on his and Paisley's marriage? The thought tore him up inside. Outraged him. Still, if push came to shove, he'd stuff down his frustrations, his pride, and humble himself and call Dad.

"You already aw-wake?" Mia's voice croaked.

"Yeah." He spoke quietly, not wanting to bother the people sleeping next to her.

"I can't wait to get back to my own bed. This cot is miserable." She ran her hand over her hair, smoothing it out. "What's the plan?"

"Nothing." No plan of his involved her.

He sat up. Rubbed his palm over his scruffy face. What would Paisley think of his unshaven—he sniffed himself—bad smelling condition? How many days had he gone without shaving or showering? Three? She used to say she liked it when he let his whiskers grow out on the weekends. That it made him look wild and carefree. Maybe she'd be attracted to his appearance. Although, not his odor. He chuckled.

"What's with the grin?" Mia's voice was soft.

"Nothing, really." He needed to watch what he said around her.

He slipped his feet into his shoes. Stood. Pulled on the secondhand coat. He checked the item in the pocket—the only thing that went right yesterday. Then he smoothed out the blankets on the cot. Hopefully, he was all done sleeping here.

At the table laden with coffeepots and platters of donuts, he filled a cup and picked up a maple bar. James Weston was already there. His expression looked downcast.

"Something wrong?"

James took off his glasses, wiped his hand over his eyes. "I've been standing here trying to figure out how to get back to my house. They say we can't return for a few more days, but I've got a list of things to do. I've had all I can take of sitting and waiting."

"Any solutions come to mind?" If James figured out a way to get back home, maybe he could catch a ride.

The older man rocked his thumb toward the gym doors. "Take a gander at that."

Judah stared through the glass on the doors. Dark gray clouds loomed overhead. Hard raindrops fell. The trees swayed in the wind. "Oh, no."

"Storm." James put his glasses back on. "Ruins my plans."

Judah's too, maybe. Why did one thing after another seem to be preventing him from getting to Paisley?

Lord, could You make a way where there doesn't seem to be a way?

He took a sip of his hot drink, contemplating the storm and how it might affect his return to Basalt Bay.

"Hi, guys." Mia's voice.

"Morning." James stepped over near Judah. "How long do you suppose this will last? I'm worried about my place. The thought of looters makes me see red."

"Me too. Maybe someone has access to the news. Let's find out how the road crew is doing. This weather will impede progress, I'm afraid." Judah leaned closer to the other man, trying to keep his voice quiet enough that Mia wouldn't hear. "Before, when you spoke of going home, what were you thinking about doing?"

"You know the old road to the lighthouse?"

"Yeah. It's nearly impassable."

"Thought I'd drive the long way around, come in farther north of where the guards are stationed." James nodded at another fellow approaching the table. "I heard a couple of guys talking of doing the same thing last night."

"That right?" Judah could walk that far, from the lighthouse to Paul's. Easier than hiking across the dunes.

"No one can keep us from protecting our property." James clenched his fist in the air. "We have rights."

The men guarding the entrance to town might take exception to that, but Judah didn't say so.

Mia stepped between them. "What are you two plotting with such serious faces?" She sipped her coffee, grimaced. "I can't wait to stop drinking this awful watered-down brew."

"No one's forcing you to drink it, young lady." James scowled.

"I just prefer my regular coffee. Don't you?" She smiled and patted the man's arm as if to smooth out his ruffled feathers.

"I suppose that's true." James nodded, his voice changing to a more pleasant tone.

"How long have you lived in our lovely town, sir?"

"I've lived in the same house my whole life. Paul Cedars and I attended grade school together." James's chest seemed to puff out with pride.

Mia grinned again. "You must be one of our town's most upstanding citizens."

James chuckled. His face hued red. "Don't know about that."

Judah couldn't believe how Mia's schmoozing changed the man's countenance. She had a way with men. Or pure manipulation. Had she treated Judah that way before?

"I was telling Judah how I plan to get back to Basalt Bay." Uh-oh. James was rambling.

"That's fascinating." Mia leaned closer to him. "How will you do that?"

Judah stepped in before James said anything else. "I think the storm may hinder us from doing much today." He nodded toward the entryway, drawing James away from Mia. "Let's take another look."

"Nice chatting with you, miss." James lifted his cup in her direction.

"Same here." She tugged on Judah's coat sleeve. "You're staying put, right?"

"We'll see." He avoided giving her any details. He followed James back to the door. Peered outside. The weather appeared the same as before. Not good. A strong gale would make a sea journey difficult, although not impossible. And the skiff's owner might not let them use his rental in these conditions.

"Such a shame." James groaned. "Maybe I'll drive north tomorrow."

"If I don't find my own way out of here today"—Judah hated even saying that—"could I catch a ride with you?" He wanted to keep his options open. In the meantime, he'd pray for the storm to let up.

"Sure, sure. Would enjoy the company." James patted him on the shoulder. "Nice girl you work with." He nodded toward the coffee table where Mia conversed with a couple of other men. "Anything going on between you two?"

"What? No! Nothing like that." He held up his left hand, displaying his wedding ring. "Still married."

"Uh-huh." James nodded. No doubt he'd heard the gossip in Basalt Bay. "Paul and I go way back."

Oh, right, Paul. Judah drank down the rest of his lukewarm coffee in a big gulp. "I think I'll get ready for the day." He shook the man's hand. Then dropped his Styrofoam cup in the garbage on his way to the restroom.

After washing up, he was leaving the facilities when Brad Keifer entered the gym. The man tugged the front door closed with both hands, the winds fighting his hold. Judah walked toward him.

Brad shook off his hat. Brushed rainwater from his coat. "It's terrible out there."

"So I see. Any word from your friend?"

"He's not answering his phone." The fisherman rubbed the soles of his boots against the mat, then stomped toward the coffee table. "Probably doesn't want to speak to me."

Judah didn't blame the guy for being leery of Brad's temper. "Do you think he'll let us rent his skiff in this weather?"

"Who knows? I'd rather not do business with the scum."

"Have any other plans for getting back to Basalt Bay?"

"Wait for a break in the storm, I guess." Brad scooped up an apple fritter. "Although, I'm sick of waiting," he said around a mouthful.

"Me too." Judah bit his lower lip, willing away frustration. Too bad he didn't listen to himself. His thoughts rushed headlong through the things that troubled him. His inability to get back to his wife. His dad's interference in his life. Mia's constant hovering and flirtations. And where was Craig? Why had he disappeared and stayed away?

"About the boat. There is another idea." Brad gazed around the room furtively. "Not that I would stoop to such a low, you understand."

"No, of course not." Wait. What did the fisherman mean?

"How badly do you want to get to the bay?"

"Badly enough." Judah glanced over his shoulder, making sure Mia wasn't within earshot.

"I say, weather permitting, we take the skiff—borrow it. Pay Richard later." Brad bit into another donut. "I doubt anyone will go out in these winds, other than you and me. Besides, he said we could use it this morning."

He had, but— "Just take it?" That went against everything honest in Judah, even if Brad used the term "borrow." What about his integrity in the community? What if word got out that he took a skiff? Mia might spread tales. Did Judah's need to get back to Paisley justify such actions? This *was* an emergency. There were extenuating circumstances.

"What do you say?" Brad flicked donut crumbs from his beard.

Judah gulped. His moment of truth. Or temptation. The boat owner said they could use the skiff. And he did undercut their plans yesterday. "I think you should call the guy again. Leave a message. Go to his house. We should do everything in our power to contact him before we borrow any of his equipment." Even if that meant Judah wouldn't get to see Paisley today. He felt the weight of his decision all the way to his toes. The disappointment that their plans might fall through, again, felt crushing.

Brad glared at him for about twenty seconds. "Fine. But I don't know how the cheat stays in business."

"Me, either. But two wrongs don't—"

"Yeah, yeah." Brad hauled his phone out of his pocket. Stared at the screen. Held it up higher as if checking for bandwidth. "Useless phone. C'mon." Brad grabbed another donut then trudged toward the door.

Judah glanced over his shoulder. Mia lifted her hand in a wave. He nodded and scrambled after Brad, bracing for the wind and downpour just beyond the door.

Lord, please help me get back to Paisley.

Fourteen

Wind and rain beat hard against the boarded-up window in the child's bedroom where Paisley had slept, reminding her of the harrowing night she spent in Dad's bathroom during the hurricane. A bad memory still. Except for those moments when she and Judah linked pinkies beneath the door. She smiled at that remembrance. Then, it felt like not only were their pinkies touching, but their hearts too. She'd never forget that—the sweetness of his hand resting against hers all night, feeling connected with him again after those years of hurts and sorrows. And especially after the earthshaking kiss they shared. Those mental pictures were stuck in her thoughts like super glue. If only she could print them out as photos for the mantle.

Sigh.

Noises reached her from the kitchen. Pots rattled. Cupboard doors opened and closed. Was Craig searching for breakfast food?

Groaning, she realized she had to face him again. Last night after she came into Piper's room and found the door didn't have a lock, she propped a chair under the handle the way she'd seen characters do in suspense movies. Now, she stood and ran her hands down her clothes to smooth them out. She was thankful for the sweatshirt she found in the gallery yesterday. And the leggings she unearthed in Paige's drawer were thick and comfy. She shoved her feet into a pair of hiking boots she discovered in her sister's closet.

For a moment, seeing the child's bed, the stuffed animals on a low shelf, the dolls in the corner, she imagined what Piper was like. Her photos showed a blond toddler with the cutest grin. Maybe dimples. Seeing her, Paisley wondered again if Misty Gale, the sweet infant she miscarried at six months, four years ago, would have resembled her cousin. The old ache burned in her. The longing to know her daughter, to hold her, to kiss her soft cheeks, to watch her grow up. Would that pain, that feeling of loss, ever go away?

She shoved the chair out from its tipped position beneath the doorknob. Then, opening the door, she trudged down the hall to the kitchen, her heart still tender following her recent thoughts. The rain pounded on the roof like pebbles falling overhead, a perfectly depressing start to another day. Would the downpour swamp the road into town again? At this rate, it could be days before Judah reached her. Would she be stuck in this house with Craig until then? She shivered.

No, this thing with him hanging around, acting like he and Dad were best buddies, must end. Or, if he stayed, she'd leave. Maybe go to Dad's. Um, well, the front window was still broken. Everything was soaked. A tree leaned against the roof, could crash through at any time. No place to sleep other than the pantry. No thanks. She could just order Craig to leave. Insist that he vacate the premises, despite the disaster, and stay away.

As she entered the kitchen, natural light flooded the room. Someone had removed the plywood from the window. Craig's doing? See how he was endearing himself to Dad? Paisley groaned.

Thankfully, her father, and not their guest, opened and shut cupboard doors. A tomato-based casserole, probably thawed out from the freezer, rested on the counter, billowing delicious-smelling steam. Mmm.

She went straight to Dad and wrapped her arms around him. "Good morning, Daddy." Even though he didn't return her embrace or comment on her endearment, she was determined to keep taking chances, especially considering the discouraged funk he was in yesterday. She wanted to reaffirm her gratefulness that he was alive. That she appreciated this second chance to reconnect. "Nice to see you up and about. You look ready to tackle the day."

"Craig and I decided to rustle up some grub." Dad opened a can of garbanzo beans with a hand-crank can opener. He dumped the food into a foil packet. He did the same thing with a can of mixed veggies.

"Are you going to heat this on the grill?"

"Yep." He splashed in a little olive oil, salt and pepper, then crimped the top of the foil. He set the packet on a plate. "Craig's our grill guy. Good thing he showed up, huh?"

Yeah, yeah. Lucky them. She turned away so Dad wouldn't see her grimace.

The taller man burst through the doorway, shaking raindrops from his hat. "Good news. Weather's supposed to improve by mid-afternoon." He glanced at her. "Oh. Good morning."

The muscles in her chest contracted. How could she get used to him walking in and out of the house as if he were part of the family?

"Glad to hear it." Dad handed him the plate.

Craig spun around and went back outside. The two of them sure seemed chummy. Had they even spoken before yesterday?

The C-MER employee's words about the weather report suddenly blasted through her thoughts. "Wait a second. How does he know when the storm's going to pass? He said his cell phone's out of power."

"Beats me. I don't own one."

"You never replaced your old phone?" Momentarily distracted, she remembered how Dad dropped his archaic folding phone into the ocean before she left home.

"No reason to pay the bill since *no one* calls anyway." He shot her a pointed glance.

Guilt swept through her, again.

He opened the lid of a bottle of apple juice, then poured three short glasses full, his hands shaking slightly. "Besides, landline works fine."

Not now. She thought of the dead phone line at his house.

"How did the old place weather the hurricane?" He moved the glasses away from the edge of the counter.

Was he well enough to handle bad news? "Not so well, I'm afraid. The stairs collapsed. The flooring is ruined. Some windows are broken. The big tree in back fell on the roof."

A shadow crossed his face. "Guess we'll have a lot to do to fix it, huh?"

We'll?

"Yes, we certainly will."

"When's Judah coming back?" Dad took down three turquoise plates from the shelf by the sink.

"Yesterday, I wish."

"Impatient as always." At least he remembered that much

about her. He'd made some mental progress since yesterday. His eyes seemed clearer, too.

"Craig says the weather and the bad roads will keep him away another day or so." Dad set three slices of bread on the counter next to the casserole.

"What does he know?" The weather could change any second. Anyone who lived on the coast knew that.

Dad was going all out on this breakfast. She should tell him to ration the food. Who knew when they might find more supplies? But seeing him doing something so enthusiastically seemed miraculous. And she was hungry. They all had to be.

A few minutes later, Craig reentered the room carrying the steaming vegetable mix. Paisley preoccupied herself with rearranging dirty dishes in the sink, avoiding eye contact. After the men dished up their food, she fixed hers. She dropped onto a chair at the kitchen table, scooting closer to Dad, creating more space between her and Craig as she set her plate down.

"I'm glad your sister had food in her freezer." Dad scooped up a spoonful of the casserole.

"She must enjoy cooking," Craig contributed.

If so, that was news to Paisley.

Dad waved his fork with a noodle on it. "Since Piper came along, she cooks more."

"Makes sense." Paisley ate a bite of the pasta. Not bad. If Paige made this, she was a better cook than Paisley. Although, even Judah cooked better than her. She preferred opening a can or heating up packaged food in the microwave.

"Do you enjoy cooking?"

It was hard to ignore Craig's direct question with her father sitting there scrutinizing her. She chewed dramatically, stalling.

Then she remembered what he said earlier. "How did you hear about the weather?"

He took a long time swallowing his food this time. "On my cell."

What? His cell phone worked? Her hackles rose like antennas protruding from her skull. "You lied to me? You said your phone didn't work." Did he say that to keep her from contacting Judah? So much for thinking she might have misjudged him. That he might be a nice guy, after all. He was a snake. As soon as this meal ended, he was out of here.

"Uh, well." His cheeks turned crimson. He squirmed in his chair. "I thought the battery died." He guzzled from his glass. Blinked fast.

If her glare could strike him with lightning, he'd be on fire.

"Next time I checked, the weather icon flashed for a second." He shrugged. "Then it died."

Hmm. She pondered his explanation, and some of her rage dissolved. The other night when she was hiding—from him, no less—she got bursts of cell power before the phone died, enough to send Judah a couple of texts. Craig's explanation might be plausible, but she had doubts about anything he said. Once a con, always a con, right?

A twist of discomfort in her chest reminded her that she too had been misjudged by others. Maggie. Miss Patty. Edward. Aunt Callie. Even Dad.

Was she judging Craig the same way? Wait a second. Didn't he come to her father's home late at night, uninvited? Saying "Peek a boo, I see you." Calling her "Little Miss Riding Hood." Not to mention the stuff that happened three years ago. No, she hadn't misjudged him.

She finished eating in silence, then stood. "We need fresh water to wash dishes. Heated would be nice." She stacked her plate and silverware. "Any ideas about where to find clean water?"

Dad shrugged. "Beats me. Saltwater is plentiful."

Craig rubbed his index finger and thumb over his overgrown chin hair. "There's a creek not too far away. Saltwater may have backed into it during the storm, so it isn't potable. Okay for dishes. Flushing the toilet. I can take a couple of buckets over and check."

"Fine." So they were still dependent on the scoundrel. When he came back, she'd tell him to leave. She and Dad could get by on their own. Even if Judah didn't show up today, they'd be okay.

"It's still raining out." Dad stood, then bent over, shuffling things around in a cupboard. He handed Craig a large metal bowl. "Why don't you put this outside to collect rainwater?"

"Good idea." Craig left through the back door.

"You don't trust him. Why not?" Dad adjusted his glasses, peering at her the way he did when she was young and backtalked.

She piled up the dishes and carried them to the sink. She couldn't explain the whole situation to her father. And nothing less would do.

"I saw it in your eyes." He followed her, then stood next to the counter, watching her.

She'd have to answer, say something, anything. "Okay, I don't like him saying Judah can't make it back today. Who's he to spread gloom and doom?" That was partly the truth.

"Are you going to give him another chance?"

"Craig?"

"Judah."

"I haven't decided." A small mistruth. And another topic she didn't wish to discuss with him.

115

"You could have done worse than marrying a man like him, even if he is a Grant." He wiped the counter with a paper towel.

Her dad's affirmation of Judah surprised her as much as his chatting and puttering around the kitchen did.

"It's complicated." She dried her hands on a dishtowel.

"Of course, it is." He shuffled toward the living room. "What would you expect after you left him for three years?"

She would have followed him and defended herself if Craig hadn't entered the kitchen.

He wiped rainwater from his face. "Where would I find buckets?"

Paisley yanked open a couple of cupboards. "Dad! Where's a big pot or bucket?"

"Under the sink. Might be two."

She leaned down and opened the doors beneath the sink, not liking how Craig also bent down, peering over her shoulder. She spotted two matching red buckets, grabbed them and eased away from him. She set the pails on the table instead of handing them directly to him.

"As soon as I get back from the creek, I'm heading out." He shuffled his feet. "Judah might not understand my being here."

"No kidding. I don't understand it, either." Although, he did help her father in his crisis, which meant in some small way he helped her. She hated acknowledging that, even to herself.

He tugged on his hat. "I think Judah might be on his way here." He grabbed the buckets and strode toward the door.

"Wait. How would you know that?"

He paused, didn't face her. "I may not have been entirely honest before."

"May not?" Her heart pounded hard against her ribs.

116

"I'm leaving. Look out for your dad's health. Make sure he does his testing, okay?" The door closed behind him.

She peered out the kitchen window, watching the tall man speed walk across the yard and turn at the corner. What couldn't he explain? What secret was he hiding?

Dad shuffled into the kitchen with his coat buttoned up to his chin, his wool cap pulled down over his ears. "Thought I'd take a look-see at the beach."

"It's still stormy out." She heard the sharpness in her tone, a leftover reaction to her conversation with Craig. She cleared her throat. "Do you feel well enough for a walk?"

He shrugged. "It's my favorite time at the seashore, you know that."

They used to walk together at the beach, hunting for treasures following storms. Once, she found a Japanese glass fishing float in perfect condition. "Want some company?"

"Sure." He stuffed his hands in his coat pockets. "Just like old times."

Something warm and powerful filled her chest. Who cared if it rained? Who cared if Craig's strange disclosure unsettled her? Right now, the most important thing was spending time with Dad.

"Let me check Paige's closet for a coat. I'll be right out." She grabbed a flashlight and hurried down the hall to her sister's bedroom. Rummaging through the closet, she found a thick sweater and a raincoat. Good thing she and Paige were similar in size. On the top shelf, a plastic tub held hats. She picked out a gray knitted one and pulled it on, tugging it over her ears.

She marched back down the hall, dropping off the flashlight on the kitchen table. Dad waited for her by the back door, shuffling his feet as if he were antsy to get going. His bright eyes and his eager smile brought joy to her heart.

Thank You that he's doing better.

Without talking, they exited into the rain. She followed him down the driveway, along the sidewalk. They crossed the street, then veered onto the trailhead which led to the beach. She heard the breakers crashing against the rocks. Smelled the salty, musty scent of the seashore. *Her ocean.* Sharing it with Dad made it even more special.

As they broke free of tree cover, the wind churned against them, pushing them back. She squinted out toward the water. The waves pounded the beach, the sea spray whirling into the air like a giant beater mixed it. White foam rushed up and down the sand. When Paisley was young, she ran barefoot through the dancing foam, feeling the spray rush up her legs. Now, she and Dad stood huddled together, both with their hands tucked into their coats, their shoulders bent slightly forward, bracing into the wind.

"Did you notice the missing boulders out on the peninsula?" She spoke loudly, trying to be heard over the roar of the pounding waves.

"Won't ever be the same." Dad shuffled his feet. "It'll need repairs. Wouldn't want tourists walking out on the point and falling in."

She couldn't wait to go out there again, even with the damage. When C-MER resumed operations, they'd probably post signs warning people to stay off the rocks until the completion of repair work. She wouldn't pay attention to such signs.

"You be careful too." Nice to hear the fatherly concern in his voice. He knew she liked to sit out on the point. He'd done the same thing when he was a boy. He'd told her so plenty of times.

Facing into the wind, she blinked against the raindrops. They walked slowly down the beach, trudging toward Paige's building.

"What was Paige's gallery like before Addy hit?"

"Her pride and joy." She heard the smile in Dad's voice. "She and your mama used to talk and talk about their art gallery ideas."

She didn't remember such discussions. Maybe that's what they spoke about when Paisley and Peter were out playing on the beach, fighting their imaginary dragons.

"Too bad Mom didn't get to see that dream come true." He scrubbed the back of his hand beneath his nose.

Emotion stuck in Paisley's throat. Her mother's last words to her crept through her thoughts. *You are an ungrateful daughter!* Was she? Had she ever understood her mother? Had her mom ever understood her?

"What about you? Have any dreams?"

His voice drew her from her contemplations, from her confusion. "Not so much anymore."

"And Judah?"

"What about him?"

Dad tugged on her arm. "You're still married to him, aren't you?"

"According to the law." Their last kiss flitted through her thoughts. *Maybe more than just according to the law.*

"You know Mayor Grant isn't my favorite person."

She bet a lot of townspeople felt that way, her included.

"You could have picked a better father-in-law." Dad chuckled. "But he comes with the package deal. Pastor Sagle says everyone has at least one redeeming quality. I wonder what the mayor's might be."

Her thoughts leapt to the night Edward yanked her away from Craig. How he stepped into a volatile situation and rescued her. Was that a redeeming quality? But didn't he cancel it out when he paid her to leave his son? Or did that fall on her since she followed his wishes? *Sigh.*

"Look!" Dad thrust his finger toward the sea, holding down his hat with his other hand.

"What is it?" She squinted toward the breakers, didn't see anything unusual.

"A skiff! Wait. There it is!" He shuffled to the midpoint of the rocky shoreline.

Judah? If so, Craig was right about his arrival. "Can you see who it is?" She followed Dad, stepping around a couple of large rocks.

"The sea's too rough for a beach landing here."

"Judah would know that." Oh, there. The bow of a skiff rose beyond the foaming waves. It fell, disappearing into a trough. One person manned the boat. It could be him. Still too far away to tell.

Dad leaned forward, peering through his wet glasses. "Think it's him?"

"I don't know." Whoever it was faced powerful breakers just ahead. Dangerous ones. Why was he even landing here?

Plodding to the edge of the tideline, they watched the skiff battling turbulent waves. The way the guy steered the skiff, how he tipped his head down, bracing into the wind with the top of his head, reminded her of Judah. "It might be him." If so, he was coming to her by way of the sea. A lightness she hadn't felt in days filled her. Made her grin like a teenage girl with a crush on a boy.

Unless it wasn't him. But who else would ride into town in a skiff on such a blustery day? In waves that could capsize him. It had to be Judah.

Fifteen

Judah had already dropped off Brad at what remained of the old cannery dock. Now, he was steering the skiff through heavy rain toward the beach at Basalt Bay. Not the best landing place. In fact, one of the toughest. But it was the most direct approach to town. If he could get past the breakers separating open waters from the cove, he'd pull the skiff onto shore, anchor it, then rush over to Paul's. His only goal, his one desire, was to see Paisley, to hold her in his arms and make sure she was okay.

He was soaked through, thanks to not having on his usual rain gear. With each slam of the bow against the waves, his teeth rattled. More water sprayed over him, adding to his soggy condition.

Despite his eagerness to see his wife, he needed to stay focused and get through the next battle with the sea. Strong winds and gusting rain had made traveling from Florence to Basalt Bay challenging. Judah and Brad, being experienced boatmen, didn't express doubts or any inability to navigate through the rough waters. Still, Judah recognized the clenched-teeth grimace on the other man's face, a man who'd weathered plenty of storms and rough seas. They'd taken a risk. Fortunately, they made it this far.

Judah steered into a trough, keeping the boat angled slightly west. The craft rose on the crest of the next wave, and he had a quick glimpse of the beach. He turned the bow, aiming for the smoothest section of shoreline. Not far ahead, a large boulder was hidden beneath the water; he'd seen it at low tide many times. He had to carefully veer around that rock. Sea spray splashed over the boat, sending foam splattering onto his shoulders, his face. He tasted saltwater. Spit. He scrubbed the back of his hand over his eyes. The salt burned. No time to pause.

On the next rise, for just a sec, he thought he spotted someone on the beach. The boat dropped into a dip and a wall of gray water shielded him from seeing the shore. Coming up again, he stared hard at the shoreline. Two people! Was one Paisley?

The boat plunged. The waves blocked his view. He rode it out, rose on another crest. That might be her, but who was the guy? Craig? *No way!* Judah steered crosswise into the next wave. His wife would not be anywhere near that man.

The boat dipped harshly. Water poured over the side. *Yikes.* He picked up the bucket and bailed fast. With his other hand, he steered through another wave, praying it didn't capsize him. He perused the bubbling white water of the breakers ahead. Clenched his teeth. Stared down the waves, hoping to get through them without trouble.

He held the steering mechanism tightly. The craft jerked left. Water arced over the bow, spray hitting him full in the face. He spit. Bailed. Not much farther. Down the trough; ride the wave. More water poured over the gunwales. The boat was about a third full of seawater now. With all this water rolling over the skiff, he was relieved the engine didn't stall. One big wave could sink him. He wouldn't let that happen, if he could help it.

The skiff ploughed heavily through the surf, but Judah angled shoreward. More pounding waves splashed over the back of the skiff, over the engine. He spit. Wiped his eyes. Kept bailing.

He caught another glimpse of Paisley—it had to be her. She waved at him with big movements like she was doing the motions for the "YMCA."

The boat rose then dropped, jarring his teeth. He groaned. Seawater inside the skiff reached the midpoint of his calf, soaking his wound.

Suddenly, the keel rammed into something. The engine sputtered. The skiff lurched sideways. He held on and turned the tiller to avoid a second strike. Had he miscalculated the rocks? The bottom of the engine scraped along whatever the boat crashed into before he had time to lift it.

The motor glug-glug-glugged. Died. Waves struck the side of the skiff, turning it east, hurling it west. Any second the next wave could pound over the sides, tossing him into the sea. He dropped the bailing bucket. Held onto the gunwales with both hands, riding it out. There wasn't time to try to restart the engine.

A couple of days ago, in a different location and with a different skiff, he was forced to jump into the sea to save himself and his employer's boat. If it came to that, he knew what to do. Still bobbing in the merciless thrashing of waves, he yanked the oars out of their clasps. One by one, he plunked them into the oarlocks. Fighting to regain a directional bead on the shore, he reefed on the oars, groaning with the exertion of moving the weighted skiff.

"C'mon." He groaned, pulling hard on the oars. *Pull. Pull.*

His injured leg was numb to the burning sensation he experienced earlier. Because of the lack of pain, he worked harder, exacting more strength and stamina from himself.

He let up on the oars, hoping the next rush of water would propel the craft onto the wet beach like a rocket. Utter failure. Instead, a wave crashed against the port side. Judah didn't have time to react. The boat jerked upward, tipped nearly on its side, sliding him into the sea like hot butter off a chunk of crab. Ice-cold seawater rushed over him, over his head. Submerged him.

He jackknifed his boots off the bottom of the sea floor. As he came up gasping for air, he reached out for the skiff, but it was already too far away. He couldn't lose it now. Taking a long draw of air, he swam hard toward the boat bobbing with the waves.

"Judah!" Paisley's voice.

He lunged for the skiff, kicking his shoes hard in the water. He pulled against the frigid waves with his arms, swimming determinedly. The boat was being swept toward open waters by the tidal force and the strong winds. He had to pursue it.

"Judah, come back!"

He glanced over his shoulder between breast strokes. She was in the water now, too. The waves hit her knee-high. He wanted to tell her to stay back, to stay safe. Instead, he kept swimming against the current, kicking with all his might, knowing the conditions were too cold for him to be in the water much longer.

Finally, he reached the half-sunken boat and grabbed hold of the starboard gunwale. He drew in great gulps of air, trying to catch his breath. He moved his hands along the top edge, gripping closer and closer to the bow until he reached the floating rope. With the line in his left hand, he swam on his right side, scissor kicking as hard as he could, slowly pulling the resistant boat. At times if felt like he wasn't making headway at all. The water chilled him. Made his movements stiff and clumsy.

Then Paisley was on the other side of the boat, holding on to the rope, swimming and pulling the craft, too. Even though seeing her in the rough surf made him concerned for her safety, he was thankful for her assistance, encouraged by it. Her jumping in the sea with him, unreserved, was typical of her. She wouldn't be afraid to fight the waves with him.

He swam until his shoes bumped into muddy ground. He stood on wobbly legs, spitting out water, coughing. He gripped the side of the boat, tugged on it. Paisley did the same. The wave action worked in their favor, now, pushing the skiff toward land.

"Falling into the sea is becoming a habit with you." She tossed him a cute grin, her hair dripping wet, but then she slipped. She landed on her knees in the water, flailing out her hands.

"Paisley!"

She stood quickly. "I'm okay. My b-boots s-stuck in the m-mud." Her teeth chattered as she grabbed the port side of the skiff again.

Keeping an eye on her, he shuffled to the stern, shoved hard against the weighted boat.

That's when he saw the other person on the beach was Paul. Not Craig! His father-in-law swung his arms to his right as if directing Judah where to land the skiff. Paul waded into shallow water too, helping them drag the boat in, but his movements seemed clumsy and stiff. Probably due to the cold.

Judah shoved; the other two pulled. It took all three of them to get the half-swamped boat through the mud and mostly out of the surf.

As soon as he dropped anchor, Paisley splashed through the water toward him, dove into his arms, her wet arms wrapping around his shoulders like an octopus, clinging to him. He laughed, fighting for balance, and returned her embrace—boy, did he ever. He nearly got knocked over by the next wave. She was laughing too, reminding him of how they used to play and have so much fun in the ocean when they were younger. He wanted to kiss her, but with her dad standing right here watching, he held back. Besides, they were both shaking from the cold.

"I'm s-so g-glad to see you." She slid out of his arms, stepped back, lowering her gaze. Was she uncomfortable being close to him? Because of her dad watching?

"Me too." But they were freezing. He had to secure the boat. Find dry clothes. She did too.

He lifted his hand to wave at Paul. The older man was shaking, also.

Paisley scurried over to where her dad extended the towrope as if checking its length. Judah knew the approximately twenty-foot rope wouldn't reach any boulders where it could be tied. He'd have to find longer rope. Until then, he hoped the anchor would hold the boat when the tide rolled back in.

He scooped bucket after bucket of water from the inside, dumping it on the sand.

"W-where've you b-been all this t-time?" Paul shivered and adjusted his wet glasses.

"Dad—"

"I tried to get here yesterday." Judah glanced at Paisley. She scuffed the toe of her boot against a broken crab shell. Was she avoiding his gaze? "Mia drove me north and—" He briefly explained yesterday's events while he kept bailing. He couldn't ignore the awkward silence. The tight look on Paisley's face. Because he mentioned Mia?

"C-come up to Paige's house. W-we all n-need dry clothes." Paul's teeth chattered.

"So, Paul, were you the one who showed up the other night? The one who made Paisley and me scared out of our wits?"

Paisley shook her head harshly at him. A warning? What did he say to elicit such a dark look?

Paul scratched his nose, his hand shaking. "I d-don't know w-what you're t-talking about. Haven't been h-home since the s-storm." He wrung his hands. "S-so c-cold."

"Let's go, Dad." Paisley draped her arm over her father's shoulders, shooting Judah another strained look.

He'd been out of touch with her nuances for a long time, but it seemed she expected him to know something. Or maybe his brain was too foggy after his icy swim.

Paisley and Paul shuffled down the beach. Paisley's arms encircled her father's shoulders like she was trying to shield him from the cold. Was something wrong with him, other than him being wet and chilled? Something seemed odd, out of sync. But Judah's landing had turned out weird, anyway. Not the home-coming he envisioned.

He kept bailing but watched over his shoulder. Father and daughter stopped. Paul gesticulated, seemed agitated, pointing back at Judah. Paisley shook her head, then resumed her gait across the sand.

So Paul hadn't returned to his house since the storm? How could that be?

Wind gusts pounded against Judah's wet back, chilling him. His teeth chattered as he worked, but he didn't stop until he dumped out most of the seawater.

After he checked the anchor, he tromped across the mud flat, his shoes sliding in the wet muck as he followed Paisley and Paul. Since his gimpy leg was still numb, he was able to push it, although he might be sorry later. He veered around partially filled sandbags that had been torn up and displaced by the waves. He grabbed a collapsed lawn chair in his path and tossed it up on the rocks so it wouldn't get swept away by the tide. The metal frame clattered, but the roar of the sea overpowered the noise.

He trudged across the wet sand, making a quick perusal of the seashore like he would if he was on the job. The beach needed a major cleanup. At the peninsula, a gaping hole remained where the five-foot boulder he labeled Sample D used to sit. He recalled the night of the storm and how the geyser of water cascaded over the old breakwater. How he feared Paisley might be out there. Thank God she wasn't. Samples B and C were missing too. As was a section of the point. C-MER and the town council would have decisions to make about reconstructing the harbor's protective barrier.

Thanks to Paisley and Paul's snail-like pace, he caught up to them at the beach parking lot. She glanced up with a startled expression. The sound of the ocean waves and the wind must have muffled his footsteps.

"Hey." He dared to take her cool hand in his. "I want you to know that I couldn't wait to get back to you. I went crazy with worry. Tried everything I could think of to get back here. I'm sorry it took me so long."

She withdrew her hand from his. "Me too." Her other hand was linked in her father's arm. She seemed to be pulling him forward.

Judah sighed. "Any idea where I can find some clothes?"

He doubted Paige had anything his size at her house. He gazed at the beach houses up ahead. "I might have to break in somewhere."

"Hard to believe you would consider doing such a thing." Her frown almost made him laugh. As if he said he was going to rob a bank.

"I'll leave a note. I doubt anyone will mind since it's an emergency."

"True. My dad's going to need some—"

"No, I don't," Paul interrupted her. "I have overalls at Paige's for when I work on things there."

"Why didn't you tell me that yesterday?"

Paul shrugged.

"I doubt Paige has any rope," Paisley said. "You'll have to search elsewhere for that, too."

He'd nearly forgotten about the rope. "Thanks for the reminder. I'll come over to your sister's after I get the skiff situated."

"You know where she lives, right?" She squinted at him as if asking some other question.

"Sure, I've been there before." He'd visited their niece. Was invited to her second birthday party. Piper called him *Unca Dzuda*.

"Okay. See you later."

"Pais, is something wrong?" Even though they were freezing, trudging along in the rain, he had to know.

She shook her head, shrugged, didn't meet his gaze.

He sighed. Now probably wasn't the time to push for an answer. "I would have been here for you if I could. You know that, right?"

"I want to b-believe that." Her lip trembled.

He longed to take her in his arms the way he thought of

doing down on the beach. Kiss away her doubts. Tell her how their separation ate away at his patience, even his faith, a few times. All that seemed a lifetime ago now that he stood beside her. Yet, something was amiss. An invisible brick wall had risen between them.

Paul coughed.

"We have to go." Paisley walked away with her arm draped over her dad's shoulders.

Frustration pounded through the icy places in Judah's heart. They were separated for three years. Together as a couple—if he could even call them that idyllic term—for less than twenty-four hours. And in the last two days, he lived and breathed the hope of reuniting with her. Them starting where they left off after the storm. Now, this.

Chills overcame him. He needed dry clothes. A coat. Maybe a comforter to wrap up in.

Then, could he and Paisley sit down and discuss whatever had caused such a great divide between them?

Sixteen

Judah stood on the sidewalk in front of James Weston's beachfront house. Piles of shingles, kelp, and displaced items were scattered across his yard and the neighbors' yards. All the windows on the five homes facing the sea were covered with sheets of plywood. The same was true of the houses across the street, except for Paul's. At his father-in-law's, Judah would have to climb a ladder to reach the second story, and with his leg aching as it was now, he'd rather not do that if there was an alternative.

Since he'd recently been in contact with James, that man's house seemed the best option for breaking into. Surely, Paul's friend and neighbor would understand Judah's need for dry clothes and rope.

Judah's coat and jeans dripped seawater. He was shaking almost uncontrollably. If he didn't find a change of apparel soon, he might be in danger of hypothermia. Bolstered by the adage about "desperate times calling for desperate measures," he trudged across the wet lawn toward James's back porch. As he moved, his wet, stiff pant legs made a scraping sound against each other. Every time he lifted his knee, the firm fabric tugged against his stitches where the bandage had come loose while he was swimming. Hopefully, the stitches were still okay. He'd have to search for another bandage and a first aid kit.

He hobbled up the steps, tugged on the doorknob. Locked, of course. He shoved his arm and shoulder against the door to test it. Nothing happened, other than his leg aching and throbbing with renewed vigor. He grabbed hold of the doorknob with both hands and shook harder. Nothing gave.

He groaned.

This break-in attempt wasn't such a great idea. And James was a bit of a curmudgeon who might even be upset about Judah trying to break down his door. However, this was an emergency. Judah's health depended on getting out of these drenched clothes.

One more try. Taking a breath, he planted the foot of his injured leg as solidly as he could against the porch. Then he lifted his other foot and rammed his heel against the wood near the lock, the weakest spot on the door. Pain ricocheted up his sore leg. He groaned, held his breath, waiting for the tremors in his calf to cease.

Nothing on the door broke free, either. Time for Plan B.

He hobbled down the steps, contemplating how he could climb the ladder at Paul's and enter through the bedroom window he exited two days ago. He limped across the flooded street, noticing the large pile of shingles and garbage in the front yard. Paisley did a lot of work here. Good for her!

Where was that ladder Craig used? Judah trudged around the left side of the house, sloshing over wet muddy ground. The backyard was still swampy but mostly cleared of shingles and garbage. No ladder here. He backtracked to the front and checked the right side of the lot. Two days ago, Craig didn't take it when he rushed Judah to the ER. Since then, had he come back for it?

Judah swallowed a lump in his throat. What if it was Craig who came here the other night? The person Paisley feared. Was that why she freaked out when he questioned Paul about it, earlier?

There he was jumping to conclusions. It could have been his own father. But wouldn't Paisley have mentioned that? Someone obviously took the ladder. Looters?

Seeing his truck that was slammed against Paul's front porch during the hurricane, he remembered that he sometimes kept work-related supplies in there. Maybe even rope. Since the driver's door was jammed against the porch, he opened the passenger side, then released the front seat to see into the back compartment. He shoved a container of tools on the floorboard out of his way. Checked under the seat. There. A tangled-up wad of rope. Perfect!

What was in the black garbage bag next to the rope? He tugged on the plastic, tore it open. A pair of grubby jeans and a stained sweatshirt tumbled out. He nearly wept. He forgot all about the clothes he stored in the truck for doing messy work at C-MER. He grabbed the items and headed for the porch.

He pulled himself onto the floorboards, opened the front door—good thing it wasn't locked—and trudged inside. The apple tree didn't protrude through the gaping front window the way it did during the storm. Instead, thick plastic sheeting covered the opening. He noticed the neat line of nails. Paisley's work? Or Paul's? That's right. Paul said he wasn't here. If

Paisley could put down a straight row of nails like this, she'd be a great asset when it came time to fix their beach cottage.

He hobbled into the kitchen, stripped down and checked his purplish wound—the stitches were still intact—then gently pulled on the jeans and dry sweatshirt. He'd like to ditch the wet socks and shoes. Maybe find a coat. He shuffled around the damp house, looking for any kind of outerwear. He checked inside the dryer. Scrounged through some cupboards, keeping in mind his need for a bandage, too. Came up empty. He wished he could climb into the gaping hole, up to the second story, and find what he needed. Although, he knew he wore a different shoe size than Paul.

As he shuffled past the back door, he saw several empty alcohol bottles in the garbage can. Whose were those? *Oh, no.* Was Paisley drinking again? Was that the reason for her aloofness? Thoughts of how erratic she became when she drank excessively in the past barreled through his mind. He didn't want to go down that road again. Prayed it wasn't happening. Just seeing the bottles, and contemplating what they might mean, rattled him.

Sighing, he walked across the wet floor, assessing the damage. The carpet would have to go. As would the wet, lower portion of the sheet rock. Getting heat flowing into the room was essential, the sooner, the better. Unfortunately, that couldn't happen until the electricity came back on. He trudged toward the pantry, the room he knew Paisley hated as a kid. She'd never explained why, just said she despised it. He opened the narrow door and stared into the semi-darkness. A colorful rumpled towel was spread out on the shelf. Is this where she slept? In this tiny dark room that was little more than a closet? He hated to think of her being alone in here.

Canning jars lined the top shelf. A couple of long skinny

boards lay on the middle shelf. Was this where she hid when she talked to him on the phone? When she told him someone was here? He suggested she grab something to use as a weapon. Did she hold these two sticks? He tried to picture it, recalling the fear in her voice. The pounding horror he felt in his own chest. He gulped. Then thanked God for keeping her safe, for being with her. For His help in getting Judah back to town, also.

He lumbered into the living room, his leg wound cramping with each step. The bare walls had discolored rectangular shadows where pictures used to be. All the paintings were on the floor, some face down. It was disheartening to see so much ruined art that had been his mother-in-law's passion when she was alive. The whatnot shelf lay on its side. Broken glass and porcelain pieces were scattered on the rug.

Maybe he'd come back tomorrow and clean up. Remove the carpet. He and Paisley could work on this together. Might give them time to talk. Maybe she'd be more communicative away from her father. And Judah could explain why he rode in Mia's car.

He shuffled to the porch. The deep ruts and mounded ridges where a vehicle drove through the front yard were obviously a truck's. Dad's rig? When the mayor tried to get Paisley to go up to his house, did he drive across the grass? Or did he come back later? Scare her.

Judah groaned. It was hard on him, not knowing. Second guessing everything.

He lowered himself from the porch to the ground, using his truck as leverage. He opened the passenger door, then climbed into the cab and scooted across the seat to get behind the wheel. Hopefully, the truck was in working order, even though it had been hurled around during the tidal surge. The key was still in the ignition. The engine gagged, coughed, barked. Water around the moving parts needed expulsion, no doubt.

He revved the engine several times until it sounded better. He put the truck in four-wheel drive, turned the steering wheel sharply, and gave it a little gas. The bogged-down tires inched forward in tiny jerks. He pushed harder on the gas pedal, and the vehicle lurched ahead, crunching over a couple of branches in the yard. Once the truck reached the street, Judah veered around several downed trees. Turning west, he headed toward the community church. There, he cut across the parking lot, steering slowly through the subdivision west of town. He had to drive across a few sidewalks and yards to bypass garbage, a motor-cycle on its side, and a sailboat smashed into a roadside tree.

Finally, he reached Paige's single-level blue house and pulled into the driveway behind Paul's VW parked sideways. Did the storm surge do that? No plywood sheets lined the windows, here, like on the neighbors' houses. It appeared as if some post-storm cleanup progress had been made.

He tried the driver's door. It wouldn't budge, so he scooted across to the passenger door, shoved against it, then slid to the ground. He winced at the ripping sensation in his leg. Too bad he decided to ram himself against James Weston's door like a thug. All that rowing and swimming in the sea didn't help, either. Sigh. He scooped up the rope. He'd walk down to the skiff as soon as he talked with Paisley.

He plodded through the wet carport, then he saw her standing near the back of the house, her arms crossed, her eyes narrow slits. Was she warning him to keep his distance?

Not likely. "Hi." He strode right for her, forcing himself not to limp. He didn't want her feeling sorry for him, thinking of him as an invalid.

What had she gone through to put that icy look in her gaze? The caution. He smiled, trying to reassure her that he was happy to see her, to finally be here with her. Couldn't they put the past days behind them and hug again, the way she greeted him in the surf when he first arrived?

"I see you found some clothes." She raised her eyebrows. "Wasn't there anything better to steal?"

"Nope. I found these oldies in my truck." He wanted to sweep some strands of hair off her cheek, but he kept his fingers at his sides. "I tried breaking into James's. Couldn't do it. It appears I'm a failure as a thief. So I went over to your dad's."

"Oh? How did it look?"

"You've been there, right?" He pictured the plastic nailed to the front window. Would she tell him about the liquor bottles if he asked? Probably best not to discuss that right now. Not when she already seemed to have a chip on her shoulder. Or a grudge, or something.

"Not since—"

"Not since what?" He took her hand. With the fingers of his other hand, he dared to stroke back a clump of hair from her face, his fingers pausing near her ear. What wasn't she telling him?

Be patient. The two words resounded in his brain. Hard to do when he wanted things to progress faster between them. He wanted reconciliation and healing. For them to move on to the being married part. *Give it time, Grant.*

"Nothing." Her lips clamped shut. She stepped back, removing his fingers, denying them access to her cheek.

Inwardly, he groaned. Had his inability to get back to Basalt Bay caused this rift?

She took another step back. "My dad's sick. I'm distracted. That's all."

"What's wrong with him?"

"Diabetes. He had a high blood sugar incident." She lifted her shoulders. "I didn't even know he was ill. He wasn't taking his medicine. Depressed. Acting like he wanted to die."

"Wow. Sounds like he needed an intervention."

"Yeah, he was in a bad way."

Her gaze flitting anywhere other than looking him in the eye shouted something was wrong that had more to do with him than Paul's sickness. What? Maybe he shouldn't press her, but hadn't he pledged to not let things go unspoken? Didn't he plan to pursue his wife, pursue her heart? And yet, the only thing he needed to know right now was that she was okay.

"How are you doing through all of this?" He kept his tone soft. And he kept his distance, assuming that's what she wanted.

"I'm fine."

He knew, saw, she was anything but fine. And he also knew she didn't want to talk about it. Her body language spoke volumes.

"I'm heading down to the beach to secure the skiff." He held up the rope. "Care to join me?"

"I should stay with Dad. He might need my help."

"Right. Okay, sure." He watched her go inside. Disappointment raked through him. His dreams of arriving in Basalt Bay as her rescuer, as the husband who she was eager to see and be with, wilted and died.

What had happened to Paisley in his absence to cause this chill?

Seventeen

Paisley felt warmer thanks to her sister's supply of clothes. Too bad that warmth didn't quite reach her core. Instead, agitation churned in her gut as she fingered the soggy items in the freezer. Everything appeared thawed, lukewarm, and ruined. She grabbed the trash can and dragged it across the floor. Yanking out the items from the upper compartment, she hurled them into the can, enjoying each of the thudding, crashing sounds. Next, she bent over and emptied perishables from the fridge in the same grab-and-slam manner.

Where would she find more food? Dad needed sustenance for healing and getting stronger. Where was she supposed to find healthy food? No fresh vegetables in town. She hated the thought of breaking into people's houses. She did plenty of mischievous stunts in her youth, including a few break-ins that she still had to make amends for. She didn't want to add to that list of wrongs.

Dad shuffled into the kitchen in overalls. "Anything good in there?"

"No. Couldn't you sleep?"

"Nah." He ran his fingers through his gray hair. "Did I hear Judah's truck? Is Craig still around?"

Ugh. What if Judah ran into him here? Was the other man even in town? Or did he slither away the way he came?

"It was Judah."

"Where's the boy now?"

The boy? Judah was hardly a boy. That Dad thought fondly of him still surprised her.

"He's down at the skiff tying it up." She dropped a half-gallon of milk into the trash.

Why had Judah asked Dad whether he was the one who showed up the other night? If he didn't know that it was Craig, perhaps hadn't seen the text—she swallowed hard—then he probably didn't know the rest, either. All these days, she thought he knew that she told him she loved him.

Then, when she saw him flailing in the waves, thinking of his injury, she rushed into the cold water after him. Would have done anything to help him. And when they brought the skiff to shore, she jumped into his arms, thrilled to be able to do that, knowing he knew she loved him. But something was wrong. She didn't see that special gaze in his eyes that she was looking for. Instead, he seemed to be asking her questions that she couldn't answer in front of Dad.

And she had questions too.

Why did it take so long for him to get back? Sure, he was injured. But two days? She was desperate for him to return, for him to share in the struggles she experienced after the storm, and he hadn't. Instead, she had to accept another man's help. Just the thought of having to tell Judah about that made her tremble.

And what about Mia? Why did her name slide so easily off his lips? They were coworkers, but the woman was trouble. Paisley knew that from the first day she met her. Even now, thinking of the flirty blond made her slam things into the trash a little harder than necessary.

"What's going on here?" Dad stood next to the can, watching, probably thinking she was acting childish.

"Sorry." She threw in a head of rotten lettuce.

One of Dad's eyebrows quirked. "What happened between you and Judah?"

"Not much." She dropped a glass dish of moldy peaches into the trash.

"You don't have to throw the bowl away too."

"It's gross. I don't want to wash it." Cleaning this one with its gray, fuzzy peach chunks stuck to the sides, in cold water, would be awful. Dad probably thought she was being childish about this too, but she'd always hated washing dishes, especially messy ones.

He leaned over and dug out the bowl. "I'll do it." He shuffled to the sink and set the dishware on the counter next to the pile of dirty dishes. A few cups and plates already soaked in sudsy water. Craig's doing, no doubt.

She continued emptying the fridge while Dad scrubbed the bowl.

"Are you going to tell me what's going on with you two?" Dad spoke over his shoulder.

"Nothing like washing dishes in cool water, huh?" She changed the subject.

"It's a kindness that we can wash dishes at all, thanks to Craig."

Yeah, yeah. Everything good around here is Craig's doing.

Dad poured water from the red bucket into the sink to the right. Then dipped clean dishes into it. "There's a little rainwater in the bowl Craig set outside. Not enough to do anything with."

Paisley pulled out a couple of containers from the fridge. "And there's only one bottle of water left. We'll have to find more today." Where? City Hall? Maggie Thomas's inn? An unholy glee rose up in her at the thought of breaking into that woman's establishment. Maggie might even be the type to have a stockpile of food and water. Only, did Paisley want to stir up more angst with the innkeeper who had a reputation for spreading gossip? They already had a history of disagreements and accusations between them.

"I have a few bottles at my house." Dad rattled silverware in the sink.

She thought of the other kind of bottles over there, too. The ones Craig said were Dad's. "Judah and I used those water bottles during the storm."

"Oh. How about at the gallery?"

"That's a good idea." She remembered seeing juice containers when she was there yesterday. "I'll walk over and grab an armful."

"Maybe you should wait for Judah."

"Why?" She'd lived on the southside of Chicago. She wasn't about to slink around Basalt, a small coastal town, as if she were afraid of her shadow—even if she had cowered in the pantry the other night. She wasn't that scared child any longer. She was a strong woman, or wanted to be one. The only person she didn't care to run into today was Craig.

"Looters. That's my concern, Craig's too." Dad placed a couple of pans on a towel he spread out on the beige countertop in lieu of a drying rack. "They might do anything to get what they want."

So would Craig. Why did Dad act as if the man were angelic? "I can take care of myself."

"I don't doubt that." He chuckled.

At least he had some confidence in her. Whatever they needed, she would find it. They had to have water; she'd figure it out. What about the small grocery store? How difficult would it be to break in there? She could keep a tab of what she took. Write an IOU.

She and Dad worked together in silence, except for the occasional clink of dishes. She finished her task first. After she tied the knot on the garbage bag, she went in search of an outdoor trash receptacle.

The wind was calming down, finally. A gentle rain fell, unlike the downpour from earlier. She should head for the gallery. Or try to get inside City Hall or the grocery store. Both were probably bolted down. Hiking out to Maggie's would mean a half-mile walk each way, plus hauling whatever she found. She didn't want to be gone from Dad that long.

Under the carport, she found a large can and shoved the bulging bag inside. The ocean wasn't in view from Paige's house, but Paisley heard the crashing waves in the distance. They drew her, called to her like a favorite song. She wished she could go down and sit on a rock and experience the sea. For a little while, she'd like to forget about the problems that had befallen her since her return to Basalt. To focus on herself. But she could hardly do that with all the responsibility she felt for Dad's health and for finding food and water.

Judah was probably still down at the skiff. Maybe she should go by and see how he was doing.

She hustled back into the house. "Dad?" He wasn't in the kitchen.

"In here."

She strode into the living room and found him resting on the couch in the semi-darkness. "You okay?"

"Just tired." He let out a long sigh.

She hoped fatigue was his only problem, and that his getting wet at the beach hadn't made his condition worse. He was better since he took the insulin, wasn't he? Part of her wanted to stay right here with him. To watch for any changes that might signal another crisis. But if she didn't find the needed supplies, they would have another type of emergency. "I'm going to the gallery. I'll grab whatever liquids I can find."

"Good. Maybe check on Judah?" His slight smile made it hard to tell him to stop playing matchmaker.

"Get some rest. I'll be back soon."

"Okay." He closed his eyes.

She walked down the hall, grabbed a coat and a knit hat from Paige's closet. Then she marched out the door, down the driveway, and along the sidewalk toward the church. As soon as she got her first glimpse of the ocean, her footfalls increased in speed. She wanted to run straight for the peninsula, to sit on the point and lose herself in the glory of sea spray dancing over her. Although, she didn't have any desire to get soaking wet when she'd just changed, especially since there wasn't any heat source in the house.

Still, seeing the waves rolling up on the beach, hearing the roar, made her want to stand here and take it all in, even though tasks awaited.

Maybe she could take just a minute for herself.

Eighteen

Paisley closed her eyes, her hearing in tune to the sounds of the sea, the pounding rhythm of waves against rocks, the rustling of wind blowing through hollowed-out logs. Nature's melodies blended perfectly with the throbbing of her heartbeat in her ears until she could barely tell the difference between the two. She released a long sigh that felt drudged from the bottom of her lungs. In increments, her muscles relaxed from her shoulders to her ankles.

Oh, to stay in this restful feeling of being at home, at peace, next to the sea. Of life returning to normal, whatever that meant in her post-hurricane world. She had survived the ordeal of the storm. And somehow survived her enemy's presence. Surely God was watching out for her, helping her.

Breathing in the salty air, she glanced up at the sky and her thoughts turned prayerful. *Lord, thank You for keeping me and Dad, and even Judah, safe during the storm and through all that's happened since. I don't want to only pray when things go badly. I'd like to sit here*

*on the beach and talk to You every day, the way I once did. I want to find
a way back to You, too.*

She gazed toward the opposite side of the beach where Judah
was in the skiff doing something at the stern. He hadn't let the
rough seas keep him from getting back to her, had he? Even if
his arrival wasn't as quick as she would have wanted, he had
made a valiant effort to reach her.

The words she texted him the night she hid in the pantry
ran through her thoughts like lyrics. *I love you. I love you.* Her heart
picked up a stronger beat. Her chest filled with warmth. If only
he knew what she was thinking. If only she were brave enough
to walk right up to him and tell him. Dive into his arms again.
She smiled at the thought of how she met him earlier, then she
strode purposefully in his direction.

As she drew closer, she saw the long rope that extended
from the tip of the bow all the way to a rock beneath James
Weston's home. She could tell Judah was preparing for high
tide.

He glanced up, his gaze tangling with hers. This time she
didn't look away. He smiled warmly. Lifted his hand in welcome.
At the endearing look he gave her, a chilly place in her heart
melted. It wasn't a head-over-heels kind of love she felt for him.
Attraction, sure. Friendship, yes. And thankfulness that he still
wanted to be a part of her life, her husband. Yet she couldn't
say those three words stuck in her throat.

"Hey, beautiful."

Oh. She hadn't imagined him saying that.

"Nice of you to drop by and see me." He tugged on the
anchor line, probably checking its resistance, or its ability to hold
during the hours of tidal shifting to come. The waves lifted the
back of the boat, rocked it.

"I'm heading to the gallery to gather supplies. Find water." She nodded toward Paige's business, keeping things neutral. Non-romantic. Right. Like that could happen. "Not much edible food left at the house. Dad's hungry." She chattered, filling in the empty spaces.

"Hold up and I'll come with you."

"Oh, uh, sure."

"If you don't mind, that is." There was vulnerability in his gaze.

"I don't mind." She glanced up at the open window of the art gallery. Just then, someone darted past the gaping space. *Craig?* Had he been watching her? Her heartbeat suddenly throbbed in her temples. The muscles in her esophagus tightened. Intense pressure weighed on her chest. Shallow, raspy breathing. Sweaty palms. Apprehension. She hated the precursors of a panic attack.

"Paisley?" Judah's worried voice.

She didn't dare glance at him. Didn't appeal to him with her gaze as if she wanted him to hold her in his strong arms. She didn't want that, right? Facing the ocean, away from the gallery, away from Judah's watchful eyes, she forced herself to search for something to distract herself. Five things. *Focus. Breathe.*

A seagull swooped down over shallow waters; came up with a small fish in its mouth, maybe a minnow. Farther out, a salmon leaped. *Inhale, exhale.* A foaming wave crashed against the skiff, tipping it one way then the other. A child's red shoe danced in the surf, disappeared. A crab scuttled along the sand as if running from her.

There.

She inhaled a deep cleansing breath, blew it out slowly. Her heart still pounded rapidly beneath her ribs. Why did she respond so adversely to thoughts of Craig being near, when she'd already put up with him being in the house helping Dad? Didn't make sense. She shuddered anyway.

Judah's hands came around her shoulders. He pulled her into his chest, into his sweatshirt that smelled warmly of him and the sea. She sighed against him. Let his arms engulf her. No one could hurt her, here. Could they stay this way forever? No talking. Just being. Resting. Together.

"Did I say something wrong?"

She shook her head. Sighed. The caring tone of his voice soothed her. No matter that he didn't come to her aid fast enough. He was here now, holding her. She needed someone to be her calm. Her true north. *Him.*

"I thought I saw, um"—she wouldn't mention Craig's name—"someone in the gallery."

Judah swiveled toward the building with her still in his arms, his blue eyes peering pensively at the window. She noticed his several-days-old beard. Had an inkling to run her fingers over the whiskers to feel their softness. But if she did—

"You sure?"

"Huh? Oh, I thought so." She pulled back a little, but he didn't let go of her.

He lifted her chin and his fingers heated up the skin on her face where he touched. "Want me to go check?"

See how sweet he was being. "No, that's okay." This time, when she stepped back, he released her. She felt bereft of his warmth, of his tender touch.

She glanced toward the open window again. Didn't see anyone. She gazed into her husband's eyes. *Her husband.* Not her "ex" like she dubbed him for three years.

"We could go together. Grab some food and water." If

Craig was up there, surely he'd disappear before they reached the door.

"That would be great."

"A power line is down a little west of First Street. We should avoid that."

"Definitely." Judah took her hand as they strolled along the beach, linking their fingers together like they belonged. Always belonged. She felt his thumb stroke her bare ring finger as if he were checking to see if she put her ring on yet.

She gulped. *I wish I still had my wedding ring.*

His gaze caught hers. He smiled.

I love you.

Why couldn't she just say the words?

His blues shone like the reflection of the sun on the surface of the sea.

I love you.

The intensity in his gaze made her wonder if he was thinking about kissing her. Before she saw someone in the window, possibly watching them, she might have gone along with the idea of kissing him back. Of feeling his mouth hovering a breath over hers. Forgetting all the parts of their relationship that they still had to dissect and rehash. To form a bridge over the chasm of the last years. Could a simple kiss do that?

Might, if it was like the one they shared a few days ago. *Deep blue sea in the morning!* The remembrance of that passionate moment heated her up as if she were sitting next to a toasty fire. Glancing into Judah's eyes, seeing his warm look, made her think he might be thinking the same thoughts.

But her romantic reminiscing came to a stammering halt. If Craig was in the gallery, heaven forbid, everything was bound to come out about where he stayed last night. How he assisted

Dad. Slept on the couch. Judah would hate that—but she hated it just as much.

They hurried toward the rocks near Miss Patty's rental. Judah led her up the boulders, even though she used this passageway plenty of times as a kid back when she and Peter charged down to the beach through their neighbors' yards. Still, she appreciated Judah's gentlemanly actions as he assisted her up the rocky embankment that had water flowing down them from the street above. A woman could get used to such chivalry.

"It's strange not seeing anyone along Front Street." His limp was more pronounced when they reached even ground. "The town will need a huge restoration." He didn't add, "Like us," the way he did a couple of days ago.

"When will the others return?" She let go of his hand.

"Brad Keifer came back with me. I dropped him off at the cannery."

"Oh."

"The rest will return in a couple of days. There's a mudslide between Florence and Basalt Bay. Crews are working on it. And, last I knew, the entrance into town is badly damaged." He cleared his throat. "I expect someone will check on utilities soon. Have you seen anyone around?"

Other than Craig? So Judah really didn't know about the man's late-night intrusion and scare tactics?

They reached the gallery and she still didn't answer his question. He seemed distracted as he shoved open the front door that was slightly ajar.

"Looks like someone was here."

"I came by yesterday." She stepped through the foyer, peering around the room cautiously, just in case someone might still be inside. "The door was stuck open then."

"Probably from the storm surge." He shoved against the door a couple times as if his manpower could get it unstuck. "It's swollen from water damage."

"Uh-huh. Let's see what food we can scrounge up and get out of here."

Judah walked beside her to the coffee bar. The building creaked. Wind gusts coming through the gaping window made the canvas tarp on the floor rise and fall. Something clattered. She jumped. Glanced over her shoulder.

Judah opened a cupboard, dropped something. His gaze met hers. "Just me. You okay?"

"Mmhmm." She opened the cupboard where she found water bottles yesterday. She leaned down to see farther back. Six bottles of water; no juice. Several juice bottles lined the shelf before, she was sure of it. Someone must have helped himself.

"Something wrong?"

"A few juice bottles are missing."

"Looters?"

Or Craig. Maybe Brad. She shrugged.

Judah strode into the gallery, stopping at the window. His hair fluttered in the wind. His shoulders tensed. "Someone's on the beach."

"What? Who?"

"I don't know. Stay here." He marched across the gallery. "I may have discovered our thief."

"Judah, wait up!" She scooped up the water bottles, but he was already gone. She ran to the open window.

A tall, solid-looking man who resembled Craig's stature stood in the skiff. His back was to her, so she couldn't be certain. He seemed to be fiddling with the engine. *Oh, no.* Was he planning to take the skiff?

151

Paisley rushed back to the counter, found a plastic bag and threw in all the liquid and packaged food items she could find, praying the person in the boat was not Craig.

Nineteen

Judah alternated between running and hobbling down the sidewalk. He tried to catch a glimpse of the skiff between Sal's and the first beach house. Who was the guy? Brad? It didn't look like him from the gallery window. If someone was stealing the rented boat, Judah had to stop him.

He crept down the rocks they'd recently come up, being careful not to slip on the wet stones and the water pouring down from the street above. He didn't want to alert whoever it was of his approach, either.

Maybe Brad finished his tasks and was leaving early. But didn't he say he'd be busy for the rest of the day? That he planned to leave town early in the morning?

As soon as Judah climbed off the last rock and landed on the wet sand, he scrambled across the pebbled beach the best he could. At least, the rope was still tied to the rock where he secured it. Wait. Was the man—who was *not* Brad—pulling up the anchor?

"Hey, you!" Judah ran with adrenaline shooting through his veins. "Leave the anchor alone!"

The thief turned. *Craig?*

Judah stumbled.

Why was Craig in Basalt Bay? And what was he doing stealing a boat?

"You can't take that skiff, Masters. Get out of it, now!" Judah doubted the engine would even start since it stalled earlier, but it might.

Craig continued messing around with the outboard. He yanked on the starter cord a couple of times. The engine coughed. Sputtered. Died.

Why would Judah's supervisor take a skiff that wasn't his? That was like someone stealing a horse in a western movie, a hanging offense.

Craig pumped the gas valve. Pulled the cord again.

"What do you think you're doing?" Judah didn't stop when he reached the water. He plowed through the surf, the waves pounding against his knees, up to his thighs. *Man.* There went his dry clothes. "You can't take that boat. Brad Keifer needs it tomorrow." He reached the side of the skiff and gripped the gunwale. "Did you hear me, Masters?"

Craig stumbled to the bow of the bobbing craft. Drew something out of his front pocket. A knife? He planned to cut the skiff loose?

You've got to be kidding me.

"Put that knife away." Judah gritted his teeth.

Craig gazed at him with a dull gleam in his eyes.

Judah wouldn't fight him. But stop him from stealing the skiff? That he would do. He ran his hands along the gunwale, trudging through the waves toward the bow. "Don't you dare cut that line. This boat stays here."

"I'm not *shtealing* it. I'm 'borrowing' it." Craig guffawed.

What was with his slurring? And his emphasis on "borrowing?" It sounded like the verbiage Judah and Brad used when they spoke about Richard's skiff earlier. How would Craig know about that discussion?

Craig stumbled. "You been tempted to do that, r-right? Borrow something that isn't yours." He lunged toward the rope with the knife. A wave hit the boat and he tumbled backward.

"Leave this skiff alone. It's not mine." Judah groaned as another wave hit him. "You know better than this."

"I know *whooosh* boat it is. Richie won't mind. I know where to r-return it."

"It's staying here." A cold wave sloshed up Judah's hip. "Brad's taking it in the morning."

"In your *condish-shion*, you can't do anything to *shtop* me." Craig pulsed the knife blade toward the rope again, his arm outstretched, his hand flailing the air—Judah's chance to stop him. He lunged forward, reaching over the edge of the boat, and smacked Craig's wrist hard, knocking the knife out of his hand. The metal flew like a silver fishing lure, twirling to the bottom of the sea.

"Look what you did!" Craig bellowed. He slammed both of his palms against Judah's chest.

Judah stumbled backward, trying to regain his footing, but not before catching a pungent whiff of something on Craig's breath. Alcohol. Was Craig drunk? And planned to take the skiff? C-MER promoted the "Don't Drink and Drive" message for boating. Craig taught on it in seminars. He was being irresponsible now. Judah had to stop him, whatever it took.

He lunged back to the bobbing boat where Craig was fingering the knot Judah had tied to the bow. "Get out, Masters. I don't know why you're doing this, but just stop. Why are you even here?"

"Same as you." A glint of steel shone in Craig's eyes. "*Shpending* time with your *shweetie*."

Judah saw crimson. And clarity. Craig *was* the one who barged in on Paisley the other night and scared her. Despite his supervisor's condition, Judah sprang forward over the side of the skiff, ignoring the pain in his leg, and grabbed Craig by the front of his coat. His knuckles itched to connect with the man's jaw, but he demanded self-control of himself. "Why have you been hanging around Paisley, my wife?" Thoughts of what might have happened blurred his boundary lines of nonviolence.

"You mean, were we 'lone? Cozy?" Craig flung up both elbows, disengaging Judah's grip. "Why else would I come back?" He belched a foul-smelling breath. "She doesn't wear a wedding ring. An' she *likesh* me."

Even though Judah knew that to be a bald-faced lie, a bitter roar bellowed up from his chest. With both hands, he shoved downward with all his weight on the gunwale. The skiff tipped sharply toward him, then rocked in the opposite direction.

"Wa-a-a—" Craig stumbled backward, toppled over the edge of the boat, his hands flailing the air as he plunged into shallow water.

Judah charged around the skiff, its unanchored stern making it a deadly force in the churning waves. Craig leaped up and his fist collided with Judah's left cheek before Judah had a chance to do anything. The force landed him on his backside in the water. Craig's hands shoved against his chest, pinning him beneath the waves. Judah held his breath. Kicked at Craig. Slugged him.

Finally, he wrenched free, probably due to the other man's weakened state. He scrambled to his feet, shoving Craig away from him, gasping for air. "You weasel!" Judah wiped seawater off his face. Glared at the guy who he once thought of as his friend. Hate. Revenge. Retribution. All rose up in him. Had Craig harmed Paisley in any way? Because if he did—

Judah thought of the distance he felt between him and her. Was this why? "What have you been doing with my wife?"

"Sang her a love *shong*." Craig spit. "An' she loved it."

"You're a scum. And a liar."

"I was here when she needed a man. *Shtrong* man like me." Craig thumped his chest that already seemed puffed up with pride. Water poured down his face from his wet hair. "Where were you? Oh, yeah. Hanging out with the *workplashe* hottie."

Judah winced. "You know where I was." He jabbed his index finger at Craig's chest. "Stuck in Florence, thanks to you."

"Judah! Judah!" Paisley shouted at him from the shoreline. When did she get here? How much had she heard?

Craig must have lifted his fist to strike Judah again because Paisley screamed at him. "Craig! You moron, stop!" She plunged into the water, kicking up sea-foam, somehow wedging herself between Judah and Craig. "Don't listen to anything he says. Get out of the water. Now." She put her arm around Judah's waist, leading him toward shore, glaring at Craig. He liked that— her siding with him, casting surly looks at the other guy. She thrust out her hand toward Craig, who seemed as surprised as Judah to find her here. "Just stay back! Never come near me again, you hear?"

Craig squinted at Judah. "You're fired!"

"I quit!"

"Can't quit when I already fired you." The man stomped up the beach, swayed sideways, stumbled.

Judah never wanted to work for the sleaze again, anyway. Although, he couldn't believe that after eleven years of employment at C-MER it had come to this. Ended like this.

"Look at you." Paisley glowered. "How could you fight him?"

"But I—" Judah never even threw a punch. But he'd wanted to. Now his face hurt. His leg hurt. He was freezing. And what was she upset about? He had been defending her. Them. "Didn't you hear what he said about you two?"

"Doesn't matter." She crossed her arms over her middle. "He's a jerk. He doesn't have to open his mouth for us to know that. He's not worth fighting when you're already injured. What were you thinking?" She whimpered and the sound gripped him in his gut. "You didn't know, did you?"

"D-didn't know what?" He gazed at her, recognizing the pain emanating from her dark eyes. "What is it, Pais? What's wrong?"

"Never mind. Now isn't the time. We're soaking wet, again. Let's head back to Paige's." She took off marching across the sand, didn't wait for him.

Groaning, Judah turned and watched Craig climb up the rocks near James's house. He slipped twice. Judah feared he might topple down the boulders. Hit his head or something. But he made it up to the sidewalk, then disappeared beyond the buildings. Good riddance.

Judah's teeth chattered as he waded back into the water. He pulled the stern of the skiff in line with the rope. He grabbed hold of the anchor, dropped it into the sea again. Couldn't believe all that had just transpired.

He trudged toward land, hobbled down the beach, and finally caught up to Paisley at the parking lot. She must have paused to wait for him.

"What did you mean? I didn't know what?"

She started walking again. "That Craig was the one who scared me the other night. I thought you knew."

"How would I know?" He glanced at her as he strode beside her. "I feared it was. Prayed it wasn't."

"I texted you."

"What? When?" He clasped her arms, stopping her forward motion. Even though they were cold and wet, this conversation was too important to not be facing her. "When did you text me?"

"After you said . . . you loved me . . . on the phone." Her eyes filled with moisture.

"What did you say in your text?"

"Doesn't matter." She pulled away from him.

He dodged around her, held out his hands. "Oh, yes, it does matter." Especially now that he'd heard what Craig said.

"I was scared. I needed you, Judah." Her small, wounded-sounding voice tugged on his heart.

"I know." He'd failed her. "I'm sorry I wasn't here for you. I wanted to be. I felt crazy not knowing what was happening. Knowing you could be in danger." He wanted to take her in his arms and hug her. A kiss seemed out of the question, although not far from his thoughts.

"Come on. I'm too cold for this. You are too." She tromped around him, walking up the trail.

He didn't try to stop her. But as he turned to follow her, he glimpsed the empty parking lot between him and the peninsula where her car had been the night of the storm. "Where's your car?"

"The sea took it," she said over her shoulder. "My dad saw it during low tide."

"Oh, wow. I'm sorry."

They trekked up the narrow trail single file, crossed the street, then trudged across the church parking lot.

"Can you tell me what happened with Craig that night?" he asked as soon as he could walk beside her.

She was silent for several steps. "He banged into things. Was drunk. Then he fell asleep."

"That's it?" Relief battled his disbelief, even though he guessed she was giving him the abbreviated version of the story.

"It was a lot for me to handle."

"Of course." He didn't mean to diminish her experience. "Did he, um, sing to you?"

She looked at him sharply. "Why would you say that?"

"He bragged that he sang a love song to you, that you liked it. Drove me nuts."

"He crooned some pathetic country tune. I hated it. Hated him. I was his p-prisoner." The crack in her voice struck him, a sword hitting its target.

"I'm sorry you went through all of that." Something Craig said still gnawed at him. "He mentioned that you don't wear a wedding ring. Like it means something to him."

She huffed. "He helped with Dad's insulin. He knew medical stuff." Her voice got louder. "That's the only reason, and I repeat, the *only reason* I let him come into the house."

"Wait. He was with you at Paige's?"

"Just to help Dad." She thrust out her hands, palms up.

"What was I supposed to do? Refuse the only medical help available to my father?"

"No, I suppose not."

As they walked the rest of the way in silence, a question lingered in his mind. Why was Craig making such an effort to cause trouble between Judah and Paisley?

Twenty

By the time they reached Paige's house, Paisley was shivering uncontrollably. She needed dry clothes. Maybe a couple of blankets to wrap around her shoulders until the shaking stopped.

She and Judah slipped out of their wet shoes and boots, leaving them side by side on the porch—something they used to do after beach walks at the cottage.

"Paisley. Judah. There you are." Dad shuffled into the kitchen from the living room as they came through the back door. His eyes widened. "What happened to you two? Chilly for another sea dip, isn't it?" He chuckled.

"Yes, s-sir." Judah nodded at him.

Paisley didn't comment. She waved for Judah to follow her down the hall. She didn't know what she could find for him to wear. He might have to drape blankets around himself until his clothes dried out. In this cold house, that might take days. She heard his footfall, the uneven rhythm of his steps, behind her.

They hadn't spoken in a while. His claim that Craig mentioned her not wearing her ring, as if that gave the guy permission to hang around her, was ludicrous. She'd put a ring on her finger, right now, if that alone would stop him from coming around. If she had a wedding band, that is. Unfortunately, a pawn shop in Chicago took care of that—another thing she dreaded having to explain to Judah.

In Paige's room, Paisley dug through the dresser drawers. Not finding anything big enough for Judah, she searched the closet. She nudged a cardboard box labeled "shoes" and found another one marked "fat clothes." *Fat clothes?* Paisley imagined what her sister might have looked like at nine months pregnant. She carried the box to the bed, then yanked open the top. She plunged her stiff, cold hands into the pile of garments, pulling up one after another. "This might work." She flung a pair of baggy turquoise stretch pants on the end of the bed close to where Judah stood.

He held them up, a dumbfounded expression crossing his face. "You've got to be kidding. What are these?"

"Maternity clothes." She snickered, despite her chills. He probably wouldn't appreciate her humorous take on his wearing her sister's "fat" pants.

"Just great. A p-perfect finish to this d-day." He shivered and pointed toward the box. "Find something else, please. I h-have my p-pride." He tossed the stretch pants back on the bed.

She fingered several items. Held up a flannel forest-green shirt. "This might be a man's shirt." She tossed it toward him.

"This'll w-work. Not those g-girly things." He slid his arms out of his wet coat. His shirt came off next.

Realizing she was staring at his bare chest, she averted her gaze. She rummaged through the box, distracting herself from thoughts she shouldn't be thinking—that she liked seeing him without his shirt. She picked up a pair of boxers and a navy t-shirt. "Hey, look." She tossed them on the bed, glad for something to do other than watching him undress.

"That's more like it." He picked up both items. He held the t-shirt to his chest. "Will probably fit. Anything for pants?"

"You might be stuck wearing the ones I showed you."

"No, thanks. I'll stay in my wet jeans."

"Suit yourself." Flinging the rest of the clothes from the box onto the bed, she checked a couple more items, wishing her cold fingers worked better. She saw a thick pair of black leggings. She grabbed them and read the tag. "Extra-large leggings work?"

"Seriously?"

She tossed them at him. "Good thing my sister wore big clothes at one point in her life, or you wouldn't have anything to wear. Oh, how about these?" She held up a pair of pink-floral flannel pajama bottoms. "Maybe the leggings and pj's can work together for thickness." She piled the finds on the bed. "Beggars can't be picky."

"You expect me to wear these?"

"Why not?" She glared at him, her patience wearing thin. It was time to find the things she needed. "Just be thankful for something that fits and is dry. Remember, we're in a disaster here."

His lips clamped shut.

"Come on. It's temporary. Nobody's in town to see you other than my dad and me." Unless Craig showed up, but she wouldn't mention that. "Now, I have to find some clothes for myself. I'm freezing too."

"Of course. Sorry. Thanks for, um, these." He held up the pj's and grimaced.

She scooped up the clothes, stuffing them back in the box, then rummaged through Paige's drawers. Finding a thick sweater, underclothes, and jeans, she headed for the door.

"If you see any large bandages, I could use one."

"Sure thing." She left the room and closed the door to give him privacy.

Ten minutes later, Judah trudged down the hall with a begrudging expression. His squinty eyes warned her not to say anything. "My father would have a cow if he saw me in these." Bright pink flowers decorated his long legs. Above his bare feet, at least three inches of his ankles were exposed. She wanted to snicker; his glare kept her from doing so.

"Where shall I put these wet things?" He held out a wad of dripping clothes.

She pointed toward the bathroom. "Over the shower rod. And I found a first aid kit. It's by the bathroom sink."

"Thanks." Judah left the room.

Paisley dropped onto the couch next to Dad, wrapping an afghan from the recliner around her shoulders. The light streaming in was an improvement over the previously dark room.

"Good thing Craig was here to help take down those boards, hm?" Dad nodded toward the large window.

"Uh-huh." Too bad he mentioned Craig's name. Judah might hear and—

"Craig?" Judah strutted into the middle of the room, his hands empty. "What was he doing here?"

She shook her head at him, trying to convey that she'd explain later. He stared right back at her, demanding answers, now.

"He helped Dad, remember?"

Judah squinted at her.

"He's been doing a few things around here since he stayed over." Dad sounded pleased with that fact.

"As in, he slept here?" Judah braced his hands on his hips. "You didn't tell me he stayed here, Paisley."

Like this was her fault?

"Sorry." Not her sincerest apology. This wasn't how she would have told him about Craig's overnighter. But seeing Judah standing here in all his male bluster and pride, wearing hot-pink maternity clothes, glaring at her as if she were to blame for the whole problem, caused a snicker to rise in her throat. She covered her mouth and snorted, but his sour-grapes glare toned down her mirth. "I told you he helped us. I didn't want to be in the same room with him." Oh dear. Now she revealed information in front of Dad that she didn't want said. She could almost hear the wheels turning in his mind.

"What's the problem here?" Dad adjusted his glasses. "Craig's been nothing but helpful to me and has been fixing things up for Paige. What's wrong with him pitching in?"

"Right. Desperate times and all that." Paisley tried to appease Dad while appealing to Judah with an imploring glance. "Can we talk about this later? We have more important things to discuss."

"More important than getting to the bottom of what Craig's doing here? After all the stuff he's done?" Judah's voice rose. "You defend him now?"

"Just let it go, will you?"

"What does he mean?" Dad's voice sounded thick and scratchy. His eyes seemed foggy. His shoulders slumped. He'd tested himself and taken his insulin today, right? "What did Craig do?"

"Nothing for you to worry about." She threw another glare

in Judah's direction. If he didn't take the hint this time, she'd grab his arm and march him back into Paige's room. Give him a piece of her mind. Who did he think he was stomping in here and making demands? They were in a calamity, for goodness's sake.

A scowl crossed his mouth, but he didn't say anything else.

Dad leaned forward and pointed at Judah. "That how you got the shiner? From Craig?"

Paisley didn't notice a bruise. She gazed at his cheek. Oh, my, he had a doozy. "They fought like schoolboys, that's what." She winked at Judah, hoping he'd drop his grudge and keep things light.

"That's not fair." He thrust his index finger toward her. "You didn't hear what he implied about you two."

"You and Craig?" Dad peered at her intensely.

"A misunderstanding, that's all." She glowered at Judah. "Can I speak with you privately?" She leaped from the couch, then strode outside with the afghan still draped around her. The garbage strewn across the backyard—another task to be dealt with—seemed symbolic of all the garbage she was still dealing with in her life. With Dad. Craig. Now Judah.

At the sound of him shutting the door behind her, she whirled around. "What was that? You come back, fight with Craig, and blab to my father, who I haven't explained things to yet, about stuff I don't want him asking about?"

Judah clomped down the two porch steps in bare feet. She forgot that he didn't have dry shoes to wear when she chose to come outside.

"I'm sorry, okay?" He didn't sound sorry. "Why didn't you tell me Craig was here as soon as I arrived?" He shuffled toward her, almost nose to nose.

"I thought you knew! I told you that."

"Because of the text." He sighed, rubbed his forehead with his palm. Groaned. "Well, I didn't." Moisture flooded his eyes. "I . . . I wish I had."

Seeing his tender, perhaps regretful, expression, some of her anger dissipated. Her throat clogged with emotion. "Yeah, so do I." Then he'd know what she texted him, even the part where she said she was sorry for hurting him. If he knew, would his gaze be softer? Would he pull her into his arms, kiss her like a man who loved his wife and knew she loved him back? Instead of standing here looking wounded and miserable. "If you had known, what would you have done differently?"

"I don't know. I was stuck in Florence." His hands smoothed down his wet hair. "I did my level best to get back. Couldn't walk all the way. Couldn't seem to make anything go how I wanted it to." He groaned. "I need to know what else happened those nights with Craig."

"It's over now."

"Is it?" He tapped his chest. "In here it isn't." He cast his finger toward the ocean. "A man I highly respected as a friend and colleague is now a louse and a scum to me. I can't tolerate his disregard for you or for our m-marriage."

The tremor in his voice spoke to her heart. All his ranting must really be about his deep feelings for her. His love. She could melt into that kind of caring and affection. Would, if things were different between them. But they weren't. Would they ever be again?

"This thing between us"—he rocked his thumb back and forth—"I'll do anything to protect that, even when it seems we aren't moving forward at all. I mean it, Pais."

"I know you do." A powerful wave of longing hit her. Made

her want to fall into his arms, press her cheek against his chest and listen to the beat of his heart.

And yet, when he opened his arms to her, inviting her to bridge their emotional gap, she was stuck in the mud of indecision. Should she turn away from what he said about protecting what was between them? Protect her own heart by waiting until they cleared the air between them. Or should she step into his arms? Accept him for who he was. Who they were together, with their troubled past and their unknown future. To do what she told him to do. *Let it go.*

His hands lowered. Did she wait too long? Taking a gulp and a leap of faith—*God, help me make the right decision*—she stepped forward. Her arms slid easily around his waist, her hands clasping together at his back. Sighing, he pulled her shoulders in, snuggling her against his chest. His chin came to rest against her head. Her cheek caressed the soft fabric of her sister's shirt where Judah's heart beat a powerful rhythm beneath her ear. Some of the ache she'd carried ever since he rode away in Craig's truck to get medical help, and Craig's return and all the problems that followed, eased.

"I'm sorry I wasn't here for you when Craig showed up." He whispered near her ear. "I would have done anything to be with you. To protect you from him."

"I know."

"Did he . . . did he hurt you in any way?" He stroked his fingers down her back.

She shuddered. "No." Not in the way he meant.

"I'm glad." He held her without speaking. Then, "I've messed up in a million ways over the last years."

She had too. Tears flooded her eyes, and she blinked fast to combat them.

"But you have my word that I'm sincere about loving you. About wanting to be a good husband for you. About not wanting to let our marriage go. I want 'us' back. If there's any way for that to happen—and I believe God has a way—we'll find it together."

I love you, Judah. Why were the words so hard to say?

He leaned back. Stared at her, smiling. He glanced at her lips, into her eyes, back at her lips. His tender look seemed to be asking if she was ready for romance. For love. Was she?

The moment passed, and he stepped back. "I know you explained some of what happened that night. I'd like to hear the rest, if you don't mind."

"Okay."

"After you told me on the phone that someone was at your dad's, what happened?"

He deserved to hear the details, so she explained. Occasionally, he asked a question, giving her his full attention. At some point, they walked up on the porch to get out of the rain.

The only thing she kept back was the message in that second to last text. Because when she said those words, they would be her commitment to him. Her promise to keep loving him for the rest of her life. A vow that she too wanted their marriage rescued. That would be a gigantic step for her after three years of thinking they were finished as a couple.

And she had a question too. "From the second our conversation got disconnected, what happened with you?" Playing with the buttons on his shirt, she gazed into his eyes. She wanted to hear about Mia, but she wouldn't bring up the woman's name.

Judah shared about his experiences over the last two days. She heard the frustration in his tone. His worry, not only about their recent separation but his dread over not knowing how she'd fared for the last three years. He mentioned Mia's name

170

on his own, with no prompting from her. When he explained how the C-MER receptionist admitted to thinking he was attracted to her, his cheeks reddened. He looked uncomfortable, but his honesty was important to her. Even so, a spark of jealousy twisted in Paisley's heart. Hadn't she witnessed Mia's overt flirtations? Even at the emergency town meeting before the storm, Mia flirted with several guys, Mayor Grant included.

"Finally, we were able to rent a boat and head home." He sighed. "I wish it would have been sooner, but I'm grateful that you and your dad were okay."

"Me too. And I'm thankful you're here now." She turned in his arms to better see him. Not for her lips to line up with his. Although, that's what happened. She blinked a few times, waiting for him to narrow the gap. Wishing he would; afraid he wouldn't.

He cleared his throat. "What shall we do before it gets dark? Clean the yard?"

"Sure." She glanced away, hiding her disappointment. "Better not get those clothes wet. They're the only things left in this house that fit you."

He chuckled. "Wouldn't want to have to go without."

"No, we wouldn't want that." Uh-oh. Did they just cross into husband/wife flirting? Time to go inside and check on Dad.

Judah clasped her hand as she retreated. "Sorry. I was just kidding." He gave her that endearing smile she used to love. Still loved.

She gulped. Slipped her fingers away. Hurried to the door.

He scooped up his wet shoes from the porch. "I'm going to work out here for a while."

"Okay." She stepped into the kitchen, leaned against the door, took a couple of deep breaths. Something sweet was happening between them. But the kissing, sharing intimacies like a married man and woman, she didn't think she was ready to take that step. *Ugh.* Then why was she disappointed that Judah hadn't kissed her?

In the living room, she found Dad napping on the couch. She covered him with an afghan. Then she went back to Paige's room and grabbed a coat. Judah was probably cold too. Was there anything in Paige's closet that might work for him? Something to go with the pink pj's, perchance? She snickered.

When she was about to give up on finding anything, she spotted a thick item rolled up on the far end of the shelf. She pulled it down. Unrolled it. A letterman's jacket from the Siuslaw High School in Florence? Whose old coat was this? It had a Viking mascot patch. Another patch, perhaps a name tag, had been torn off the front, leaving a bright rectangle of color.

Was this part of Paige's secret? A piece of her past?

Paisley groaned. She had enough secrets of her own without trying to figure out her sister's. She scurried back outside and handed Judah the jacket. "Look. I found this in Paige's closet."

"Thanks." He pointed at the patch. "Go, Vikings!" They shared a grin since they'd both attended the same high school. He slipped on the jacket, snapped the front closures, sighed as if instantly warmed.

They worked together for about an hour, cleaning up the back and front yards. When Judah scooped up a pile of seagrass and kelp, winking at her as he walked past her to throw his armful of stuff on the trash pile, her heart flip-flopped. On his way back, he put both his hands, one on top of the other, over his heart. He grinned at her and winked again. Swoon-worthy stuff.

Was this what working with him on rebuilding their cottage, and the town, would be like in the coming days? If so, she couldn't wait to get started.

Twenty-one

Judah rolled over onto his side on the lumpy couch where he slept last night. His shoulders ached. So did his neck. He grimaced at the discomfort. At least, he was under the same roof as Paisley. Although not as close as he'd like to be. He was here in the living room. She was sleeping in Piper's room with the door closed, probably locked.

He chuckled at that, even though he would never intrude on her space if he thought she didn't want him there. And she hadn't given him any reason to think she wanted him to be closer. Other than the way he found her watching him a few times yesterday. Her eyes wide. The way she blinked slowly in his direction. He remembered a couple of times when he winked at her, how she smiled back. Seemed slightly out of breath.

That gave him hope she wasn't completely unmoved by his romancing. And he couldn't forget the way she dove into his arms on the beach. Even if things got icy afterward, he had that sweet memory to cling to.

His stomach growled. What he wouldn't give for a hot cup of coffee and a pile of pancakes.

Today was foraging day. His prey would be packaged food, canned goods, and bottled water. Maybe some coffee grounds and an old percolator. Would that work on the grill? He'd search for supplies anywhere he could get in—Paul's, City Hall, the cottage. Paisley mentioned Maggie's. He preferred to keep a wide berth between him and the grumpy innkeeper who chased him off her property with a broom a couple of times in the past.

He groaned as he sat up. Felt the swollen place on his cheek with his fingers. "Thanks a lot, Craig." Ice would help. But without electricity, he wouldn't find any.

He heard a rumble coming from somewhere outside. Machinery? Sounded like large motors. Perhaps the road crew would get through today. Soon, neighbors would be showing up, joining in the work of getting the town back to normal.

He stood, grumbling at the tug in his stitches along his calf. He quickly put on the shirt and jacket Paisley unearthed for him yesterday. The emblems on the letterman's jacket caught his attention. Basketball. Football. Drama. Interesting combination. Just seeing the jacket brought back memories from his high school days.

He slipped the pajamas over the leggings, and the bright pink fabric shocked him, still. Today he would find, had to find, something masculine to wear, preferably a pair of jeans.

The back door squeaked opened. Paisley entered carrying two buckets of water. He hurried into the kitchen and took one from her grasp.

"I didn't know you were awake." He set the bucket on the floor by the sink. "I would have helped you carry these."

"I don't mind hauling a few buckets." She set the other one down. "I've been to the creek twice already. The first time was for water to flush the toilet."

"Oh man." He'd shirked his duty and it wasn't even seven a.m. yet.

"My growling stomach woke me up." She smiled.

"I know the feeling." He rubbed his flat belly. "I could use a bucket of coffee."

"Don't mention that word! Just thinking about missing my morning brew makes me crazy." She pointed to three cans of food on the counter. "That's breakfast."

Judah read the labels. "Peas. Garbanzo beans. Carrots." He hid his internal reaction of *blech*. "Mmm."

"Not worth starting up the grill for." She opened each can, then evenly distributed the contents into three bowls.

Paul shuffled into the room. "Morning." He ran his hand over his hair that was sticking up.

"Good morning."

"Hey, Dad." Paisley smiled at her father, then frowned. "Rough sleep?"

"Uh-huh."

Judah glanced at Paul. Dark shadows lined his eyes. His whiskers were scraggly. But so were Judah's. He ran his hand over his face, feeling his chin and cheeks that he usually kept hair free.

"Here." Paisley handed each of them a bowl.

Paul muttered something about preferring biscuits and gravy.

Judah chuckled but didn't say anything that might get Paisley's hackles up.

They ate their portions of bland vegetables silently. Food

was food. But this unappealing, cold meal made Judah more eager to find a decent supply of canned goods.

"What's the plan?" Paul's voice sounded gravelly, dry.

"We'll hit the places we have access to. Your house." Judah nodded at his father-in-law. "The cottage. If we can't round up enough grub between our places, we'll try some of the others like we discussed."

"The cottage is a mile away." Paisley scraped her bowl. "Is your leg up to that long of a walk?"

"Sure." Even with his injury he could make it a mile, maybe two, coming back. "We need the food. And I need real clothes." He did a pirouette, pulling the pajama fabric out to the sides.

Paisley snickered.

"I heard some motors." Paul shrugged. "Might be fixing things up at the junction."

"Yep, that's what I think too. Won't be long now." Judah set his empty bowl in the sink. "Thanks for breakfast."

He used the facilities and checked his bandage. Then he scooped up his wet shoes from the porch, dropped down on a kitchen chair, and tugged them on. The wetness bled through the thin socks Paisley gave him. Another reason to head out to the cottage.

From down the hall, he heard Paisley questioning her dad about taking his insulin. He told her he didn't need a nursemaid. She and her dad seemed to disagree a lot, not unlike Judah and his own father.

"Ready?" Paisley charged down the hall and exited the back door without waiting for him.

"Hey, wait up." He followed her out, but she trudged past several houses before he caught up with her. "I see you're in a hurry this morning."

"My dad was so sick when I got here. I'm still worried about him, but he won't talk about his testing and injections. Or let me help him. Not that I know anything about it, but I want to help." She swung her arms as if thrashing the air with her stride. "For a while I thought, well, Craig said my dad might be an alcoholic."

"Craig said that?" His anger toward that man exploded inside of him way too easily. "Why would he say such a thing?"

"He said he found Dad's stash." She slowed down her pace. "Apparently, he drank his share of it that first night."

Stash? Was she talking about the bottles in the garbage can at Paul's? Those were her father's? What a relief. But obviously not for her. He touched her arm. "Do you still think that might be a possibility? That your dad's drinking excessively?"

"I don't know. But I can tell you this, if we find liquor at his place, I'm dumping it all out!" She threw him a vehement glare.

"Maybe Craig found more of it at your dad's yesterday."

"What do you mean?"

"When he slugged me and tried to steal the skiff, I smelled the sauce on him."

She stopped walking. "He's horrible when he's wasted. That's probably why he hit you. Why he acted so stupid. You didn't say anything. Let me blame you for—"

"It doesn't matter." He may not have thrown a punch, but he'd certainly wanted to.

Paisley walked faster again, crossing the church parking lot. "Dad's first, right?"

"Yep."

"Maybe we'll find enough food there to last a couple of days." She pushed a branch out of the way with the toe of her boot. "We wouldn't have to walk out to the cottage today."

Mary E Hanks

"If you don't want to hike that far, that's okay." He rolled his eyes, attempting a comical expression. "I, on the other hand, am getting into my man-clothes today."

"Oh, come on." She grinned, the previous tension fading. "Pink isn't a bad color on you."

"Right."

She pointed at his floral pajamas. "Too bad we don't have a camera."

"Yeah, too bad."

As they approached the Cedars's two-story house where he and Paisley waited out the storm, he noticed the squaring of her shoulders, the slowing down of her footfall, the frown on her lips. Was she nervous about going inside?

He laid his palm at her elbow, tugging her to a stop. "Shall I go in the house alone? I can bring stuff out on the porch for you to sort. You don't have to go inside if you don't want to."

"I'm not some frail flower."

"I would never think that." Sometimes he couldn't win. Even when he tried to be caring and loving toward her, he wound up saying the wrong thing. "You'll do just fine." He stood quietly beside her for a couple of minutes, gazing at the front yard. "You did a great job making that pile of shingles and debris."

"Thanks." Her shoulders shook. Her jaw clenched.

He put his arm lightly over her shoulder, trying to show his support. "Good work covering the front window with the plastic, too."

She jerked away from him, staring at the house. "That wasn't me. The last time I was here the apple tree protruded through the window. Must have been . . ."

Craig.

His name, even unspoken, lingered between them.

178

She groaned, then marched toward the porch.

He caught up to her in a few footsteps. He helped her get up onto the porch, even though he knew she didn't need his help. Where were the steps, anyway?

He climbed onto the porch floor, easing his sore leg up. Then he stood and followed Paisley into the still-damp house. In the kitchen he found her opening and slamming cupboard doors. He went straight for the freezer, tugged it open. The smell of rotten food hit his nostrils. "Phew."

"No kidding." She lined up jars and cans on the countertop. "Know where any trash bags are?"

She pointed at a lower drawer.

He opened it and grabbed a black bag. That's when he noticed his wet clothes were still on the counter from yesterday. Not wanting Paisley to take care of them, or to go through the pockets, he grabbed the pile and strode across the living room. "I'll be right back." He stepped onto the porch, then flung the shirt, pants, and coat across the railing. They might even dry out here. He dug the small package out of the coat pocket and stuffed it into the letterman's jacket. One day he'd show her what he bought. Not until she was ready, but soon, he hoped.

He returned to the freezer. While he filled the black bag with thawed meat and warm stuff from the fridge that had to be thrown away, he listened for unusual creaks overhead. Nothing sounded threatening or made him think the house was unstable. The tree on the roof would have to be cut down soon, or else it might fall and hit power lines—or worse, injure a bystander.

He hauled the smelly bag out to the front porch and tied a knot in the top. When he returned, Paisley was filling a garbage bag of her own, her movements less jerky. Maybe she'd let off enough steam about being back here, about Craig having been here again.

"What did you find?" His stomach gurgled. "Any coffee?"

She cast him an evil eye. Oh, right. She didn't want him mentioning caffeinated drinks.

"Chili, soup, and corned beef. Probably Dad's regular fare since becoming a widower." She shrugged. "He upgraded to a coffee machine that uses K-cups. No use to us without electricity."

"The rest sounds good." He'd get the grill going as soon as they got back. "Here, let me carry that."

She squinted at him as if declaring her independence. He kept his hands outstretched, and she finally handed it over.

"I didn't find any water." She trudged across the wet floor. "Just a couple of juices."

He followed her into the living room. "Do you want to go out to the cottage with me? I still need to find clothes."

"If we could access the second floor, you'd find plenty of stuff here." She paused and pointed at the hole in the ceiling.

"The ladder's gone. I checked yesterday."

"Seriously? The one Craig used was alongside the house." She marched out the door, shoulders back, like she was on a mission.

He knew she wouldn't find the ladder, but he didn't say anything. He supported the bottom of the heavy bag as he walked out on the porch and shut the door.

In a few minutes, Paisley came around the side of the house. "You're right. It's gone."

"Craig probably took it, since it was his." Judah bent his knees and lowered himself from the porch.

"Mr. Weston! *Mrs. Thomas?*" Paisley's voice rose dramatically.

Judah glanced up. James trudged along the sidewalk,

stumbling over branches and garbage, grumbling over his shoulder. Maggie Thomas wasn't far behind him, looking frazzled, her grayish hair in disarray. She scowled at James, muttering something that sounded derogatory.

"Hey, James!" Judah waved and strode across the street, joining Paisley.

James nodded at him, but his gaze fell on the disaster in his yard. His jaw dropped. He spread out his hands. "What happened here?" He stopped next to his tent trailer that was on its side in the watery grass, gaping at it.

"Hurricane Blaine happened, that's what," Maggie snarled. "Everywhere we've walked it's been the same, *Mr.* Weston."

"I can see that, *Mrs.* Thomas," James shot back at her.

The two weren't getting along, that much was obvious.

"I'm surprised to see you both here." Judah shuffled the bag in his arms. "I mean, it's good, great, to see you made it back okay. Welcome home."

"Okay? You call *this* okay?" Maggie thrust her hands toward her muddy shoes and dirt-speckled pants. "Look at my ruined pumps! I'll never be able to wear these pants again. I hardly made it back unscathed." She glared at James. "Besides making me walk through miles of debris, this man can barely see to drive. His archaic truck rumbled over so many downed limbs and trash I'm bruised from the jolting ride."

"Now, hold on." James jabbed his index finger at her. "You've yammered at me for three hours straight. I'm sick to death of it!"

"Insufferable man." Maggie harrumphed. "Won't listen to advice, even if kindly given."

"Kindly given? This, this woman"—James shuddered— "wouldn't stop yacking the whole way from Florence to here."

Maggie gasped. "You couldn't see the trash in front of you, right in front of your eyes. What were you thinking driving over that bicycle?"

"You drove over a bicycle?" Judah stared back and forth between the two.

"Yes, he did!" Maggie plopped one hand on her hip.

Judah glanced at Paisley. Her hand covered her mouth, and her shoulders shook with suppressed laughter. Seeing her reaction, it took all his self-control not to chuckle, too. He couldn't imagine how heated Maggie's and James's disagreements must have been on the drive back from Florence.

James stomped his foot. "The bike was smashed already, so what's the big deal?"

"Was that any reason to make me suffer while you crushed the whole thing? The man is unconscionable." Maggie wiped her brow with the back of her hand and whimpered.

"So, did you come down the alternative road?" Judah decided to redirect the subject.

"Alternative road?" Maggie huffed. "Is that what you call it?"

James spit. "Only way in. I abandoned my vehicle well before the lighthouse, thanks to fallen trees on the old road. Impassable, really."

"Sorry to hear that."

"Shouldn't have come that way at all." Maggie rubbed her hand over her hip. "Could have killed me. Then he forced me to walk. Without water. I'm about to die standing right here. Any emergency services? I might need oxygen."

"None yet, Mrs. Thomas." Paisley's snicker turned into a snort. She was obviously still trying to suppress her mirth and failing.

182

Maggie's glare froze in Judah's direction. Her mouth dropped open. She pointed at his pink-clad legs. "Why, I never. What happened, young man?"

Oh man. He forgot all about his apparel.

James coughed like he was choking on something.

Judah's face must have hued as rose colored as his clothes. "Pink's the color of the day." He tried to make a joke of it.

"Another terrible decision in a line of bad choices." Maggie squinted accusingly at Paisley.

Inwardly, he groaned.

Paisley stepped behind him; her snickering vanished.

"I think I've made some great choices." He glanced back at his wife, winked.

She gave him a panicked look.

Maggie made a disgruntled snort.

Time to change the subject again. "James, at least your place fared better than some, huh?" Judah rocked his thumb toward Paul's property. "Still, a lot of work to be done around here."

"That's for sure." The man heaved a sigh.

"I have to get back to my inn. See what terrible things have befallen me. My life's work ruined by the sea." Maggie sniffed, her face crumpling as if she were about to break down emotionally. She squinted at Judah. "Are you capable of driving me home, young man? Do you have any pity left for your fellow neighbors, or are you as hardnosed and selfish as your father?"

He felt badly for her situation, but her demanding tone and mean attitude grated on him. "Roads are littered with downed trees and mud and junk. I can drive you part way, but it will be a rough ride."

Maggie groaned. "I have to sit down." She tromped across

James's yard, trudged up the steps, then dropped down on the bench. She covered her face with her hands. "I don't know if I'm going to make it. I'm so tired."

Under normal circumstances, Mrs. Thomas was a force to be reckoned with—stubbornly strong-willed and opinionated. Seeing her like this, wilted, whiny, and seemingly giving up, Judah hardly knew what to think, what to say to the woman he'd feared and avoided for most of his life.

"What's this?" Maggie lifted the corner of a blanket as if it were filthy.

"Oh, that's my—" Paisley stepped forward, stopped. "My blanket."

"Why is it on my porch?" James's voice turned harsh; his tone judgmental.

"It's a long story." Judah stepped in so Paisley wouldn't have to explain. He walked to the porch, controlling his limp, and held out his hand. Maggie passed him the blanket, a scowl on her face. She probably had her own thoughts as to why his wife's blanket might be on a neighbor's porch. He wasn't clarifying anything. "Thank you."

Hearing Maggie's long, weary-sounding sigh, he felt compassion for her. She probably needed a glass of water. A dry place to put up her feet. Maybe even to take a nap. Perhaps, there was another solution, other than her going out to the inn and facing whatever problems the hurricane had created, alone. "Maybe you should stay here for a while and rest."

"Here? Why?" Her eyes bugged.

"She can't stay here. Huh-uh." James stomped his boot, sending mud flying. "We're already in a war, her and me."

"I didn't mean that you should stay here, exactly, Mrs. Thomas." Judah adjusted his foot to ease the tension in his leg. "Without electricity or water, is it a good idea for you to be half a mile away from all of us, alone at the inn? You might need help with something, and you couldn't call anyone for assistance."

Maggie whimpered again. "What else can I do? I want to go home."

Judah glanced at Paisley. Would she mind terribly if he offered the older woman a place to stay for the night? His wife had past issues with the innkeeper, too. Could she set those aside, considering the hardships Maggie was facing?

Paisley squinted at him. Shook her head. Did she guess what he was thinking? They should be willing to provide shelter for anyone in need, right? Even Maggie Thomas. "You could . . . stay with us." He gulped.

Paisley's sharp intake of breath coincided with Maggie's. "Judah."

"Stay at Paul's?" Mrs. Thomas put her hand on her chest. "Why, I couldn't."

"Not at Paul's. We—that is, Paisley, Paul, and I—are staying at Paisley's sister's in the subdivision." He jostled the black bag in his arm. "We have food for dinner. James, you're welcome to join us, too."

"I have my own supplies." James picked up some trash.

"Judah—" Paisley tugged on the bottom of his shirt.

He didn't dare meet her gaze. "What do you think, Mrs. Thomas?"

"I don't know. I'm so, so tired." She sighed.

"You probably need to relax for a few minutes."

Paisley gripped his arm above his elbow. "We have to talk, now."

"Oh, I do, I do." Maggie probably didn't hear Paisley's plea. "I don't know if I could take another step, truth be known."

Paisley tugged on Judah's arm again, this time more force-fully.

He met her gaze. *I'm sorry.* He cleared his throat, preparing to address the innkeeper. "I'm going to get my truck. I'll be back in a few minutes."

Maggie sagged onto the bench and seemed exhausted. Judah's heart went out to her. But he felt equally concerned about his wife's pale face. Her wide eyes. That scared-deer expression. She stared at something over his shoulder, probably fighting a granddaddy of panic attacks at the mere thought of sharing a room, a house, with the woman who accused her of stealing Maggie's heirloom pearls.

He clasped Paisley's hand, willing her to look at him. To find strength in him. But she didn't even meet his gaze.

"Every yard's a disaster. Never seen it so bad." James talked as if unaware of the emotional undercurrents. "Houses that have been in the neighborhood my whole life are ruined."

"It's sad, but we'll recover if we stick together. Help one another." Like inviting Maggie over. He remembered something else. "Oh, James, I tried getting into your house to find some clothes. I kicked the door."

"You what?" The man stared at his house like it might collapse.

"Don't worry. I was unsuccessful."

"Good. I'll take your help as repayment." James eyed him sternly.

"I didn't hurt anything, honest." Judah sighed, realizing James was serious. "What do you need help with?"

"Assistance with taking down the plywood from the windows, for starters."

"I can do that." Not that he considered it repayment.

"What about me?" Maggie yelped. "Are you leaving me stranded with this awful man?"

Having her cantankerous attitude in Paige's small house was going to be problematic. But he could hardly go back on his word, despite Paisley's tugs on his arm.

"I'll be right back after I get my truck." He waved to the other two, hoping they could be civil to each other until he returned. With his free hand, he clasped Paisley's. Her expression said it all—he should not have invited Maggie without her express permission.

Which, of course, she never would have given.

Twenty-two

Paisley strode into the backyard, her thoughts churning as she replayed Judah's excuses for inviting Maggie over. *"We have to help our neighbors through this disaster. Even if it is Maggie Thomas."* Dad would go through the roof. He and Maggie had never gotten along, even when Mom was alive. Maybe he couldn't stomach the woman's gossiping, or her snickering and whispering with Aunt Callie and Miss Patty, either.

Judah said he wanted to do the Good Samaritan thing, to do what was right. Paisley told him, as sweetly as she could, that it was okay he'd made a mistake. He could just uninvite the woman. Which he refused to do.

Now, she had to break the bad news to Dad. Judah volunteered to come in the house and explain, but she told him no. She'd take care of it, even if he was the one who caused this added turmoil in their lives. How was she going to smooth things over with Dad?

"Paisley." The gruff male voice interrupted her thoughts, stunned her, kept her from proceeding up the steps.

She swiveled around.

Craig sat on a chair on the patio. He stood slowly. Stuffed his hands in his coat pockets. His dark eyes peered at her with wariness.

"What are you doing here?" She shuffled backward. She didn't need this, his showing up here again, now.

"I've been waiting to talk with you. Can I carry that bag? Looks heavy."

"I'm fine." She readjusted the weight of the canned goods in the bag. "I don't want your help. Never did, other than with my dad." She had enough on her plate without him hanging around and causing trouble with Judah. Besides, he put her on edge. Always would, probably.

"I'm trying to help you guys get through the crisis, that's all." He took a step closer. His eyebrows formed a tight V in the middle. "I hauled more water for you. Came by and checked on Paul."

"And now you want my thanks?"

"No."

"Then, what?" She imagined herself hitting him with the bag of cans if he dared to reach a finger toward her.

"I'm doing my job. Being neighborly."

"You're off duty. C-MER is closed." She gripped the bag tighter. "Just stay away from me, will you? And my father. I'm taking care of him now." She stomped up the porch steps.

"Then why isn't he taking his insulin?"

"What?" Her heart thudded to the floor. She turned back, met his gaze. "But I thought, I was sure he did."

"He didn't." His face looked deadly serious. "He hasn't tested himself or taken any insulin since I helped him the last time."

"No way." That couldn't be true. She asked Dad about the insulin several times. Although, he argued with her about it just this morning. Told her to mind her own business.

"You'll have to push him until he sees the benefit for himself." There he was telling her what to do again, taking charge, butting his nose into her family's business. He drew the bag from her arms. For some reason, maybe because she didn't want it to burst in a tug-of-war, she let him. But she didn't need his help. His intrusion. However, it seemed Dad still did. Just wait until he heard Maggie was coming. He'd blow a gasket.

"I don't mind helping him." Craig strode into the kitchen ahead of her. "Like I said, I don't mean any harm for either of you."

"What about Judah?" She followed him, still irked. "Did you *not* mean harm when you held him under the water? When you punched him?"

"That's none of your concern."

"Excuse me, but if it involves my *husband*, it is my concern."

He set the bag on the counter. "Just watch out for your dad, okay?"

"I am!" Oh, she wanted to throw something at him.

"Can I help with anything else while I'm here?"

"No. Just . . . just go. Please." All she needed was for Judah to return and find him here. Or for Maggie to walk in and see Paisley alone with him. The rumor mill would explode with tales. Why did Judah have to invite that troublemaker here?

Paisley scooped up the bag to move it to the opposite side of the sink, felt the bottom give way as she hefted it into her arms. Cans and plastic jars thudded to the floor in a cacophony of noise. She groaned. Craig jumped right in and had most of the cans in his arms before she picked up three.

"Craig, you're still here." Dad entered the kitchen with a grin on his face. He didn't seem as fatigued as he had earlier.

After Craig set the cans on the counter, the two men shook hands like long-lost pals.

"I'm just helping Paisley." He made himself sound like her rescuer. As if she needed him, which she did not.

She picked up a juice bottle and opened it. She poured some into a glass and handed it to Dad, eyeing him. "Feeling better?"

"Fine as rain in a storm." Dad sipped the drink. He shuffled to the counter and fingered a can of chili. "From my house?"

"Yep."

"Good. I'm hungry. Let's fire up the grill, Craig."

"Of course." Craig winked at her.

She wanted to scream at him as they tromped outside, laughing and chatting about camping trips and mismanaged fire rings.

This was bad. Judah could show up with their guest at any moment, and Paisley still hadn't told Dad about her arrival. She followed him to the patio. "Dad, there's something I have to say to you."

Craig glanced at her, a shadow darkening his face.

"Yes?" Her father's smile faded.

"Maggie Thomas is coming over. She's going to spend the night here." She delivered the words quickly.

Dad's eyes bugged. "You've got to be kidding. Why on earth would *that* woman come here?" He removed his glasses. Glared.

"Judah, he, um, invited her. He felt she shouldn't be alone out at the inn." She took a breath. "Makes sense. You know, looters, whatever."

"You just uninvite that backstabber." His eyelids scrunched to small slits.

"I'm sorry, but I can't."

"I won't stay under the same roof with Maggie Thomas." Dad shuffled toward the door with jerky movements.

"Dad, it's an emergency. We're in a disaster. Isn't that what you said about him"—she jabbed her thumb toward Craig— "staying here? Let's be Good Samaritans and all that." She thought of Judah's explanation.

Craig cleared his throat loudly, then rattled something with the grill.

"I don't care if there's a Hurricane Catherine and a Cyclone Frank on their way. That Thomas woman is not welcome here." Dad scuffed his shoes on the mat in front of the door. "After what she said about your mother? About you?" He coughed a couple of times. "How could you let her darken this door?"

"I didn't. But Judah thought—" Paisley sighed. So she wasn't the only one burned over things Maggie had spread around town. "I'm sorry this is hurting you." Another apology. "But he's trying to do something good, okay? We don't have to like it. But I'm afraid, for tonight, we're going to have to put up with Maggie. For Judah's sake, if not for hers."

"I disagree."

"Well, maybe it's time to bury the hatchet." She heard the gruff sound of her own voice.

Dad's jaw dropped open.

Craig cleared his throat loudly this time. Was he pointing out her hypocrisy? If she could bury the hatchet with Basalt's biggest gossip, why not him?

"Forget the wrongs she's done against us?" Dad wagged his index finger at her. "Against you? Isn't that why you ran?"

A breath lodged in Paisley's throat. The man behind her was a huge part of why she ran.

"She was partly to blame." And Mayor Grant. Miss Patty. Aunt Callie. How could she forget the gossip and lies that tormented her for years? Yet the way Judah opened his arms, his heart, to her since she returned, and all his reminders about God's love for her, were changing her. Making her want to act differently. Kinder. "Forgiveness has to begin somewhere. Even between us, Dad."

He harrumphed, trudged into the house.

Craig clapped his hands. "Nice speech."

Infuriating man. She clenched her jaw and marched inside. In the kitchen, she found Dad standing by the sink, opening cans and dumping them into a pot. "I'm sorry about all of this."

He didn't respond.

"I knew you wouldn't want Maggie here. I didn't, don't, want her here, either." She tapped the counter with her fingernails. "What would you have me do? Yell at Judah and tell him Maggie absolutely cannot stay? Cause a gigantic stink in front of Mrs. Thomas and Mr. Weston? Make things worse between Judah and me?"

"James is back?" Dad faced her, his eyes lighting up as if he hadn't heard any of the other things she said.

"He is." A seed of mischief came to mind. "You know, your neighbor is the one who caused this problem with Maggie in the first place."

"How so?"

"He brought her back to town. If you're upset with anyone, it should be with him."

Dad harrumphed. But he might have cracked a smile as he went back to opening cans.

She felt a little reprieve from the tension.

Dad asked Craig to carry the pan of chili outside. Paisley pulled four bowls from the cupboard near the sink. Then remembering their other guest would probably be hungry, she added another. Did Maggie even like chili? She searched for the same number of spoons, feeling shaky. Her stomach cramped at the thought of food. She wasn't starving. Just hungry. And the lack of caffeine for several days was taking its toll on her nerves—as was the idea of sitting at the same table with Mrs. Thomas. Craig being here was bad enough.

Carrying the bowls outside, she wished she and Dad could eat alone and talk. She opened the conversation with that business about forgiveness. Did he even feel a need to reconnect with her or to forgive her?

Right now, he just seemed annoyed. And things were bound to get worse when Judah arrived with Maggie.

Twenty-three

Judah didn't want to leave Paisley alone to face her father with the news of Maggie's arrival. He offered to explain the situation to Paul, but she insisted that she'd do it. He drove back to James's house, praying the evening ahead wouldn't be too unbearable.

Instead of waiting for him on the porch like he imagined she would, Maggie sat in a chair in James's living room, sipping a drink, her feet propped up on a stool. Almost like a queen. She peered at him with the briefest of glances, then closed her eyes. Apparently, she wasn't in any rush to leave now.

Judah went outside to help James. The older man was already prying plywood sheets off his windows. It didn't take long for the two of them to uncover the first-story glass and the front door. Judah assisted James with carrying the plywood pieces to the garage for storage. He promised to return on another day to help with the second-story windows, too.

He called to Maggie from the front doorway, letting her know he was ready to leave. Then he climbed into his truck. Moments later, the loud rumble of another vehicle approached. Dad's black truck skidded to a stop in the watery muck still lingering on the road, splattering Judah's rig and his arm that rested on the window edge.

"Son."

"Dad."

The words were exchanged stiffly. His father looked slightly down on him, since his truck was taller.

"I heard you were back in town."

"Who told you that?"

"Doesn't matter." Dad grinned with his mayoral toothy beam. "Your mother wants you to come home. Eat a meal with us. We have plenty of space for staying over."

Mom wanted him home. Not Dad, hmm?

"You know how your mother is." Dad laughed, almost mockingly. "Always looking out for the kid in you. Foolishly, I might add."

Mom was a gem for sticking with Dad all these years. That his father dared to badmouth her upped Judah's irritation.

Maggie climbed into the passenger side of Judah's truck, slammed the door, glared at Edward.

"Mrs. Thomas, what a surprise." Dad lifted his hand in a slight wave.

"Hmph." She shuffled on the seat, turning her back to him. Maggie had made it abundantly clear in town meetings and in local gossip that she didn't approve of the mayor.

"Heading out to the inn, I presume?" Dad asked.

She didn't answer. Appeared to be giving him the cold shoulder.

Dad's cheeks hued red. His chuckle sounded forced. He glanced at Judah. "What do you say about heading home with me?" He messed with his phone. "You and, and your, and your—"

"My *wife?*"

"Oh, right." Dad wrinkled his nose as if smelling something repugnant. "I can run both of you up to my place. I have a generator. Hot water." He stared pointedly at Judah's chin. "A place to shave. Not to mention, grilled steaks and a perfect view."

He didn't include Maggie. Or Paisley's dad. Judah perused the road ahead, taking in the remnants of the recent disaster. Downed trees. Garbage spilled across wet yards. Outdoor furniture tossed here and there. Shingles speckling every yard on the block.

How could he and Paisley leave the others behind? For them to seek comfort—hot showers, real beds, coffee—while family and friends went without? How many times did he already say that to get through this crisis they had to stick together?

"Well?" Dad pushed.

"I don't think so. Thanks, anyway." Judah glanced at the back of Maggie's head. He invited her to join them at Paige's. He still meant to help smooth out whatever awkwardness that decision might cause. Besides, he doubted Paisley would consider going anywhere with Judah's dad, let alone leaving her own father behind.

"Interesting clothes you have on, Son."

Oh man. How could he have forgotten about those again?

"Not quite your color." Dad smirked.

"I got soaked in the drink. Had to borrow these." Judah's cheeks heated up.

"Another reason to come up to our house. Plenty of clothes there."

Judah pictured himself dressed in a pair of the mayor's slacks and a crisp button-up shirt. Would he be expected to wear a tie, too? "We should go. Paisley's expecting us."

"Finally," Maggie muttered.

"A lot of people for such a tiny house." Dad messed with his phone again.

How did he know how many were staying there? "Who told you I was back in town?" Judah returned to his earlier question.

"I'm connected." Dad lifted his phone. "It's my job to know what's going on in my town."

His town.

"You got yourself a nice shiner there. How'd you let that happen?"

Dad probably knew the answer to that, too. Was he communicating with Craig? Or Mia? Although, Mia didn't know about the fight. Unless Craig told her.

"All righty." Dad revved his truck engine loudly, then drove down the road in the direction of Paige's. Why was he going that way and not toward his house on the cliff? Judah didn't have a choice but to follow him.

"Is he coming to the house too?" Maggie's voice hit a high octave. "Because if he is, I won't go in! I promise you, I won't!"

"I don't think that's going to happen, Mrs. Thomas." What was the mayor up to? Was he planning to strongarm Judah into doing what he wanted?

To avoid downed trees, he had to swerve and drive over a couple of yards, causing the truck to lurch and bounce.

Maggie groaned and glared at him. "Why I never! What a horrible driver you are!"

The wheels bogged down in some of the flooded yards. Thanks to his four-wheel-drive vehicle, they kept moving forward, didn't get stuck. He sure got an earful, though.

"You're as bad of a driver as James Weston!" Maggie wailed.

"I've never seen more thoughtless driving in my life than I have today."

"Sorry, ma'am." He couldn't do anything about the road conditions. However, he slowed down even more to show her he didn't intentionally cause her pain.

Just ahead of him, Dad's truck veered into the church parking lot. Why was he stopping there? Judah pulled in beside him. Lifted his hands in a questioning shrug.

"What are we doing here?" Maggie shrieked. "I thought we—"

"I know. I know. Just a sec."

Dad jabbed his index finger toward the grassy knoll at the back of the church property. The area appeared littered with debris and roofing. Judah didn't see any reason for him to be pointing. Then, Paisley trudged from around the back of the church building, a bulging black garbage bag clutched in her hands. Judah shut off the engine, ready to leap out of the truck.

"We're staying here?"

"Just for a minute." He shoved against the driver's door, hoping it opened this time so that he didn't have to ask Mrs. Thomas to move. The door rattled, budged a little. He tried again. It creaked open, making a metal against metal scraping sound. He slid from the seat, his feet landing in a couple inches of water on the pavement. He hid his wince at the tug in his calf.

"I thought we were going to a house where I could rest." Maggie glowered.

"We will. Sorry for the delay." After her harping over his driving, he was relieved to step away from the cab for a couple of minutes. "Just wait here. I'll be right back."

"What else can I do?"

He strode a few steps across the parking lot, stepping over branches and rocks. He lifted his hand to wave at Paisley, but Craig marched around the corner of the church. Judah's hand froze. Outrage lit a fire in the middle of his chest. What was Craig doing here with Paisley? Judah lowered his hand and stomped across the parking lot, a few choice words churning in his brain.

"Wait, Son."

Had Dad known what was going on here? That this cleanup crew included Craig Masters hanging out with Paisley?

Judah wanted to yell out in frustration. Instead, he purposefully made the words *"Mercy and grace, mercy and grace"* repeat through his brain. But it didn't soothe his temper this time.

Before he reached Craig, Paul sauntered from behind the church with a pile of papers in his arms. "Where do you want these, Paisley?"

"Over here." She pointed to a stack of debris. Her gaze clashed with Judah's.

He recognized the trepidation in her eyes, not the reaction he wanted to promote. *Don't do anything rash.* Oh, he wouldn't do anything too crazy. Well, maybe just—

"Masters, I want a word with you!"

"Son, wait." He heard Dad tromping across the pavement behind him.

"What's going on here?" Maggie's demanding voice sounded close, like she was following, too.

He may have made a terrible mistake in bringing her along. Whatever she witnessed in the next few minutes would probably be broadcast to all eleven hundred of Basalt Bay's returning residents.

"What do you want?" Craig squinted.

"I want to talk with you. Now."

"Judah, hold up." Dad grabbed his shoulder. "Son, it's not worth a fight."

"I'm not planning to fight." He jerked away from his father's grip. "I said I wanted to *talk*."

Craig dropped the metal chunk with a clatter. He clenched his right fist as if giving Judah a warning.

Judah would gladly finish what they started yesterday. That scuffle, the way Craig held him beneath the saltwater, still burned in his gut.

"Judah—" Paisley's voice came softly. "Can I talk to you? Explain. Please."

He didn't blame her for Craig butting in where he didn't belong. He understood what she told him before, about her father needing the guy's medical know-how. That didn't mean he had to stay around her. Judah couldn't forget Craig's words about him spending time with Judah's "sweetie," either.

"You've helped my family. Thank you for that. Now it's time for you to leave."

"Or what?" Craig's eyes narrowed.

Adrenaline shot through Judah's veins. "You have no right to be here." His family, his wife, were off-limits to this man.

Craig guffawed. "You own the church property now, too?"

"Masters!" Judah's dad barked the word.

Craig's chin rose. His nostrils flared. But he lowered his fist to his side, flexed his fingers.

What kind of influence did the mayor have on this guy that he yelled one word and Craig responded?

"We're just being good neighbors—your wife and me. And Paul." Craig nodded at the older man.

His words "wife and me" twisted triple loops in Judah's chest. "I'm Paisley's husband. She and I are together again."

"That so?" Craig glanced toward Paisley.

"Yeah, that's so." Judah didn't check his wife's expression. "Stay away from her." He lowered his voice. "I mean it."

"You Grants think you own everything." His ex-supervisor thrust his index finger at Judah's chest. "Does the need to control the world run in your veins, too?"

What ran in his veins was the impulse to slug the guy in the face and return the favor of a bruised cheek. Maybe a black eye.

"Judah, please. Can we talk?" Paisley touched his elbow.

Did she give Craig permission to hang out with her? Perhaps, gave him hope about something romantic happening. *No way!* But that's what Craig wanted, right? For him to doubt her. To drive a wedge between them. But why?

"I had it right all along." Maggie cackled gleefully. "There *was* another man. Callie Cedars denied it. Wait until I—"

"No, you're wrong!" Paisley shouted.

"You don't know anything." Paul glared at Maggie, his eyes as wide as golf balls. "I told you she shouldn't be allowed in our house. Gossiper. Liar. Talebearer."

"Dad."

Craig grinned as if he thought the whole thing was humorous. Then he strode toward the garbage pile. Did he plan to keep on working even though Judah told him to leave?

Judah stomped after him. "This is the last time I'm telling you, Masters. Stay away from my wife."

"Grant men talk tough. Fight like girls." Craig pointed at Judah's pants. "Case in point. And, what, you couldn't resist wearing that old high school relic?" He nodded toward the jacket.

Judah gritted his teeth; tried to control his temper.

"There's a better way to solve disagreements." The mayor cleared his throat.

"I know your way of fighting, Mayor. Dirty." Craig picked up the metal piece he carried earlier. He hurled the chunk onto the pile. The metal clattered. He strode over to Paul who was still holding the wad of papers.

"Well, that was something." Judah's dad unwrapped a piece of black licorice. Stuck it in his mouth. "I didn't know you had it in you to stand up to Craig, Son. How about you get your gal and let's head up to the house? Put some distance between you and Masters."

Tempting thought. For about five seconds.

He'd put off talking with Paisley long enough. "Excuse me." He nodded at his father, then walked straight to his wife and clasped her hand. He drew her toward the church steps. "Why is Craig still here?"

She jerked her hand free. "He helped Dad with his insulin. He ate with us. That's all."

"That's all?" Judah's voice leapt higher. When she flinched, he wished he'd controlled his tone better. "Look, I'm sorry. I'm just . . . upset."

"No kidding. I didn't invite him. My dad did. Like you invited Maggie!" She glared at him, her angry gaze telling him she was enraged at his actions. "He helped my father. The two of them have become friends."

"I couldn't believe he was here. With you." He thrust his fingers through his hair. Frustration pounded in him. If his leg was better, he'd go for a jog. Burn off the rage. He thought he put those emotions behind him.

"All this . . . anger . . . isn't like you."

"Today it is." He ran his knuckles over his sore cheek. "When Dad pulled into the parking lot and I saw—"

"Yeah, why is *the mayor* hanging around?" Her dark gaze locked with his.

"He invited us up to their place. Hot bath. Comfortable bed. Coffee."

Her glare intensified. "Maybe you should go and enjoy the luxuries your family can afford."

"Maybe if—"

"No! I'm taking care of my dad. I don't know how you could even suggest I go with Edward when I wouldn't go with him after the storm. Even though I was all alone and desperate for help, I refused to ride with him." Her voice lowered. "You know how I feel about him."

Some of his molten fury dissipated. "But I would be with you, Pais. That's the difference." He wanted her to admit that his presence, him being close to her, would make a difference in how she felt toward his father, toward life in Basalt Bay.

"You've changed, Judah." She kicked at a rock, shuffling it in the muddy water. "I don't even know who you are right now."

"Yes, you do know who I am."

"Fighting with Craig?"

"Hey, that's—"

"Acting as if you hate him." She thrust out her hands toward him. "What's with that? You call that being a Christian, how a man professing to know God acts?"

Judah gulped, unable to refute her words. They took him from fury to humility, maybe humiliation, in about five seconds. Hadn't he encouraged her to trust God? To believe that He had a good plan for their lives, for them being together. What did he do? Blew it earlier, and now again. He wanted revenge that went way beyond just protecting his wife. He wanted Craig to take back the things he said about Paisley. He wanted to rub the man's face in the dirt. Maybe she knew him better than he knew himself.

"How could you bring Edward here when you know how much he h-hates m-me?" Her voice trembled.

"I didn't bring him here." He wasn't accepting the blame for everything. "He is my father. And you and I are still married, making him your father-in-law." He hoped she still wanted to be married to him, but so much was messed up between them since the night of the hurricane when they kissed.

"Did you forget he paid me to l-leave you?"

How could he forget that? "I'm sorry he did that to you, to us." He gnawed on his lower lip. What else could he say? Nothing he said would make amends for the wrongs of the past.

"Maybe you should go to your parents' house. That would give you time to think things over."

"After all I did to get here? To be with you?" Was that what she wanted? For him to leave. "Nothing doing. I'm not leaving you, that's a promise. Not even for a hot cup of coffee."

She may have almost smiled at that.

"I'm here for you. Always will be. As long as you'll have me." He meant that, even if he acted stupid earlier.

She sighed. "I need to go help my dad. I'll meet you and Maggie at Paige's."

He watched her walk away, her accusation "you've changed" pounding through his thoughts. He'd have to ask the Lord to help him get over the anger still swirling in his veins, in his desire for payback. He sighed. None of those things, other than prayer, mattered as much as making things right with his wife.

"Well?" Dad demanded as soon as Judah approached him.

"We're staying here."

"But we have a generator. Comfort food. Hot water."

"I know, Dad." He shook his father's hand. "Thanks for the offer."

"What am I going to tell your mom?"

"The truth." Judah walked toward Paisley. "Tell her I love my wife. She'll understand."

"Of all the—"

Judah didn't hear the rest of what Dad muttered. He followed Paisley to where she was dumping the contents of a black bag onto the garbage pile. He grabbed hold of one side of the plastic and helped empty it. She nodded at him, a softer look in her eyes.

Craig and Paul dragged some wood chunks from behind the church. Judah couldn't believe Craig hadn't left yet. He picked up a few items, dropped them on the garbage pile, but mostly he watched the other man. How long would he have to stay on alert?

As long as it takes.

Twenty-four

Paisley scooped up more trash off the muddy church lawn, stuffing cans, plastic containers, and seaweed into another garbage bag. She'd be glad when they were finished here. Maggie had gone back to sit in Judah's pickup. Her accusation that Paisley had another man in her life soured in Paisley's gut. How would she endure the woman's sharp tongue for the rest of the evening? How would Dad? She groaned.

Judah and Craig both dropped an armload of junk onto the pile at the same time. They glared at each other as if they were about to exchange heated words. Something made a vibrating sound. A cell phone? Who still had bandwidth? Edward? No, that noise came from Craig!

"What was that?"

Craig met her gaze for a half second, then yanked his cell phone out of his back pocket. He stared at the screen. "I have to take this."

"*Take this?* Does your cell work? Did it have battery power this whole time?" With each question, her voice rose higher. "I don't believe it." He was a scum. Judah was right not to trust him. She didn't trust him.

Craig turned away, his other finger to his ear. "Hello. Yeah. Uh-huh. I can hear you." He walked toward the church building.

"Can you believe that?" She whirled around to face Judah. "I could have called you."

Understanding dawned on his face. "He must not have wanted that to happen."

"He's controlling. Manipulative. Cruel."

"What's wrong?" Paul wiped his nose.

"All this time, Craig's cell phone worked. I could have called Judah."

"Would that have made any difference?" Dad shrugged as if Craig's deception didn't bother him in the least. "The road was still unusable."

"Sure. But it would have made all the difference in the world to me." If she had talked to Judah, told him that she loved him, he'd know. Everything would be different between them.

"Doesn't seem like it matters." Dad turned away, trudged toward the church.

She groaned.

Judah touched her hand as if he understood.

"Anything else I can do to help?" Edward strode by, sounding too chipper.

Yeah, go home. If he and Craig left and took Maggie with them, everything would be simpler for Paisley. The older woman wasn't going to appreciate Paige's cold house, their limited canned goods, or sleeping on a lumpy futon—although it was the best they had to offer.

Judah ran his palm over his scruffy chin. His beard made him look roguish like a pirate. She could get used to that look. She didn't smile at him, but she must have stared at his face too long.

He gave her a sweet smile, his eyes twinkling. Brave of him to do that with his father standing here watching them—and with the way she chewed him out such a short while ago. He must have taken her words to heart. He seemed more cooperative and humbler ever since.

"There's plenty of work to be done here and around town," Judah finally answered his father's question. "Neighbors helping neighbors. You're welcome to join in."

"Oh, right, sure."

Since Edward and Bess had amenities, Paisley decided to take a chance on her idea. "Edward, why don't you take Mrs. Thomas up to your house? You have spare rooms. Food." This disaster had made her bolder. Judah's eyes widened, but he gave her a slight nod.

Edward sputtered. "That doesn't s-seem r-right. Oh, look at the time. I have to go." He stomped, nearly ran, toward his truck, apparently reneging on his offer to help.

Judah chuckled.

"I guess he didn't appreciate my suggestion."

"Guess not."

With his phone lifted in his hand, Craig charged after Edward. "Mayor! Wait up. There's been a riot at the junction."

"A riot?" The mayor pivoted toward him. "Tell me."

"Vehicles are in a logjam at the road barricade. Residents are riled up, demanding access to their homes. Sounds like chaos. They need your assistance to bring order. Say a few words."

Edward stood taller. "I'll go where duty calls. Masters, come with me." He jumped into his vehicle.

Craig motioned to Judah. "Grant, let's go."

"I don't work for you anymore."

"Well—" Craig took a step toward Paisley's dad. "Sorry I can't help any longer."

"Go, go." Dad waved. "You've done plenty."

Oh, he certainly had. He caused trouble. Lied. Insinuated things. Riled Judah. Paisley was thrilled to see him get in Edward's truck and leave. After the mayor tore out of the lot, the wheels spitting mud, silence followed. She let out a relieved sigh. The air felt easier to breathe.

"Ready to head back?" Judah asked.

"I am." She tied a knot in the bag she'd been filling. Left it next to the pile. "I'll walk over with my dad."

"I have the truck."

"And Maggie." How were they going to get along with the outspoken woman? "Dad, let's go and get something to eat. You need to rest."

"Okay."

Judah cleared his throat. "Sorry about, you know, before. You were right. I have been acting as badly as Craig."

"Not *as* badly. I may have exaggerated. I'm sorry for what I said too."

"Don't be." He swallowed. "I do wonder why he seems to think there's hope for you and him."

"He's delusional and a troublemaker, that's why."

"Ready?" Dad's cheeks were ruddy and his eyes bright. He seemed to have enjoyed the outdoor labor.

She hoped he hadn't overtaxed himself. She'd keep an eye on him. Make sure he ate and drank plenty of water.

As she trudged along beside him toward Paige's, she glanced over her shoulder and watched Judah climb into his pickup. Why were constant roadblocks keeping them from finding their way back to each other? Would it ever get easier?

Twenty-five

From where she slept on the couch last night, Paisley awoke to find Judah leaning over her, grinning.

"W-what is it?" Her voice cracked as she peered up at his smiling, bearded face. "Is something wrong?"

"Nothing's wrong." His fingers brushed hair off her forehead. "Good morning, beautiful. I couldn't resist saying that for another second."

She must look a disaster, hadn't showered in five days. Still, his manly smile did wild things to her heart. Thinking of her morning breath, she pulled the blanket over the lower part of her face. "Why are you waking me up?" The room didn't seem light enough for this intrusion. He'd set up an outdoor lounge chair in the kitchen to sleep on. Maybe he hadn't rested well.

He tugged the blanket down to her chin, exposing her mouth. "I thought we could get an early start."

"For—?"

"For the cottage. To gather food. Clothes. The wind died down. It's low tide. We can walk along the beach." His eyes were wide. He seemed fully awake.

She, on the other hand, was zonked. Wanted to keep sleeping. Without coffee to start her day, staying burrowed beneath the comforter was her only wish. She yawned. "What about Dad and Maggie? I can hardly leave them alone." She thought of the squabbling duo she contended with during dinner and afterward last night. How Maggie complained about everything—the bland chili, the cold house, the dark bathroom, the lumpy futon in a child's bedroom, the company. How Dad alternated between throwing critical comments at her and giving her the silent treatment. Leaving a livid cat and an irritable dog by themselves would be safer. "Why not take your pickup?"

"Downed trees and power lines. Besides, I know how much you love beach walking." He winked at her.

"I'd love a beach walk." However, there was the matter of Dad and Maggie. And Paisley's need to stick close to her father. She sat up, brushing her fingers through her messy long hair that needed a shampoo.

"Maggie already left."

"What? When?" Paisley slipped her feet into the boots she'd borrowed from her sister's room.

"I heard her getting around this morning, creeping past me in the kitchen. She left about an hour ago, mumbling about 'getting out of the enemy's camp.'"

"I wonder where she went."

"Her inn, most likely."

"That's a long walk for her in those shoes." Paisley smoothed her hands down her rumpled shirt sleeves.

"Yep. So, what do you say?"

She wouldn't have to worry about Maggie and Dad being at each other's throats, now. "Okay, I'll hike out to the cottage with you." She stood. "First, I'll use the bathroom. Then check on my dad." She scurried down the hall, knowing she'd have to haul water later.

Without eating breakfast, they were out the door in a few minutes. She'd found Dad reading in bed. He grinned when she told him that Maggie left. He joked about them bringing back eggs and bacon for a celebration.

She and Judah walked toward the church in silence. They didn't hold hands, but she felt an emotional rope tugging them closer. Her hands moved back and forth in time with her stride, and she bumped into his arm a couple of times. She recognized a familiar longing in his eyes, like he wanted to bridge the gap between them. Maybe link their fingers together. Or their pinkies.

A low fog hung in the air above the bay, making it seem earlier than it was.

Did Maggie make it out to her inn okay? The woman was spunky, despite her plethora of grievances. Last night, besides mourning every aching joint and the "awful" food, she expressed anxiety about her property. That looters might have broken in and stolen things like "someone" did to her precious jewelry a few years back—something she still blamed that "someone" for doing. She glared at Paisley with open hostility, but Paisley didn't rise to the bait.

When she and Judah reached the parking lot near the beach, they paused.

"Skiff's gone. Brad, most likely." Was he worried that Craig might have taken it? He held up his hand to his ear. "Listen."

She heard something too. A loud truck or a machine engine. "What is it?"

"Let's go find out." He took her hand and she liked how comfortably her fingers fit with his.

Instead of heading for the beach, they strode toward downtown along the sidewalk. They had to walk through a couple of inches of muddy water, stepping over or around debris. Judah's limp didn't seem as bad today, which must mean he wasn't in as much pain.

They passed by James Weston's, Dad's, the Anderson's. She stopped and pointed at the downed power line across the street that she'd been avoiding.

"Oh man. That looks bad." Judah tugged her hand, leading her closer to the oceanside buildings, making a wide berth around the danger zone.

When they reached Miss Patty's rental, kitty-corner from City Hall, he pulled her around the building. Then he peered around the corner like a spy.

"What are you doing?" She snickered.

Before he could answer, two utility vehicles veered out of the company's parking lot. The trucks didn't go far. They stopped next door, just outside City Hall.

"That's where they're working first? Instead of in the neighborhoods?" That didn't make sense to her.

"The mayor." Judah groaned. "Takes care of himself. He'll say it's business. City Hall needs to be open for meetings." His voice took on a deeper tone like his father's. "I'm a man of the people. Go where I'm needed." He snorted. "Hogwash."

"Yep."

Judah nodded toward the ocean like he was ready to get going, then they climbed down the rocks. On the beach, Paisley kept her gaze on the wet soil and the tidal pools in case something amazing had washed up that she could collect.

"How do you think the cottage survived the high winds?" She marched around a pile of seaweed, leapt over a small stream.

Judah splashed through the water. Too bad he didn't have boots on. "Similar to your dad's place, I imagine. I didn't put plywood on the windows, either."

"I hope your stuff is okay."

"Our stuff." He gazed at her intently.

She sighed. They still had a lot to talk about—why she left, why she stayed away—before she considered the cottage and the things inside partly hers.

The sound of ocean waves lapping against the craggy beach below them was invigorating and inviting. She wished she had time to sit down on a boulder, close her eyes, and listen for an hour. To forget the chaos of the hurricane, Judah's absence, and anything having to do with Craig. The tidal rhythm might even bring her peace the way it did the day she drove into town and rushed out to the peninsula.

Too bad the sea couldn't wash away the past the same way it did sand on the seashore. She thought of how the waves scooped up dead, dried stuff from the beach, and hauled it out to sea, leaving behind a layer of smooth, unblemished sand. If God made the ocean capable of doing such a magnificent renewal process, He must be able to do that to a human heart. To her heart.

Sigh.

She stopped walking, closed her eyes, listening to the sound of the roaring surf. She didn't have an hour, even a half hour, to spend here. Maybe thirty seconds. Just a few heartbeats, really. But she'd take what she could get. She heard the rush of water, the abatement, the churning waves that created a wonderful blend of music.

"Something wrong?" Even Judah's voice sounded melodic. He touched her hand.

She didn't open her eyes, didn't pull her hand away. Maybe they could experience this magical moment together. Would he understand her need to pause? To absorb this love she had for the sea.

He linked their pinkies. Ah, he did understand.

She didn't know if his eyes were closed or not. She didn't peek. She inhaled the musty, tangy, salty odor she associated with joy. A funny scent for happiness. But perfect to her.

Judah didn't rush her. Even though they were in a hurry to get out to the cottage, find food, and get back to Dad. She needed this. Maybe he did too. She breathed in deeply. Sighed.

Then, opening one eye, she found his eyes closed. He wore a slight smile of pleasure, or peace? She felt so relaxed with him. Like they were good friends who understood each other. And they did, didn't they? She noticed his scruffy cheeks. Entertained a passing notion of running her palms over the soft bristles. How would it feel to do that again?

"Are you watching me, Pais?"

She was caught. "Maybe." She dragged out the word.

He opened his eyes fully. So did she.

Despite the weird way he acted last night, he was such a good guy. Craig could make them both act crazy and irrational. So could Judah's dad. But she didn't want to think of either of those two.

She was thankful for how Judah had closed his eyes, listening to the sound of the waves with her. He didn't tell her they needed to hurry up and get going. Didn't let out longsuffering sighs. He simply waited with her, enjoying what she was enjoying.

She met his gaze. Swallowed. His eyes spoke a volume of poetry to her heart, all in the span of about fifteen seconds. In her mind's eye, she pictured him the way he looked standing over her this morning. Calling her "beautiful." Their gazes blending, dancing.

"We should probably get going, huh?"

"Oh, sure, okay." She walked ahead of him, lest he see the confusion, the foggy unsurety, in her gaze. What was wrong with her? Why couldn't she just tell him how she felt?

"You okay?"

"I'm fine." Would be, if she could get beyond the unsaid words clogging her throat.

They trudged past the dunes on the far side of the old cannery, the powerful winds gusting off the surface of the tide tossing her hair every which way. A few strands got stuck in her mouth and she brushed them away.

They passed the sandy beach near the Beachside Inn where they ate takeout from Bert's Fish Shack a few days ago. Paisley perused Maggie's inn. She couldn't see any visible damage to the buildings. Had the innkeeper made it home all right? Hopefully, no one broke in and caused problems the way the woman feared. Paisley said a simple prayer for Maggie's safety and well-being. *New beginnings.*

They kept following the beach along the seashore, dodging tidal pools and rocks. When they finally reached the narrow beach in front of their cottage, more driftwood had been thrust onto the top edge of the sand. Seaweed was peppered over the usually tidy beach as if manually scattered—more results of the hurricane.

"That's awesome." Judah pointed at the house, chuckling.

"What is it?"

"I forgot that the front windows were still boarded up from Addy." He sounded relieved, but then he moaned. "Oh, no."

She followed his gaze. The roof above the porch had collapsed. The splintered narrow columns lay like a pile of tooth-picks in the grass. Shingles and wood chunks were mounded on the porch floor and all around the front of the house.

"What a mess." He rushed ahead of her. "Stay back."

"Why?" Like she wouldn't help him after they came all this way? She immediately scooped up boards and threw them into a pile. He didn't protest, but she noticed him watching her—not romantically, more as a protector. He didn't need to act that way. She was tough. Could take care of herself. However, she didn't mind finding his shiny gaze intertwining with hers occasionally as they hurled wood chunks and shingles. A woman could be flattered over such attention. Even if the guy doing the flirting was her husband. Or maybe, especially then.

"Uh-oh. Key's gone." Judah leaned over the place where the crab shell with the key in it used to be.

"What now?"

He rammed his shoulder against the door. The damaged entry didn't give. "I'll be right back." He strode around the corner.

She kept working, grabbing tree branches out of the driveway and hurling them to the side.

In a few minutes, she heard Judah doing something at the back door. It sounded like it was stuck, too. Kicking sounds. A few groans. A couple of minutes later, the front door scraped open. He leaned against the doorframe, his face red as if he used a lot of exertion to break in. "Welcome home, Pais."

Home. She gulped.

His goofy grin, like he offered her the world—and maybe he did—as he swept his hand into their beach house the way a maître d at a fine restaurant might, made her smile. She wasn't ready to fall into his arms yet—right?—but his sincere words, his reassuring touch on her elbow as she passed him, made her feel welcome and safe as she entered their house.

Wet papers, household gadgets, pillows, and pictures lay scattered across the floor. Mostly ruined by the looks of it.

"Wow, this place took a beating." She trudged around the soaked flooring.

Water puddled in some places. The kitchen window was busted. Water must have come in through the living room window, even though it was covered with plywood from the previous storm.

"Could be worse."

"Like?"

"I don't know. The roof gone?" Judah strolled around the room as if taking inventory. His shoulders drooped. "This will take a lot of work for us to fix."

"Sorry."

"It'll be okay." He sighed. "It's still our castle."

Or ruins, maybe?

She trudged across the wet floor and entered the guest room. Her private space. How long would it be until Judah might expect more than them just being roommates? He seemed patient, amazingly so. And for that she was thankful. She had to know her own heart before she agreed to share a room, a bed, with him. She remembered not too many days ago when she yelled at him, saying she'd never share his bed again. Now, she was having second thoughts. In the last few days, her emotions, her spirit, had undergone a transformation, it seemed.

Thinking again of Judah's sparkling gaze down at the beach when he opened his eyes made her heart somersault. Maybe love, the great heart changer, was in the sea air today.

The carpet felt squishy beneath her boots. A few things lay on the floor in the wetness, blown off the dresser or walls during the storm. The soft comforter on the bed looked inviting. She was tired of sleeping on the futon. The couch wasn't comfortable, either. And she felt sleepy after the hike. Did she dare stretch out, relax, even for a few minutes?

Without taking off her boots, she flopped down on the twin bed. Rumbled a sigh. Closed her eyes.

A moment later, Judah's footfall gave him away. She peeked through lowered eyelids. He stood in the doorway, leaning his shoulder against the frame. A smile lined his way-too-handsome scruffy face. "Kind of a small bed for two, don't you think?"

For two? "Don't even think of it." Her voice came out in a hoarse whisper.

"What do you mean?"

"Whatever it is you might be thinking about doing, don't." She should stand up. Put distance between them. But she didn't move fast enough. Or maybe she didn't want to.

"Oh, you mean—" He strode to the side of the bed. Leaning over her, one hand landed on each side of her arms. His thumbs brushed her elbows. He stared down at her, grinning his maddening grin that turned her insides to mush. Made her not think straight. "Or did you mean I might be thinking of something like this?" He lowered his face, his lips within two inches of hers. She felt his breath on her skin. What was he doing? What was she allowing him to do?

His blue eyes were amazing pools of sky and sea. She remembered how his kisses used to taste of cinnamon from his chewing gum.

She tried not to invite him closer with her gaze that might look sleepy, or softly compelling. But his sapphire eyes drew her to him, begging her to let him kiss her, despite her reluctance to cross that line. They were husband and wife. But not really, right? Not until the words were said. Not until they made promises that would last a lifetime, this time.

"Or this?" His mouth brushed her cheek whisper soft in three places, his beard tickling her skin.

Oh, my. She caught a whiff of something spicy. He must have found some deodorant to put on. The manly mix of spice and Judah was intoxicating. Soft lips she knew, had known, so well lingered near hers, not coming any closer. Seemingly waiting for her permission. But her breath was caught, trapped behind her stubborn lips that refused to move any closer to him.

"Judah," she dragged out. She shook her head slightly.

He exhaled a breath. The foggy haze of desire in his eyes lifted. He backed away. Glanced at her. One look of longing. Then he scrambled out the doorway, shutting the door behind him.

She let out her breath. Stared at the ceiling. Disappointment mixed with relief. If she gave into a moment of affection with him, what then? One toe-curling romantic kiss. Nothing would have been wrong with that. But one kiss might lead to other things she wasn't ready for.

Until she was sure beyond any doubt that she wanted everything marriage with Judah offered, passion had to be put on hold. Would her heart and her head agree the next time she felt his lips so near hers?

Twenty-six

Judah leaned his palms against the edge of the kitchen sink. *Oh man.* Did he come on too strong and push Paisley before she was ready to start kissing him again? He thought she was warming up to him, but maybe he read her wrong. What now? Did his actions just throw them back to the starting line? Back to where she kept him at arm's length.

He thrust his fingers through his hair that felt a little shaggy, unkept.

He needed to be patient. To wait for Paisley's heart to blossom into love with him. That could take time.

He opened the cupboards and pulled down canned goods and packaged food. He tugged on the fridge handle. A bad smell hit him. It worked as a distraction.

He heard Paisley enter the room. Sensed her watching him.

"Before we go, I'll have to dump everything from the fridge and freezer. It stinks."

"I can help with that." She stepped into view beside him. Gave him a timid smile. "Have any cookies around like you used to?"

"Of course. Even your favorite." He reached his hands to an upper shelf.

"Chocolate chips?"

"Are there any others?" He winked, trying to get back to the light mood they enjoyed before he noticed her on the bed. He pulled down the treat package he put on a shelf before the storm. He ripped open the container with pictures of chocolate chip cookies displayed on the top and sides.

He held out the package to her. Their fingers touched. No denying the attraction between them. Paisley picked up two cookies, her dark eyes glimmering at him. It took all the restraint he possessed not to pull her into his arms. He stuffed a whole cookie into his mouth, watching her.

She downed her cookies too.

He popped the top off a bottle of sweet tea. He offered her the container first. She guzzled half of it.

"Mmm. That was good."

He drank the rest. Wiped the back of his hand over his mouth, still watching her.

She gazed at him and cleared her throat. "I, um, I'm going to go grab my clothes."

"Me too." He rocked his thumb toward the master bedroom. His room. Which used to be theirs. The one he hoped would be theirs again someday.

"Thanks for the cookies."

"You're welcome."

Their gazes were still locked. Time seemed to stand still.

She moved away first, walked back into the guest room, closed the door.

He exhaled, hobbled into his room and changed every item of clothing, including the pink pj's. When he was dressed in a gray sweater, jeans, and hiking boots he stood outside the closed guest room door, feeling like a new man.

"You need anything?" he called to her. "How about another bag?"

"No. I have my backpack. Thanks." She opened the door, wearing different clothes too. He liked her soft-looking bulky blue sweater that hung down over dark leggings.

"I'll get started on the fridge." He nodded toward the kitchen. "Then we can go."

"Need help?"

"Sure."

It seemed she was okay with being around him. Maybe he wasn't all wrong about his thoughts of them kissing, taking their relationship to another level.

She set her pack down. "Those clothes feel better?" He heard the laughter in her voice.

"Much. I'm all done wearing hot pink."

"You may never live that down now that Maggie, Craig, and the mayor saw you in them." She snickered. "However, I thought you looked kind of cute."

"Right." Thinking he might push the flirting envelope just a little, he added, "What, you don't think I'm cute now?"

She laughed. "What can I say? I'm fond of pink."

He groaned, then dove into emptying the fridge. Paisley pulled out the items in the upper freezer compartment. They accomplished the task quickly then hauled the trash outdoors. When they returned to grab their coats, extra clothes, and the food stuff he already accumulated, she reached for the cookie bag. "One more."

He chuckled, grabbed one also, then headed for the door.

They trudged back along the beach the way they came. Kept up a steady pace, heading northwest, without saying much. As they rounded Baker's Point, her moan coincided with his.

"Tide's coming in." Judah stopped walking. The beach ahead of them was nearly submerged and would soon be impassible. He should have paid better attention. Kept track of the time.

"Guess we took too long." She sighed.

"Do you mind hiking over the dunes?" Judah gazed toward the mountain of sand to their right. The front side of the hill had a steeper than usual slope where the storm surge had eroded the dune. That might be tough climbing. He gazed toward the ocean. "Wish we had a skiff."

"Maggie does. Maybe she'd let us borrow it."

"You think since we gave her a place to stay for one night that she considers us friends now?" Judah shuffled the weight of the bag he carried from one arm to the other.

"Um, no, I'm pretty sure I'm still on her Ten Most Despised People list."

"Then the dunes it is."

They trekked across loose sand on the way up the dune, their boots sliding in the steep parts. Harder walking than crossing the beach. Tougher on his injured leg, but he didn't mention it.

Paisley was quiet, seemed to be thinking. Out of the blue, she spoke quickly. "One time I borrowed a skiff from Maggie's inn. Me and Peter."

"Borrowed?" He tried to keep pace with her, but his boots slid a few more times, causing him to fall behind.

"We called it borrowing. She called it stealing." She made a wry face at him over her shoulder. "Maggie and I disagree on a lot of things."

He could imagine that, but he was intrigued by her story. "What mischief were you and Peter up to that you needed Mrs. Thomas's skiff?"

"The good kind of mischief." She stopped walking, let him pass by her as they approached the top of the dune.

"Is there such a thing as good mischief?"

A handful of sand pelted his back. He whirled around. Jaw dropped. "You didn't just do that."

"I sure did." She cackled, dusting off her hands. She scrambled past him, leaping, her boots sliding in the sand as if it were snow and she were wearing skis.

Her sudden frolicking reminded him of the young woman he fell in love with. The one who ran and laughed and played with him many times on these dunes. He tried to pursue her now, but he had a disadvantage with his gimpy leg. And he carried the heavy bag that could fall apart at any second if he wasn't careful. Still, he couldn't resist chasing her.

He scooped up a handful of sand, thinking of some mischief of his own. When he got close enough, he took aim and hurled the grit at her backside—not hard, but he hit his target.

"Judah Grant!" She whirled around, hands on her hips. But she was laughing too. He thought she might scoop up more sand to toss back at him. Instead, she seemed to be breathing hard, staring out over the panoramic view of the ocean.

He caught up to her, laughing. Enjoying the playful interaction they had.

While she seemed entranced with the seascape, he watched her. Took in her shining, gorgeous dark eyes, fringed by equally dark lashes outlining them. Seeing her, loving her, made him want to pull her into his arms, maybe kiss her breathless. But she'd already rejected his romantic advances once today. And he was carrying this plastic bag full of canned goods. They should probably get going, check on Paul.

"We were just kids"—she spoke as if the sand throwing didn't happen at all—"determined to set crabs free from a crab pot. Neither Peter nor I could stand to see crabs awaiting their death sentence in those cages."

"So, you're a softy at heart."

She nudged him in the gut with her elbow.

"Hey."

"Can't eat crab to this day."

"Really?" He'd just learned something new about his wife. "Here I thought you didn't like the way I cooked them."

"I can't stand the whole cook-them-alive thing."

"You do have a tender heart." He expected another elbow jab. When it didn't happen, he decided to come clean too. "I was recently tempted to steal a boat."

"No way."

He laughed. "Yep."

"Tell me about it."

As they hiked across the top of the dune, their boots sliding in the sand, he shared about Richard denying them the use of his skiff. How they knocked on the door of his house the next morning, instead of taking it without asking. He liked the way her gaze kept dancing in his direction. Made him wish this time with her, trudging across the sand, could last long enough for their hearts to connect and be healed.

After they descended the dune on the opposite side, and finally reached South Road, they paused. He dug out a peach-mango juice bottle from the bag, and they both took long drinks.

Paisley's hair flew about her face in the wind. Reaching out, he stroked a few strands away from her cheek, enjoying the soft feel of her skin beneath his fingers. He recognized that sweet look in her gaze, just like earlier in the guest room, and he was tempted to lean forward and touch his lips to hers. But he didn't want to seem pushy about the whole romance thing and make her nervous, wary of him. He lowered his hand to his side.

"We should get going. Dad. I, um, have to check on him." She huffed. "We've taken enough time here."

"Of course." Despite his resolve not to push her for more than she was comfortable with, her abrupt dismissal hurt. And, maybe, thanks to his disgruntled feelings, he had a momentary lapse in judgment about his next question. "Do you know anything about the missing necklace Maggie mentioned last night?" He had been curious about that ever since the woman showed up at his workplace demanding repayment for her stolen jewels three years ago.

Paisley's jaw dropped. She glared at him. "You think I stole that too?"

"No, uh, I didn't." He pointed toward the Beachside Inn. "It's just, you said you stole the boat."

"Borrowed," she said through gritted teeth.

"Right." How could he backpedal? "I'm sorry. I shouldn't have brought up a sensitive topic. You mentioned taking the boat, so—"

"So you figured I stole other things from her too? I can understand why you wouldn't trust me." Her voice was devoid of emotion. "No one else does." She turned away, expelled a breath.

"Wait." He touched her shoulder. "I'm not judging you, Paisley. Honestly." When she glanced at him, he hated seeing the raw pain, the acceptance of his doubt, in her gaze.

"For the record, I did not take Maggie's jewels."

Moments ago, they were having fun together, laughing and being playful. How did things shift so abruptly?

He sighed. "I told her you didn't."

"You did?" Her shocked tone pierced him.

"Of course, I stood up for you. I will always stand up for you. You're my wife."

Her face puckered like she might be about to cry. "Well, thank you for that." She wiped her cheek beneath her eye. "Few ever have."

He was going to respond, but a truck engine rumbled up behind them. The mayor's rig.

"Get in the back." Judah's dad rocked his thumb toward the rear of the vehicle. "I'll give you a lift. Don't want all that sand in my truck."

Craig peered at them from the passenger side.

Judah glanced at Paisley. "What do you think?" Even though his leg hurt, and he knew she needed to get back to check on Paul, if she didn't want to ride in the mayor's vehicle, he'd politely decline. Seeing to her needs, what she felt comfortable with, was more important to him than his own ease, or going along with what his father wanted.

She glanced inside the truck, blinked a few times, then met Judah's gaze. "I'll ride in the back with you."

He nodded toward Dad. "Thanks." He strode to the tailgate, pulled it down, then climbed in and set down his bag. He held out his hand to Paisley. She could do it herself, they both knew that; however, she didn't reject his offer, probably due to Dad and Craig watching them through the back window.

Judah closed the tailgate. They dropped down on the floor. Paisley drew up her knees and wrapped her arms around them. She may have inched a little closer to him. He slid his arm over her shoulder. If they were jostled, he wanted to be holding her.

As the truck took off, she asked, "Did you find anything good for dinner?"

"Sure, we can mix stuff together. Add ketchup. Best glop in Basalt Bay." He winked.

"Ketchup was your solution to all my bad cooking."

"Hey, I happen to like ketchup."

When the truck leaped over something on the roadway, she was nearly thrown onto his lap.

"Oops. Sorry." She chuckled, sounding embarrassed.

Judah didn't mind their closeness. He wrapped his arms about her more snugly. Heard her sigh.

"We may have to offer them dinner," he whispered near her ear.

She gawked at him. Perhaps questioning his sanity. "Well, then, you're in charge of the meal."

"Just like old times." He snickered. "Dad will have news about what happened at the junction. Should be interesting."

Whether or not that warranted inviting the two in the cab to a meal, he wasn't sure. Especially when he still wanted to keep a safe distance between Craig and Paisley.

Twenty-seven

Side by side, Judah and Paisley worked on meal prep, opening and dumping canned goods—chili, stew, green beans, boiled potatoes, pumpkin—into a stew pot. While he felt confident the mix would be palatable, she stared skeptically at his concoction. He had to admit, the mixture was a shocking orange, thanks to the pumpkin base.

"Want to taste it?" He held out a tablespoon of the glop to her.

"No, thanks."

"Ketchup will fix it. I promise."

She raised one eyebrow. "You think ketchup fixes everything."

If only. He set the spoon on the counter and sighed.

A few minutes ago, when Craig announced that they ran out of propane, Paul suggested they dig a hole in the backyard and cook over a campfire the old-fashioned way. Even Judah's dad seemed gung-ho at the prospect of helping with the firepit. When had his father ever been interested in outdoor activities? At least, it kept the three men busy, working together.

His dad said he wouldn't stay long. That Mom probably had a meal fit for a king planned for him up at their house. Yet he kept hanging around. Judah noticed Paisley's stiff shoulders, her set lips, whenever the mayor or Craig stepped through the doorway. So far, his father hadn't explained what happened at the junction, a topic Judah was still eager to hear about.

Through the window, he watched Paul heading back from the neighbor's yard with an armload of wood—more borrowing. Craig dug a hole for the campfire. Dad stacked rocks in a circle around the pit. The three of them seemed to be working companionably, but Judah had detected unspoken tension between Dad and Craig ever since they arrived at Paige's house.

Paisley set mugs and spoons on a tray while Judah added a little more pepper and garlic salt to his mix. They'd barely spoken since their return, other than his ketchup jokes. He may have invited trouble when he asked his father and Craig to eat with them, especially after his invitation to Maggie just last night.

He glanced out the window again. The campfire sputtered and danced about the logs that were probably soaking wet like everything else around the bay. He grabbed the handles of the stew pot and was heading toward the back door when someone knocked loudly at the front door. He jerked, nearly let loose of the handles. A splash of orange landed on the floor, on his boots. *Just great.*

Behind him, carrying the tray of mugs and spoons, Paisley inhaled a sharp breath. "Who could that be?"

"James? Or Maggie." He set the pot on the kitchen table. "Can you get one of the guys to put this on the fire?"

"Okay."

Had James changed his mind about coming over? Judah strode to the front door. Pulled on the doorknob.

Deputy Brian stood on the porch, tapping his mud-speckled black boot, a clipboard in hand. A grizzled frown made him look older than Judah knew him to be. "Judah."

"Deputy." Judah's heart rate increased. "Can I help you? When did you get back into town?"

"I could ask you the same question." The lawman thumped the clipboard with his pen. "How many people are here illegally?"

"Illegally?"

The deputy threw a glare. "Really? You, a C-MER employee who knows how our town evacuation works, need ask that question?"

Judah gulped. Technically, he wasn't employed by C-MER now.

"How many people are present who aren't supposed to be in town, per evacuation orders?"

Judah didn't answer.

Brian thumped his pen on the clipboard. "I asked you a question, Mr. Grant."

"Okay, five. But they're not all staying here." He swallowed. "Is there a problem, Officer?"

"Other than your ignoring the evacuation notice that you issued? Is the mayor present?" The deputy's voice deepened.

"He is."

"May I come in?" His question sounded like a command.

"Sure." Judah stepped back. "The others are in the backyard." How much trouble was he in for venturing back into town before the evacuation notice lifted? Did Deputy Brian know that Paisley and Paul had been in Basalt Bay all along?

The deputy strode through the living room, then paused in

the middle of the kitchen as if analyzing the space. "Is this where you weathered the storm?" So he knew about that.

"No. I, we, that is, my wife and I were at my father-in-law's house."

"Your wife? She's back in town?" Brian scribbled something. Acted even more agitated. "And your father?"

"Is this way." Judah tried walking normally as he headed for the back door.

"How did you hurt yourself?"

He cleared his throat. "Flying glass during the hurricane."

"Exactly why you weren't supposed to be in the area during Blaine's assault."

Judah would have evacuated with everyone else, but he stayed for the best of reasons, even if Deputy Brian might not agree.

"I'd offer you some coffee if we had any." He opened the back door. "If you're hungry, we have an odd-colored stew."

"I'm here on official business. Not a social call."

As the deputy stepped onto the back porch, Judah observed the reactions of the four gathered around the campfire. Paisley averted her gaze, took a step behind Paul. The mayor's jaw dropped. Craig set his fists on his hips, glared.

Paul waved enthusiastically. "Deputy Brian, welcome! Want some dinner?" He pointed to the pot hovering over the fire, propped up by rocks.

"No, thanks." A pause, then, "Mayor? A word."

Dad and Craig exchanged a tight look.

"Now!"

That anyone, including a policeman, would speak to his father in such a forceful manner and not get a tongue-lashing shocked Judah.

The mayor grumbled about the abuse of power—like he had room to talk—then shuffled toward the uniformed man. "What can I do for you, Officer?"

"Inside." Brian jerked his head toward the door.

Dad shrugged toward Judah like he didn't have a clue what this was about. He and Brian went inside. Judah remained on the porch where he might hear their conversation.

"What do you mean, arrest me?" Dad shouted from inside the kitchen.

Arrest him? Judah inched closer to the door.

"You incited a riot, didn't you?"

A riot? His father? No way.

"There's a penalty for that." Deputy Brian's voice rose too. "You know that, *Mayor* Grant."

"I was not inciting a riot!" Dad thundered. "I was calming folks down. Helping the citizens of my town get through what many deemed an unfair situation. That's my job!"

"And is it your job to stir the mob into a frenzy?" The deputy huffed.

"That's not the way it happened, not at all."

"Then you tell me, Mayor."

Judah heard a tapping like Deputy Brian was hitting his pen against his clipboard again. Footsteps, Dad's probably, tread back and forth across the kitchen laminate.

"I stopped people from acting foolishly, from doing things they'd regret. I told them to wait for the road to be fixed." Dad's voice got louder. "Sure, I listened to their complaints. Basalt Bay is my town! A man looks after what's his own."

Judah rolled his eyes at his dad's mayoral creed that didn't extend to his own family.

Paisley stepped up onto the porch beside him. "Hear anything?"

"Dad's getting busted."

"Going to jail?"

"I hope not."

She leaned closer to the crack near the doorframe. Her forehead touched his cheek as they listened.

"What are you doing?" Dad's voice. "You're not fining me, are you?"

"I'm issuing you a citation. And, yes, a possible fine."

"Who do you think you are?"

"You may think you own the town, Mayor Grant, but you are not above the law." The officer's voice deepened to a near-growl. "None of you are supposed to be in Basalt Bay."

"You have no control over—"

"I have more control than you can imagine!" the deputy shouted.

Ten seconds of silence passed.

"Maybe I should go in there." Judah grabbed hold of the doorknob. "Try to diffuse the situation."

Paisley didn't comment, but her fingers stroked his hand in passing as if showing her support.

"Uh, Dad, could I speak with you?"

"Not now." The mayor leaned against the counter, an obstinate glare lining his face.

Brian stood in front of him, scribbling on a pad of paper.

"Dad, what's going on? What did you do?" Judah walked tentatively toward the men.

"This young authoritarian"—his father thrust his index finger toward the policeman's chest—"thinks he's the king, and we should bow to his wishes." Dad cleared his throat. "As the mayor, I tried to calm people down last night. Not incite them like this . . . this minion believes."

"Minion?" Brian cast Dad a sour look. "Getting them to chant 'Open the gates to our town' your idea of calming folks? What about throwing rocks? Is that your idea of helping, too?"

His father threw rocks at the Guardsmen? Unbelievable.

"I didn't start any of that. Or encourage it." Dad scowled, yet he seemed nervous.

"Eyewitnesses might say otherwise in a court of law." Brian flipped over a page on his clipboard. "Did you say"—he squinted at the paper—"'Pick up arms. Show them we mean business'? Did you and Masters grab rocks? Threaten our personnel in uniform?"

"Dad!" That sounded like an insurrection.

His father's face hued redder than Judah had ever seen it.

"I did not throw stones. I took rocks out of the hands of those who would have done damage." He shook his head, his lips bunched together. "Maybe I need my lawyer present."

"Maybe you do." Brian tore a form-like sheet of paper from the pad, held it out to the mayor.

Dad stared out the window, not taking the citation. "You're issuing that to the wrong person. There's your culprit." Dad pointed toward someone outside.

Was he referring to Craig standing out by the firepit? Certainly not Paul.

Brian set the paper on the counter. "Last I checked, the mayor should lead the residents in obeying the law. In following an honorable code of conduct." He stuffed the pad in his coat pocket. He met Judah's gaze with accusation. "What about you?"

"Huh?" Judah swallowed.

Brian stared at something, or someone, beyond Judah. "Paisley Cedars." By his scornful tone, he could have spit after saying her name.

"Grant." Judah glanced over his shoulder. Paisley stood in the doorway, a strained look on her face.

"I should have known. Trouble follows her wherever she goes." He lifted his chin, stared intensely at Judah. "Were you at the junction last night?"

"No, sir." Although, he felt nervous despite his lack of involvement. What did the officer mean about trouble following Paisley? How did he know her?

"Did you join in the rock throwing?" Brian's voice rose tightly.

"I said I wasn't there."

"He wasn't," Paisley spoke up. "He was . . . with me."

Brian scowled.

Judah heard her shuffle back outside, close the door.

"You've done your duty. You should leave." Dad nodded toward the front of the house. "My lawyer will be contacting you."

The deputy bristled. "You are in direct violation of public safety laws. All of you need to leave town. No one has permission to be within the city limits."

"Since we're here, why go?" Judah wasn't trying to be troublesome, but how could they even travel out of the city when the road connecting them to Highway 101 wasn't accessible? "Won't the other residents be returning soon, anyway?"

"Until utilities are fixed, and the road is cleared, this town is under evacuation." The deputy thumped his finger in a rhythmic beat against the clipboard.

"Isn't the road almost repaired? Utility workers were here today."

"Working on City Hall only." The deputy glared at the mayor.

"My offices will be open tomorrow." It seemed Dad threw down a gauntlet.

"Not unless prerequisites are met." Brian bit out each word. "I can arrest you. All of you. Plenty of room in the jail."

"A building you happen to share with me!" Dad tossed up his hands. "What do you want, Deputy? Are you just here to cause trouble?"

"I am the law in Basalt Bay!" Brian closed the gap between him and Dad, his index finger stabbing the air. "You might get away with stirring up a crowd intent on pushing their way into town. But if either of those two men who were guarding the road suffer irreparable damages, I will hold you personally responsible." He stomped across the living room, slamming the door on his exit.

Dad's chuckle sounded forced. He massaged his forehead. "Can you believe that young spitfire?"

Twenty-eight

Judah took Deputy Brian's place in front of the mayor, although not as brazenly. "Was someone hurt when you and Craig drove out to the road closure? Did you incite the crowd?"

"What? No, of course not. Son, listen. I went there intending to help. Thought I did. But"—Dad blew out a breath—"I don't know."

"Was Craig involved?"

The mayor crossed his arms, didn't answer.

"Did he start the problem?" If Craig incited the riot, that might be grounds for his dismissal from C-MER.

"I should go." Dad shuffled his shoes against the floor. "Your mother's waiting."

Avoidance—Judah recognized the trait. Grant men took evasion tactics to the level of an artform.

"Why don't you have a bite to eat before you go?" Paisley would be shocked to hear him give the invitation for a second time in the same day. "About Craig?"

"He was there, same as me. That's all I will say about it." A grimace on his face, Dad clamped his lips shut.

Judah understood Deputy Brian's frustrations. Still, they had food. He was hungry. Maybe Dad would come outside and talk. "Come on, if you want to eat something. It's up to you." He headed out the door.

"How did it go?" Paisley asked as soon as he stepped on the porch.

"Not good." He strode to the firepit. He held his hands over the warmth. Paul and Craig were still standing by the fire, eating the food from their mugs. Paisley followed him, then dished up two more cups. She handed one to him, one to his father when he approached.

Before Judah tasted his, he grabbed the ketchup bottle off the ground where someone had set it and doused his food. He took a big bite of orangish-red glop, chewed. Not bad. "Brian wants us to leave town," he said as soon as his mouth was empty.

"Not me. I'm not leaving." Paul huffed. "I told you that before the weather went to the devil."

"So you did." The mental video clip of Judah knocking on Paul's door to give his pre-storm warning and his father-in-law stubbornly declaring that he wouldn't leave town played through his thoughts.

"If Dad stays, I'm staying." Paisley lifted her chin as if she expected Judah to argue.

"And I'm staying with you, so that's settled." He smiled at her despite the tension with his father, and with Craig standing right here. He wouldn't leave her again. Come high water, or a jail sentence, they were sticking together. "If we get arrested, maybe the deputy will put us in the same cell together." He rocked his eyebrows.

Her cheeks turned rosy.

Craig cleared his throat. Rolled his eyes.

"You can all come up to my place. I doubt Deputy I'm-King-Of-The-World will drive that far to haul anyone to jail." Dad stuffed a spoonful in his mouth, gagged. "Our food will taste better than this—"

"Watch it." Judah lifted his mug. "I'm thankful for our glop."

"Hear! Hear!" Paul grinned.

"Plenty of hot water at my house, too, thanks to a new state-of-the-art generator." The mayor was still pushing his agenda. "Take it or leave it."

"Thanks, anyway." Judah took another bite of his food.

"I should go." Craig adjusted his knit cap.

"Where?" That came out before Judah remembered they weren't friends any longer. He didn't need to be concerned about his ex-supervisor's well-being, right? However, he was curious about his involvement in last night's debacle. "What's your take on what happened at the junction?"

Craig squinted. "Nothing."

The mayor set down his full mug on a chunk of wood. "It was a fiasco that shouldn't have happened, that's what. We did our best to help."

Craig snorted. Then, grumbling something indistinguishable, he strode around the corner of the house.

"I'm leaving too." Dad trudged toward the carport. "Last call for a warm place to stay with modern conveniences." When no one took him up on his offer, he said, "Give me a call if you get thrown in the pokey." Then he left.

"Guess we should let this fire die down." Paul rubbed his hands over the low flames.

Paisley sighed. "What a day, huh?"

"What's with you and Deputy Brian?"

Her jaw dropped.

Maybe Judah shouldn't have fired that question at her quite so fast.

"The deputy was her prom date. Didn't you know?" Paul's eyes sparkled in the remnant of the fire's glow.

"I guess I didn't." Was that why Brian acted so weird toward her? "Prom date, huh?"

"A really, really bad one." She glared at her father like he shouldn't have said anything.

Paul dumped a bucket of water over the hot ashes. A pillar of spitting steam rose.

A chill hit Judah. "He seemed annoyed to see you."

"He doesn't like that I know what he did on graduation night." She kicked at a rock beside the firepit. "What I got blamed for. Now that he's 'the law'"—she made air quotation marks—"it might be embarrassing if word gets out exactly who did what." Her eyes glimmered toward Judah. "Leverage for another time, hmm?"

Judah chuckled at his wife's leap to mischief, which reminded him of their sand throwing on the dunes.

"Paisley Rose, what secret do you know about Deputy Brian?" Paul squinted at his daughter.

"Things better left unsaid, for now."

"Guess we should try to get some rest." Judah used a stick to spread out the wet ashes. "And hope the law doesn't come after us in the middle of the night."

He and Paisley exchanged a look. Was she thinking of what he said about them sharing the same cell, like he was?

Twenty-nine

Paisley stretched and yawned, then remembering Judah was asleep in the room with her, she sat up and wiped her dry lips, smoothed her hands over her hair. Now why did she do those things? Judah had seen her with messed-up hair and no makeup plenty of times. Yet, his being in the same room with her overnight, after three years apart, made things seem more intimate between them than they were, even if he was sleeping on the floor several feet away from where she rested on the futon.

Last night, he made a convincing argument. If Deputy Brian showed up, Judah said he wanted to be near her, to protect her, to portray a unified front to the lawman. She agreed. But then, she woke up in the middle of the night and heard him snoring. She'd forgotten about that habit of his. She laid there quietly, listening to his breathing, thinking how nice it was to have someone else in the room, in the dark with her, even if that someone snored.

Now, tired of the uncomfortable futon, she stood and tiptoed around his sleeping form. After making her way to the bathroom, she freshened up by the dim glow of the flashlight that kept flickering. She flushed the toilet with the last of the water in the bucket, realizing her first chore of the day would have to be walking to the creek and refilling buckets. She couldn't wait until the electricity and water were restored.

They had made it to morning without the deputy pounding on the door and serving them arrest warrants. Maybe he had second thoughts. Perhaps, he realized allowances needed to be made during a disaster. And, fortunately, Judah didn't press for answers about what trouble the two of them got into at the end of high school.

Back then, they acted on dares she was sure they'd both rather forget. Brian deserved his second chance as much as she did, right? Whoa. Did she just think that about herself? That *she* deserved another chance? Well, glory be. Hope lit a tiny flame that shone brightly in her heart for about ten seconds. Then poof, her thoughts turned dark. What about her leaving Judah and not telling him where she was? What about the hurts between her and Dad? The trouble she caused in town. The uncertainties that still lingered between her and Judah. *Ugh.*

Several shallow breaths and the feeling of a hundred-pound pressure on her chest reminded her that she'd better think of something else quickly. No reason to panic. She was going to take one day at a time. Make amends with those she could, including Judah and Dad. And Judah, being the wonderful man he was, said he still loved her. So did Jesus, it seemed. And she was working on having trust and faith in both again.

When she pulled open the bathroom door, there was Judah, leaning against the wall in the hallway. A grin lined his lips, and he exuded way too much masculine charm. How did he do that without saying a word? He ran his hand through his messy hair. Smoothed it over his scraggly beard.

Her thoughts leapt to imagining her palms smoothing over his whiskers. Her lips touching his. But, no, she wasn't ready for that. Hadn't she already made that decision? She gulped. "Oh, um, good morning." They had lots of work to do today. Water buckets to fill. Drinking water to find. No time for standing here gawking at the man like he was eye candy.

"Morning." His gravelly voice flip-flopped her heart.

His eyes were shimmering pools of light a woman could swim in. Paisley figured she could stand here all day staring into his blues and never tire of it.

"My turn?" He pointed toward the bathroom.

"Mmm-hmmm." She heard the dreamy sound in her voice, cleared her throat to hide it. "Let me get out of your way."

He winked as he passed by her. Leaned in as if he might be thinking of kissing her good morning, too. Would, if she let him. *Deep blue sea in the morning!* Why didn't she just nod? Or lean in herself? But didn't they have too much rubble between them to just start kissing again? Too much past to dive into a future with him without weighing the cost.

A few blinks later, he shuffled into the bathroom and closed the door. She hurried down the hallway, bucket in hand. Chores awaited. Even if her thoughts were whipping up a delightful interlude with the man. *Settle down, my heart.*

"If you hold up a sec, I'll go with you to the creek and help haul water."

She whirled around. He stood in the kitchen doorway, still looking sleepy and handsome.

"Sure. Okay." If she kept standing here gawking at him, she

might do something foolish. Telling herself she was one love-starved puppy, she hunted for the other bucket. That's right, they used it outside last night. She'd scoop it up on the way to the creek. She perused the food items Judah brought from the cottage. Finding another peach-mango juice, she removed the lid and took a long guzzle.

He walked straight toward her. She tensed, anticipating something might happen between them—her primal reaction to the way she felt toward him, not because of anything he did. Silly girlish heart. But it was a strong beating womanly heart. Not a dead one like she thought she had for so many years. Maybe she was more ready to kiss him than she even imagined. *Maybe?*

He held out his hand for the juice container. That twinkle in his eyes shone brightly. Like he knew how she felt. Recognized her longings. She wasn't that transparent, was she?

She handed him the partially filled bottle. He took several swallows. Intrigued, she watched his lips moisten. When he handed the container back, she fumbled it in her hands.

"Thanks." She took another drink, distracting herself from his probing blues.

"We have to find more drinking liquid, hopefully clean water, today." He moved away. He grabbed a knit hat from the table and pulled it onto his head, covering his soft, messy hair. Hair she wouldn't mind strumming her fingers through. Taming it a little.

She cleared her throat. Stared at a black spot on the flooring. Glanced at the ceiling, looking anywhere but at him.

"Water's a priority for survival."

"Uh-huh." So was kissing. Linking pinkies. Telling him she loved him.

"After we secure that, we can tackle the next thing on the list."

"Which is?" What were they talking about?

He thrust his arms into his coat. Arms she wished would wrap around her. Forget water.

"I thought we should work on your dad's house. Or the cottage. We'll need our own place to stay once Paige and Piper return." He rocked his thumb toward the bedroom. "A decent bed is another priority."

Right. Beds. Her cheeks felt hot. He didn't say anything wrong or suggestive. Yet her mind leapfrogged to married life with him, perhaps sharing a bedroom.

"Ready?"

She gazed into his eyes. "For what?"

"For . . . hauling water." He stared back at her, his eyebrows making a V. "You okay?"

"Of course, water. Yep, I'm ready." She picked up the bucket and hustled out the door. Time to get going and stop daydreaming about married love. Wow, her heart was changing so fast it was hard to keep up.

"What did you think I meant?" His voice had a funny twinge to it.

She glanced over her shoulder. He was grinning. He knew, didn't he? Or thought he knew. She groaned, then walked to the firepit and grabbed the other bucket.

"Even though we'll be busy today, we should do something fun, too." He pulled one of the buckets from her grasp.

Their fingers touched. She may have held his hand for just a second in the exchange.

"Like?"

"Something lighthearted. Just you and me." His inviting grin was followed by a wink. "We could walk down to *Peter's Land*. With all the damage, we can't hike out on the peninsula, but we could take a look."

That he used her nickname for the rocky outcropping pleased her. "I'd like that."

He swung the bucket back and forth, making her think of them being like Jack and Jill going to get their pail of water.

"Me? I'd rather do something more adventurous."

"Such as?" She stepped over a cluster of branches on the sidewalk.

He gazed toward the ocean as if he were looking at it, even though they couldn't see the water yet. "Mmm. Go for a boat ride with you."

"And where would you get a boat?"

His face sobered. "I don't know. Now that I'm not working—"

"Maybe Craig wasn't serious about firing you." She swallowed, knowing this might be a touchy subject for him.

"Yeah, he was." As they approached a downed tree, he gently touched her elbow, leading her around it. "I tried to quit. He jumped in and fired me. Just as well, though."

"I'm sorry. I know how much you love your job." She turned at the corner and walked up the street toward the creek. "What about Mike Linfield?" She thought of the company manager who told her at a Christmas party how much he appreciated Judah's work ethic. "Couldn't he veto Craig's decision?"

"I doubt it."

They reached the creek that was overflowing its narrow bank from the flooding and the heavy rains during and after the storm. Bending over, they each submerged their buckets into the cold water.

"Got mine." Judah stood, hefting his full load.

"Same here." She groaned as she stood, lifting the weight of the bucket. "How many times will we do this before the crisis is over?"

Judah smiled again. "I'd walk here with you to get water for the rest of my life if it meant we could spend time talking like this. Sharing our hearts."

She knew what he meant, but she thought she would keep things light. "When did you become such a romantic?"

He grabbed his chest with his free hand. "You wound me. I've got plenty of romance for you, sweetheart." He stroked her cheek with the back of his fingers.

So much for keeping things light.

"Where is all this dreamy talk coming from?" Was he trying to say the right things, to be more romantic, in order to get her to move in with him as his wife?

He set down his bucket. Took hers from her hand and set it down next to his. He gazed into her eyes with such a depth of caring, or love, it made her feel breathless, but in a good way.

"You need to know this, Paisley Rose Grant." He stroked a strand of her hair back, his fingers lingering near her left ear. "With every fiber of who I am, with every beat of my heart, I love you."

She swallowed down a lump in her throat as dry as swallowing cotton.

His eyes, gazing into hers, shone like the brilliance of the sea on a summer day with a burst of sunlight on it. "I know you aren't ready to say those words to me yet. And that's okay. But I'm going to keep loving you and romancing you and showing you how much I want us to be a real couple for as long as it takes. That's a promise you can count on."

I love you too, Judah. The words danced in her spirit. In her throat. Why couldn't she tell him? Her pride? Was she holding onto grudges? Their past?

"You've been through a lot." His palms stroked her upper arms. "So have I. But I believe God is doing a work in both of us. He'll help us with the whole restoration thing. There's no rush. We can take our time." He leaned in and his mouth brushed her cheek. She felt his whiskers touch her skin briefly.

Just tell him.

"Until you're ready for more, I'll wait. But if you think I'm being a phony in the way I feel about you, you're wrong." His gentle smile took any sting out of his words. He picked up both buckets of water, then limped down the sidewalk toward Paige's house.

When did he become so vulnerable and willing to talk about stuff that he would have clammed up and run for the hills over in the past? And talk about romantic. She was about to melt at his feet after listening to his sweet declarations.

"Wait up." She ran after him. "I'm perfectly capable of carrying one of those."

"I know. Let me be the tough guy this once."

"Okay, fine."

The tangy scent of the sea wafting on the wind tempted her to forget the day's work. She looked forward to whenever they could take a break and go down to the peninsula. She pictured the waves bursting against the rocks, sea spray billowing into the air. She imagined her and Judah searching the beach for treasures like she did hundreds of times as a kid. Her idea of fun. That Judah understood that about her was part of their history together. Part of their love story.

She pondered what he said about his willingness to wait for her to be ready for their marriage to be restored. Did he mean that he would wait for her no matter how long it took?

Thirty

Judah was removing items from Paul's living room, relocating salvageable furniture into the kitchen, throwing others outdoors, and discarding ruined knickknacks and memorabilia into the trash, in preparation for pulling up the soaking wet carpet. Suddenly he heard a series of loud rumbles. "Listen to that."

"What is it?" Paisley held several of her mother's flood-ruined paintings in her arms.

"Heavy equipment trucks, I think." He moved to stand near the couch. "Not long until the road opens."

"Good. Maybe Deputy Brian won't haul us to jail."

"Unless he does so out of spite, or mere legalities. I think he's met his match if he tries dragging you down to lockup." He teased her as he lifted one side of the couch, testing its weight.

"Yeah, just let him try." She grinned one of those smiles that had a way of wrapping around his heart.

Ever since he told her that he'd wait for her however long it took, it seemed she was gazing into his eyes differently. More intensely. Like now.

"How about helping me haul this couch outside?" He pointed at the last large piece of furniture left on the soggy carpet.

"Sure." She set down the paintings on the wooden coffee table he'd already moved.

Paul entered the living room from the kitchen. "What's this doing in the pantry?" He held up a beach towel—the same one Judah saw on the shelf the other day.

"Oh, uh." Paisley's face flushed. "It's what I used for bedding the night I stayed here."

Just like Judah thought.

"You slept in the pantry?" Paul's eyebrows knit together above his glasses. "Why would you do that?"

It seemed a serious message passed between father and daughter. Paul shuffled his feet and averted his gaze. Was he feeling awkward about the topic or about her pointed glare?

"That was the only dry place I could find." Her voice rose. "I hated it. Have always hated the pantry. But you know that."

Should Judah step in? His and Paisley's relationship needed healing, but so did Paul's and hers. They required their own time to work things out between them without his interference. Still, he'd stay close in case she needed him. He trudged to the other side of the living room, gazing through the plastic-covered window, giving them a few moments to talk. He prayed for them too.

Paul mumbled something about women and things men would never understand about them, then stomped into the kitchen. Judah turned and witnessed the towel his father-in-law had been holding sail through the air and land on the washing machine.

Paisley's boots thudded as she followed Paul into the other room. "Why didn't you ever c-come for m-me?" Her voice broke, sounding small and child-like.

Paul shuffled boards that fell from the stairway during the storm.

"Dad?"

Paul kept working. Evading conflict? Judah empathized with that emotional cop-out. Although, he learned the hard way that it never solved a thing.

Lord, help them see that they still have each other. Touch Paisley. Heal her heart. Heal all of us.

"I w-wanted, n-needed, you to rescue m-me." Her voice broke. "To save me from the d-darkness. From Mom's unjustified wrath." She expelled a breath, like the telling was wrenched from her soul. "You never came. Not once. Never got involved. Why not?" Her voice rose with a demanding tone, then fell. "D-didn't you l-love me enough?"

Oh, Paisley. Save her from what darkness? Judah knew about her fear of the dark. That she preferred to keep a night-light on. She used to lay close to him after he turned out the light, as if she couldn't bear to be alone in the dark. He swallowed hard. All those nights by herself in Chicago, two-thousand miles from him, how did she cope?

Knowing she was never out of God's sight had comforted him during their years apart. He prayed for so long for her to come back. And here she was. Full of hurts. All of them were. But Judah knew who to turn to. Was Paisley aware of her heavenly Father opening His arms of love to her, even if her earthly father seemed uncaring, even cold, now?

"Aren't you going to answer me?"

"Nothing to say." Paul picked up a couple of handrails, tossed them on the pile.

"Nothing?" Paisley's face blanched.

Judah wished Paul would step up and be honest, even if that meant admitting to his own hurts, failures, disappointments, whatever.

"After all we've been through? The storm. Your illness. Me putting up with Craig so that you could have the medical intervention you needed?" She nearly yelled that last part.

A knot twisted in Judah's gut. He shouldn't have questioned her interactions with Craig. Her words dissolved any doubt. She had put aside her animosity toward that man so she could care for her ailing father. A sacrificial act of love in her daughter's heart.

"We need to clean this up," Paul said sternly. "That's all that matters now."

"No, that's not all that matters!"

"We have to get the house livable." Paul shuffled into the living room, scooped up the pile of paintings Paisley collected earlier. "I'll spread these outside to dry. Might save a few."

"Please, don't walk away." She followed him, a crushed look on her face.

"Why not?" Paul paused by the door they'd propped open. "That's what you did. What you're good at." His words were like a judge's gavel striking a sound block. He shuffled the canvases in his hands, then trudged onto the porch.

Paisley blew out a harsh-sounding breath. "Fine. If that's the way you want it." She covered her face with her hands.

Judah strode to her, intent on wrapping his arms around her, comforting her. "I'm so sorry, Pais."

She thrust up her hands, blocking his embrace, or his coming any closer. Her face was red. Her mouth drawn into a tight line. "We have work to do. Survival. He's right about that." A gritty look replaced her previous vulnerability.

Judah kept his hands at his sides. She needed space; he'd give her that. "Is he still angry that you left?"

"And that I missed my mom's funeral." She gnawed on her lower lip. "Can't change the past."

"He'll come around. He loves you. Always has."

She eyed him skeptically.

"Anything I can do?"

"Let's move the couch. Get this over with."

"Okay." He strode to the other end of the water-logged piece of furniture. "Might be heavy. We'll lift, then shove."

"I got it." She raised her end quickly. She undoubtedly had a load of adrenaline pulsing through her. A crash was inevitable.

He lifted his end slowly, wishing he bore the greater weight. He cringed at the tug in his leg but hid his reaction by tucking his head down. Backing up, he led the way toward the front door. When he reached the opening, he set his side down. It took some maneuvering to get the old relic on its end, then shuffled out the door. They heaved it off the porch and onto the soggy grass near the recliner Judah already threw out.

"Guess I'll need new furniture." Paul's mouth drooped into a deep frown. He rubbed his forehead with the back of his palm like he was tired. Maybe emotionally exhausted.

Judah felt badly for him too. He patted the man's shoulder. "You and half the town." He nodded toward Paisley. "Let's pull that rug, then take a break."

The atmosphere tense, the three of them worked at yanking up the carpeting, then they tore out the foam underlayment.

Throughout the process, Paisley and Paul didn't speak to each other. They hauled the wet mess outdoors and made a giant pile. Paul found the tools they needed to pry up the tack strips. Once that was done, he went outside. Paisley disappeared around the corner, into the kitchen.

Relieved the job was finished, Judah checked over the floor that was still soaked. Some of the wood was warped and would have to be replaced.

He heard voices coming from outside. James and Paul chatted back and forth across the street. Judah watched through the doorway as Paul trudged over to his friend's property. The two men shook hands.

Maybe he could get Paisley away from here for a while. She stood at the kitchen sink, staring out the window as he approached.

"I'm curious about the engine sounds. Want to take a walk and check?"

"Sure. Why not?" She spoke in a monotone.

"Would be great to get some fresh air. Stretch our legs."

"I said, 'sure,'" she said sharply.

"Okay."

She shot out the door faster than he could get out and climb from the porch. Finding the old steps, or making new ones, was high on his list of things to be done. It took effort for him to wade down the flooded street, and Paisley had gone half a block before he caught up to her. By then, she was walking on the sidewalk on the opposite side of the street. Without talking about it, they made a wide berth around the downed power line.

When he held out his hand toward her, she raised an eyebrow as if asking him "*really*?" He dropped his outstretched hand.

Two steps backward.

He couldn't even walk beside her for some of the way, since they had to step over so many branches and piles of shingles. The place reminded him of a war zone, like an explosion went off. It was astounding what catastrophic damage high winds and tempestuous waves could do. He hoped they never had another hurricane on the west coast again. Although, if it did happen, he wanted to be one of the people warning folks as he did with Blaine. That's the main reason he loved his job. The company's mission to help neighbors in a disaster or crisis meant a lot to him. Too bad things had gone south between him and Craig.

He sighed as they walked past the art gallery.

"Something wrong?"

"Just thinking about the storm and all the damage."

"Me too. What a mess, huh?" She kicked a rusty can out of her way. Flexed her shoulders. Sighed.

He shifted a little closer to her. "It'll take the whole town working together to fix it up. All of us helping each other."

"We'll need a leader too."

"You mean other than the mayor?"

"Yes. Other than him." She lifted her chin, a sparkle returning to her gaze. "You could use your C-MER experience to help as a regular citizen, Good Samaritan, whatever."

It was nice of her to think of him as a leader in the community.

They passed by Miss Patty's hardware store, the floral shop that was closed after Hurricane Addy hit, and Bert's Fish Shack. He couldn't believe how wrecked the front of Bert's was with that boat smashed into the front. He imagined the owner, who had called him "Sonny" since he was a kid, being overwhelmed, possibly discouraged, by the reconstruction ahead of him.

Paisley had gone quiet, and he remembered the words spoken between her and Paul. Hurtful words that probably replayed in her mind, eating at her.

He draped his arm across her shoulder. Taking a risk. "You okay?"

She tensed. "Why wouldn't I be?" Her glare was a forcefield telling him to get his arm off her shoulder.

He stuffed his hands into his coat pockets. Okay, she still needed space. But he wanted them to be able to talk, share their hearts, get past the walls. Which meant he had to keep pushing a little.

"Can you tell me what's going on with you and your dad?"

She stopped in front of the old cannery and thrust out her hands. "Isn't it obvious? I've failed everyone. Dad. You. My mom. Paige. Aunt Callie. I'm a walking, breathing, stinking *failure*." She reminded him of a teapot boiling over with steam and unspent energy. "How did I ever imagine I could come back to Basalt and make things right? Miss Humpty Dumpty is not only busted up, she's shattered b-beyond r-recognition." Her voice broke. "N-nothing c-can fix that."

Was she speaking of herself? Their marriage? Her relationship with Paul? He didn't know what to say. Which part to address. He was afraid to say or do anything for fear it would be the incorrect thing, again. He stood there, watching her, wishing he knew how to make everything better.

"You're not going to talk to me, either?" She squinted at him.

He felt the pain in her gaze pierce his chest, rush through his lungs. "It's not that at all. Of course, I'm going to talk with you. I'm just so sorry. Stymied, really." He reached out. Pulled his hands back. "I'm not sure what to say. Or do. I don't want to say the wrong thing."

She kept glaring, so he kept talking. "You and I have plenty of stuff to talk about, believe me, I know that. But I think, right now, you're more upset about your dad and your past with him, than with me."

"I'm such a mess." She covered her face like she did earlier. "Oh, help. Why did I even come back to Basalt? How did I ever think this would work?"

Surely that outcry was his cue. Taking another chance, he stepped forward and slid his palms around her elbows, drew her against his chest. When she didn't pull away, he wrapped his arms completely around her, held her to him as closely as she allowed. "It's going to be okay, Pais," he whispered near her ear. "You're going to get through this. We both are." He kept murmuring reassurances, feeling her relax. "I'm so thankful you came back. That you're here with me now. Everything's going to get better, even if it happens in tiny increments. We're going to stick together and face everything as a couple, okay?"

He was determined to let her know, again, that he was here for her, for as long as it took for her to feel comfortable with him. He leaned his cheek against her head, thankful for the chance to be holding her. "I love you, sweetheart. Will always love you, no matter what."

She sagged against him. Stayed almost limp in his arms for several minutes. He didn't hear her crying. He listened to her breathing, checking for any irregularities. That part of her seemed okay. She let out a deep sigh. And an anguished whisper. "Where were you with your strong arms and kind words when I needed them?"

Which time frame was she referring to? "You mean when you were in Chicago?" They still needed to talk about that time in both of their lives.

"When I was locked up in the pantry." She spoke in that small girl's voice again.

Something gripped him in his chest. "You were locked in the pantry?" That's why she was so angry with her dad? He leaned back enough to see into her gaze. Swept a few strands of hair from her cheeks. A couple of teardrops. "In the dark?"

She nodded slowly.

That explained her nighttime fears. Some of her other insecurities too.

"My punishment. To this day I hate the dark."

"I'm so sorry." He pulled her to him again. Rubbed her back. Wanted to protect her from anything bad ever happening to her again.

"He never came to my rescue." She sniffed. "But you did."

"When did I do that?" He'd wanted to rescue her when she was stuck in Basalt Bay and he was in Florence. Thought he failed epically.

"You rescued me on the peninsula when I came back."

Oh. The day she fell on the rocks and he feared she might slip into the sea before he reached her. So much had happened since then.

"And you rescued me when you landed the skiff on the beach three days ago."

"I finally made it back to you."

"Yes, you did." She touched his cheek, stroking her palm down his whiskered chin. She was initiating contact between them. His heart pounded like heavy rain on a tin roof in his ears. "And now," she whispered.

"Now?"

"Your strong arms around me. Your faithful love. Gentle words. You've rescued me all over again, Judah. How did I ever live those years without you?" She glanced up at him with tears in her eyes, looking at him so sweetly.

"Oh, Pais." He felt humbled. And when her hand stilled on his cheek, her gaze mingling with his, an unexpected bucket of hope poured through him. It took everything within him not to bridge the narrow gap between them and kiss her the way he wanted to for days. Not to push for more than she was ready for. But what if she was ready? What if her shining eyes gazing up at him were proclaiming that she wanted him to kiss her? He leaned his forehead against hers, waiting.

He made the mistake of thinking she was ready before. He didn't want to make the same error again.

When she slipped her arms around his neck, leaned in closer, he thought his heart might stop. Her fingers played softly with his ears and fireworks exploded in his chest. He rested his hands lightly at her waist. Snuggled her closer. He lifted her chin with his finger, still taking this slowly. Watching for any sign that she wanted him to step back, to not kiss her.

"Sometimes a girl needs a hero."

"Yeah?" He heard the husky sound of his voice.

He watched as she glanced at his lips. Into his gaze. Back at his lips. A breath hitched in his throat as she smiled at him the way she did on their wedding day. Like the world was theirs, just the two of them in their own perfect bubble, and her gaze invited him to dance with her.

Just like now.

Oh, Pais. It seemed the earth trembled beneath his, their, feet.

Her lips drew closer to his, maybe an inch away. "Judah?" Her breath on his mouth was warm, inviting.

"Yes?"

"I've been wanting to tell you something."

"Okay."

"That night when I texted you about Craig—"

Wait. Why was she bringing up that man's name?

Thirty-one

Paisley saw the way Judah squinted at her when she mentioned Craig's name. She hoped she wasn't completely ruining their romantic moment. But she had to revisit the incident, five days ago, when she desperately tried to send Judah a message. "I'm sorry to even say his name, right now, but that night there was something important I wanted you to know."

"Okay." He leaned back slightly.

She smiled up at him. Did he see the love in her heart? That she wanted his kiss, needed it like she needed air, but she felt compelled to say this first.

"What was it, Pais?" His knuckles smoothed down the side of her cheek.

"Before I texted you that it was Craig"—ugh, she mentioned his name again—"I told you something else. A very important secret from my heart to yours."

"What did you tell me?" His words were whisper soft.

She leaned her cheek against his jacket, listening for his

heartbeat. There. Strong and steady. She pulled back and gazed into his beautiful blues again. "I texted you . . . that I love you."

"Really?" A wide smile broke across his lips.

"Really."

"All those days ago, you told me you loved me?"

She nodded slowly.

His mouth opened, then closed. He chuckled. His mild-sounding mirth turned into full-on laughter. Then she was laughing too. "Oh, Paisley." He cleared his throat like he was trying to suppress his amusement. "I was so worried that I ruined everything between us by not getting back to you. Why didn't you just tell me when I got here?"

"I thought you knew. When I realized you didn't, I was afraid to tell you. To expose my feelings."

"Ah, c'mere, sweetheart." He pulled her into his arms again. "And now?"

His gaze drew her closer, said she could trust him with her heart.

"Now? I love you, Judah. More than ever."

She heard his small inhalation of breath. Moisture flooded his eyes. The tender look he bestowed on her was so sweet, so magical, she wanted to weep.

Finally, their lips met softly, tentatively, almost like a cautious first kiss. Then, everything she remembered about kissing this man came flooding back to her. Their kiss deepened, becoming more demanding and consuming as each of them expressed the love that was lost to them, then found, incredibly found. Who knew who made the first move? His lips claimed hers with fiery passion, or hers claimed his with wild *deep-blue-sea-in-the-morning* abandon. Either way, her lips were caressing Judah's with all the love in her heart. She was claiming her man, her husband.

A kiss of a lifetime. One she'd never forget. One she hoped he'd never forget.

He broke away first, his lips trailing her cheek, her neck. Then he stepped back, his warm gaze dancing with hers, their hands clasped. With a soft groan, he pulled her to him again, his head resting against hers. "Pais, my sweet."

She heard the happiness in his voice, in the way he sighed. She smiled, too ecstatic to do anything else.

They were standing at the edge of town. Basalt was still desolate. Destruction everywhere. But love was taking possession of places in her heart that she once thought dead.

"I love you." His breath still had a little catch in it. "I've waited so long for this. For us. God has answered my prayers."

"Mine too."

She heard quiet whisperings, like he was praying, thanking God for this miracle. She closed her eyes and did the same.

After a while, he spoke. "I know there are still things we need to talk about."

"Like Chicago?"

He nodded. "I need to tell you about the day I went there."

She pulled back. "You went to Chicago?"

"I did." He sighed, seemed slightly troubled.

"I thought you said you bought a ticket but didn't go there."

"I'm sure we both have things we need to say to each other." He blinked slowly, his moist eyes staring back at her.

"True." A few thoughts came to mind. Her reasons for leaving him. Their losses. Her not calling him for three years.

"But first, there's something else I want to say to you." He looked so serious.

"Is there any way it could wait?" She wanted to hold onto this goodness, this loving feeling, a while longer. "I hate throwing cold water on what we just experienced by talking about the past."

"I agree. That's why—" He dug into his coat pocket. With his other hand he clasped her right hand. Slowly, he knelt on one knee on the muddy sidewalk in front of her.

"Judah?" What was he—

"Paisley Rose Grant, will you do me the honor of marrying me again?" He grinned up at her, his blue eyes shining.

She'd imagined them saying vows to each other privately. But this—

"Oh, Judah." She dropped down on both knees in front of him, in the mud. His eyes widened as she closed the gap between them and initiated a deep kiss. There would be no mistake about who started this one. "Judah Edward Grant"—she whispered against his mouth—"yes"—she touched her lips to his one more time—"yes, I will marry you again."

He slipped a ring onto her finger. She held up her hand, amazed by how easily he did that. "Why, it looks just like—"

"I tried to match your other one."

Sadness over the lost ring and intense joy over this gift meshed together, making tears flood her eyes. "I love it. When did you get it?"

"In Florence, before I left." He grimaced, his leg probably aching. They held hands and helped each other stand.

Her knees were mucky and wet, but she didn't care.

"What does this mean?" She stared at the topaz jewel surrounded by clusters of exquisite tiny diamonds. "Do you want to have a real wedding this time?" She thought of their previous elopement. Of her vow to him: *I promise to love you 'til the end of time.*

"I do. Whenever you're ready."

He was being so sweet. She hated to say anything that might disappoint him. And yet— "I'm sorry to have to mention this, but I sold my wedding set. For rent and food money."

He nodded. Didn't seem upset or saddened. "I figured that might be the case. I got a wedding band for you, too. Your set will still match mine."

She threw her arms around his shoulders. "You're the best husband a girl could wish for."

He chuckled. "A guy could get used to hearing that. I do have one other request."

"What is it?" She gazed into his sparkling eyes.

"I don't want to rush you, but can we have a short engagement?"

She chuckled. His smile was just too tempting to ignore. She leaned into his mouth, kissed him again. "Yes, please."

Thirty-two

Pinkies linked, Paisley and Judah walked back toward the center of town, following the hum of engines that sounded like ten motors were going at once. A logging truck rumbled down Front Street with eight or nine trees piled on the flatbed. The giant truck stopped in the middle of the road, and Paisley watched as a long metal arm swung out. The boom crane scooped up the last of the downed trees on the street, dropping them one by one onto the pile.

"Look!" Judah pointed up at a couple of utility poles.

She glanced up. Two linemen stood inside waist-high, cage-like platforms that were extended high into the air from utilities trucks. Two other men had climbed up the poles using spurred climbing boots. Other workers assisted from the ground, hoisting up new wire with the help of long ropes. At the pole they'd been avoiding, a backhoe nudged it upright, while several utilities employees labored to stabilize it.

"They're making progress. Maybe we'll get that coffee

before the day's over." Judah pushed a branch out of their way with the toe of his boot.

"Just think, if we can have coffee, then we'll be able to take hot showers, wash our clothes, and eat a cooked meal that doesn't have pumpkin in it." She chuckled.

"Miracles can happen."

"Oh, yes, they can."

They gazed into each other's eyes, and for a moment, she felt lost in his blues, lost in his love. Or maybe at home, finally, here in Basalt with him.

She still needed to face some things. Getting back together with Judah hadn't erased that. But something compelled her to focus on the man beside her. To make amends here. With him.

She glanced at the shining ring on her finger that represented a new beginning for them. A glorious start.

"Listen." Judah tugged on her hand, walked faster in the direction of City Hall.

"What is it? Where are you going?" She matched her speed to his but didn't like where they were headed.

"I heard a horn honk that didn't sound like one of the big rigs." He lifted his free hand, waving at someone. "See! Over there."

Paisley glanced toward the government building across the street. Mayor Grant stood in the parking lot. Was Judah going to tell his father that he proposed to her? Was she ready for that leap back into the Grant family?

A dark gray sedan pulled into the parking lot in front of City Hall. That must have been the car Judah heard honking.

"The road's open!" His voice rose. "Do you know who that is?"

"No." Should she?

Edward walked straight to the car, opened the driver's door. A woman with dark hair stepped out. She leaned into the back doorway, then drew out a young girl with blond hair and held her in her arms.

"Paige?"

"Yep." Judah lifted Paisley's hand with the ring on it. "Can't wait to tell her about this."

Paisley laughed despite her trepidation. This would be the first time she saw her sister in over three years. The last time they spoke they exchanged harsh words. How would Paige feel about seeing her now?

This would also be Paisley's chance to meet Piper. Her heart spasmed with internal thoughts of her own daughter who she missed terribly. Yet, joy flooded her too. She was an auntie. She wanted to meet her niece. Hold her. Play on that swing set with her.

"Paige!" Judah hollered. Waved.

Paige lifted her hand and smiled. Then, as if realizing it was Paisley with him, a troubled look crossed her face. Her hand lowered.

Paisley slowed down. Felt Judah's tug on her hand.

"Wait." She stopped.

Someone else stepped from the shadows of City Hall. A tall man with broad shoulders.

Craig?

She heard Judah's groan.

Craig lumbered forward, a wide smile on his face. He embraced Paige and Piper in a group hug, the way a family would.

Paisley's breath caught in her throat, choking her.

Craig leaned in and kissed Paige, whether on the mouth or her cheek Paisley couldn't tell from here.

She felt Judah squeeze her hand. He didn't know about this, did he?

Craig took up the child in his arms, bouncing her. The little girl who looked like a cute dolly giggled, patted both his cheeks as if that were the most natural thing for her to do.

A horrible glug settled in the middle of Paisley's stomach. Her jaw seemed to hit the ground. She glanced at Judah. He had the same disbelief on his face.

Was Craig Piper's father?

If you enjoyed *Sea of Rescue*, or mostly enjoyed it, please take a minute and write a review wherever you purchased this book. They say reviews are the lifeblood for authors. Even one line telling what you liked or thought about the book is so helpful. Thank you!

~ ~ ~ ~

I took many creative liberties with Basalt Bay, my imaginary town on the Oregon Coast. To all those who live nearby, please forgive my embellishments. I enjoy the Pacific Ocean and the Oregon Coast so much that I wanted to create my own little world there.

~ ~ ~ ~

Check out Part Three, *Bay of Refuge*—available now!

~ ~ ~ ~

If you would like to be one of the first to hear about Mary's new releases and upcoming projects, sign up for her newsletter—and receive the free pdf "Rekindle Your Romance! 50+ Date Night Ideas for Married Couples." Check it out here:

www.maryehanks.com/FREE.html

I want to say a heartfelt *"Thank you!"* to everyone who helped with this story.

Paula McGrew . . . Thank you for your editorial critique and for helping me deepen the characters and the plot. I appreciate your comments and encouragement so much.

Suzanne Williams . . . Thank you for taking on my cover ideas, and for being willing to tell me when something doesn't work. By doing that, you made this design more beautiful than I imagined.

Jason Hanks . . .Thanks for being my sounding board and for helping with mechanical questions. And thanks for encouraging me to follow my dreams.

Kathy Vancil, Kellie Wanke, Mary Acuff, Beth McDonald, Joanna Brown, and Jason Hanks . . . Thank you for being A+ beta readers. You each found different things to encourage, challenge, and critique with this story. I love that! Thank you for saying "Yes" to being beta readers for me.

Hanna Hanks . . . Thank you for critiquing and offering advice about the medical intervention in this tale. I know you were busy, yet you took the time to help me out. Thank you!

(This story is a work of fiction. Any mistakes are my very own! ~meh)

Daniel, Philip, Deborah, & Shem . . . For all the days of my life, you are my dreams come true. Traci, my first daughter-in-law, thanks for being a part of our tribe and putting up with our shenanigans.

www.maryehanks.com

Books by Mary Hanks

Restored Series

Ocean of Regret

Sea of Rescue

Bay of Refuge

Tide of Resolve

Second Chance Series

Winter's Past

April's Storm

Summer's Dream

Autumn's Break

Season's Flame

Marriage Encouragement

Thoughts of You (A Marriage Journal)

Youth Theater Adventures

Stage Wars

About Mary E Hanks

Mary loves stories about marriage restoration. She believes there's something inspiring about couples clinging to each other, working through their problems, and depending on God for a beautiful rest of their lives together—and those are the types of stories she likes to write. Mary and Jason have been married for forty-plus years, and they know firsthand what it means to get a second chance with each other, and with God. That has been her inspiration in writing the Second Chance series, and, now, in the Restored series.

Besides writing, Mary likes to read, do artsy stuff, go on adventures with Jason, and meet her four adult kids for coffee or breakfast.

Connect with Mary by signing up for her newsletter:
www.maryehanks.com/FREE.html

"Like" her Facebook Author page:
www.facebook.com/MaryEHanksAuthor

Made in the USA
Monee, IL
08 February 2022

90937024R00163